Bolan grabbed the man's slick and spasming hands

Despite his best effort Bolan could only watch as one of the thin black cylinders squirted out between their entwined fingers. The assassin's thumb came off the detonator button and it fell from his hand, trailing its connecting wire.

Bolan still retained hold of the man's wrists. He turned and rammed his hip and shoulder into the suicide bomber and threw him cartwheeling through the air back into the elevator. Bolan leaped to one side. He blinked in surprise as no blast came. His eyes flew wide as he heard the twin clicks and hiss of fuses lighting.

Bolan was dead.

MACK BOLAN ®
The Executioner

The Executioner
Don Pendleton's®

NIGHT OF
THE KNIVES

A GOLD EAGLE BOOK FROM

WORLDWIDE®

TORONTO • NEW YORK • LONDON
AMSTERDAM • PARIS • SYDNEY • HAMBURG
STOCKHOLM • ATHENS • TOKYO • MILAN
MADRID • WARSAW • BUDAPEST • AUCKLAND

First edition October 2004
ISBN 0-373-64311-X

Special thanks and acknowledgment to
Chuck Rogers for his contribution to this work.

NIGHT OF THE KNIVES

Printed in U.S.A.

The first law of war is to preserve ourselves
and destroy the enemy.
> —Mao Tse-tung 1893–1976
> *On Guerrilla Warfare*

Power politics is the diplomatic name for the law
of the jungle.
> —Ely Culbertson 1891–1955
> *Must We Fight Russia*

Some people use politics to advance their personal
causes. When that involves slaughtering innocent
citizens, they should prepare to meet their
personal executioner.
> —Mack Bolan

THE
MACK BOLAN
LEGEND

Nothing less than a war could have fashioned the destiny of the man called Mack Bolan. Bolan earned the Executioner title in the jungle hell of Vietnam.

But this soldier also wore another name—Sergeant Mercy. He was so tagged because of the compassion he showed to wounded comrades-in-arms and Vietnamese civilians.

Mack Bolan's second tour of duty ended prematurely when he was given emergency leave to return home and bury his family, victims of the Mob. Then he declared a one-man war against the Mafia.

He confronted the Families head-on from coast to coast, and soon a hope of victory began to appear. But Bolan had broken society's every rule. That same society started gunning for this elusive warrior—to no avail.

So Bolan was offered amnesty to work within the system against terrorism. This time, as an employee of Uncle Sam, Bolan became Colonel John Phoenix. With a command center at Stony Man Farm in Virginia, he and his new allies—Able Team and Phoenix Force—waged relentless war on a new adversary: the KGB.

But when his one true love, April Rose, died at the hands of the Soviet terror machine, Bolan severed all ties with Establishment authority.

Now, after a lengthy lone-wolf struggle and much soul-searching, the Executioner has agreed to enter an "arm's-length" alliance with his government once more, reserving the right to pursue personal missions in his Everlasting War.

1

Lagos, Nigeria

The Executioner checked his range card. He nodded to himself and settled into his prone firing position. The view through the scope of his FR-F1 was crystal clear, the bipod rock steady. The French sniper rifle was mid-twentieth-century technology and antiquated compared to the latest sniper weapons, but it was solid. If traced, the rifle would be found to have been reported stolen from one of neighboring Cameroon's arsenals. The rifle had been spirited to Virginia, where John "Cowboy" Kissinger had brought the battered weapon back up to spec, and it had been waiting for just such an occasion.

Mack Bolan put the vertical post of his crosshairs on the target and spoke softly. "EDICT."

Gary Manning lay three feet away, spotting through his laser range-finding binoculars. "Elevation—247 yards. Deflection—wind, one klick left. Indication—center target on veranda."

Bolan took a slow breath. "Confirmation—seen."

"Time to fire." Manning checked things through his binoculars a last time. It was a beautiful morning in West Africa. Conditions were postcard perfect for sniping. "Fire."

It was a very bad day to be Ransome Uwaifor.

Uwaifor had ridden the recent wave of African heroin smuggling and ridden high. He had paid off the local magistrates and police in his home province in northern Nigeria. When they had demanded too much money, he simply had them all killed and had himself elected magistrate. The local police and councilmen were all his own men. He had given up bribery entirely, except what was being directed his way, and had gone straight for the more direct means of murder, torture and intimidation. He had raised himself from magistrate to state representative. He had the enviable position of having a monopoly on the heroin trade in his district, as well as being a "respected" member of the civil government. He had gone from a settlement drug lord to a legitimized warlord of his own state. As a "devout" Muslim he was widely suspected of supporting and giving sanctuary to Islamic Jihad terrorists throughout West and Central Africa.

But none of that brought the Executioner to Nigeria.

When a Canadian photojournalist began documenting Uwaifor's atrocities and probing his terrorist ties, he had promptly had the woman kidnapped. Canada had no tangible assets it could put in place to deal with the situation in Nigeria. Intelligence led Bolan to believe that Heather West was still alive and relatively unharmed. Uwaifor was waiting until evening. He had invited guests, and he needed more of his men to show up. Ransome Uwaifor was planning a party. The party would culminate with the videotaping of the execution of the Canadian journalist, then anonymously putting the film on the Internet for the Canadian press and the rest of the world to download.

Bolan began taking up slack on the FR-F1's trigger.

Ransome Uwaifor thought he was invincible. However, he had made two mistakes. While he despised the heroin addicts who had made him his fortune, he had developed the habit of taking coffee and smoking cocaine through a Turkish hookah out on the veranda of his English colonial-style house every morning around ten.

His other mistake was that the woman he had kidnapped happened to be a personal acquaintance of the big Canadian lying near Bolan. Uwaifor would have been a righteous target any day of the week in Bolan's war book, but today's mission happened to be extremely personal.

Gary Manning's eyes were slits of cold fury as he observed Uwaifor.

Bolan let out half of his breath as his finger continued to take up the slack on the trigger. Kissinger had tuned it to a four-pound, glass-rod break. The way Kissinger tuned a trigger the rifle would almost go off by surprise. Bolan kept—

"Stop." Manning peered even more intently through his optics.

Bolan let up on the trigger as two men walked out onto the veranda.

Ransome Uwaifor looked up, red eyed from his water pipe. He was a small man with the physique of a bantamweight boxer, and his hair was shaved very close to the skull. He wore a half-open, white silk bathrobe, and his dark musculature had become even more carved and lean with his increasing cocaine use. The man at the table beside him was a bald mountain in an impeccably tailored Armani suit and mirrored sunglasses. Tunde Addo was Uwaifor's right-hand man and had risen through the ranks right beside him, going from street-corner bone-breaker to highly efficient assassin. He was also rumored to be the brains of the outfit. More and more so, as Uwaifor's increasing cocaine use reduced his functional ability to that of political and charismatic figurehead. There were also four men in police uniforms carrying AK-47s. The bodyguards.

The two men walking out onto the veranda were anomalies. They had appeared from nowhere, which meant only God knew what other holes there were in the already sketchy intelligence Bolan and Manning were working with.

One of the strangers was dark-haired with a beard and

mustache and appeared to be Arab. He carried a briefcase. The other man was a large blonde, perhaps six foot two or three, and wore a white tropical suit.

Manning slowly shook his head. "Where the hell did they come from?"

Bolan grimaced. "Intel said nothing about any houseguests."

"So who the hell are they?" Manning asked in frustration.

"I don't know." Bolan let out a long breath. The plan had been simple. Whack Ransome. Whack Addo. Through observation they had deduced that there were perhaps ten to fifteen hitters on the premises, but with both heads of the organization cut off, the muscle could be expected to scatter. Bolan and Manning would move in, retrieve Heather West and extract by boat to Benin.

The plan was starting to go south.

Bolan never took his eyes off the primary target. The blond man pulled a thin wooden case from inside his jacket and handed it to Uwaifor. The drug lord took it and exposed his gold teeth with obvious delight. "Your call. Abort?"

Manning didn't hesitate. "We either get her out, or we avenge her. No way we leave her behind."

Bolan peered through his telescope. "EDICT."

"Elevation—247 yards. Deflection…" Manning paused a moment. "Zero. Indication—center target on veranda."

"Confirmation—seen."

"Time to fire." They watched as the two men shook hands with Uwaifor and Addo and sat down to coffee. Uwaifor seemed to be entranced with the case. He stroked the blond wood with his hand and began opening its twin brass latches.

Slowly, Bolan began to take up the slack on the trigger once more.

Ransome Uwaifor's head exploded like a melon. Crimson gore splattered everyone at the table as his skull failed to contain over two thousand pounds of energy. The French rifle recoiled as Bolan flicked the bolt and put his crosshairs on his secondary target. Everyone at the table screamed or froze, save the blond man. He dived from his seat and rolled across the tiles of the veranda toward cover with a pistol in his hand. Bolan swung his scope onto Tunde Addo. The giant was starting to rise from his seat and claw beneath his jacket for a weapon. Bolan squeezed the trigger and the big man sat down as a weeping hole appeared in the center of his colorful necktie. Bolan worked the bolt and raised his aim slightly to confirm the kill. The big rifle roared, and Addo's mirrored sunglasses snapped in half and flew off to either side. The strongman slumped facefirst onto his breakfast tray with the back of his head blown out.

The blond man was nowhere in sight. His companion had pulled a Russian AKSU carbine from his briefcase. The weapon would be useless at his distance but the 30 mm grenade launcher mounted beneath it could reach out and touch Bolan if the man was observant.

The French rifle bucked against Bolan's shoulder, and the man staggered. Bolan flicked the bolt as the man's face went pale and his weapon sagged in suddenly nerveless fingers. Bolan's second round rocked the man's head like an invisible right hook and laid him supine next to Addo.

Screaming and shouting within the villa began in earnest. Bolan swept his scope across the veranda and quickly around the grounds. People were running in all directions. Bolan abandoned his sniper rifle and rose.

Manning was already up and moving downslope at a run toward the house. Bolan scooped up the FAL assault rifle on the tarp beside him. He clicked a NATO fragmentation rifle grenade onto the launching rings and dropped to one knee. The four guards were still on the veranda, firing their AKs on full auto in all directions. Bolan's rifle bucked, and the grenade looped through the air and detonated on the veranda. Windows shattered, and the four gunmen jerked and shuddered as the shrapnel tore through them.

Bolan spoke into his headset. "Where are you, Gary?"

"I'm in the trees along the drive. Three hundred feet and closing. I'm taking the back."

"According to intel, Ransome has a regular torture tomb below the house. I'm guessing your friend is either in the bedroom or the basement. I'll come in through the front. Don't go below until we link up."

"Affirmative, Striker."

Bolan fixed another grenade onto the muzzle of his battle rifle and sent the CS tear-gas round through the already shattered windows that opened on the veranda. He put another grenade in place and began loping down the hillside. People were running out of the house in all directions. Most of them were half-dressed and clutching assault rifles of various makes. The door of the carriage house was torn off its hinges as someone drove a Land Rover through it. Half a dozen men with machine guns ran out of the house and piled into the vehicle. The Land Rover fishtailed on the gravel drive and lunged forward as its wheels suddenly found purchase. A woman with a kerchief on her head and wearing an apron ran screaming and crying from the house. She still clutched a wooden spoon in her hand. She ran into the middle of the drive and waved both arms desperately at the men in the Land Rover. The vehicle did not stop for her.

The man behind the wheel gunned the engine and ran her down.

Bolan knelt and flicked the ladder of the grenade sight to one hundred meters. He aimed the grenade between the two panels of the Land Rover's windshield and fired. The glass punched in and an orange light flashed within as all of the windows blew out. The engine died and the vehicle slowly veered off the drive and crumpled its front bumper against a tree. Black smoke snaked out of the shattered windows.

Bolan flicked the FAL rifle's selector to full auto as he rose and closed in on the villa. "Manning, what's your status?"

"I'm at the back door. Have deployed CS on both floors. Five hostiles down. About seven made it past me, but they were all hired muscle and they're beating it for the trees."

Bolan did some math. There were supposed to be no more than ten to fifteen gunmen in the house, and according to Bolan's calculation most were accounted for. Of course, the morning had already proved to be full of surprises. "Any sign of Blondie?"

"No." Manning was silent for a moment. "Striker, I don't like that guy. He didn't blink when Ransome went headless. He moved. He moved like lightning, and he's still MIA and on the premises."

Bolan didn't like the blond man, either. "I'm approaching the front," he said. Bolan came out of the trees and gunned down two men with a burst from his rifle. The front door was standing wide open with a grayish-white gas billowing out of it.

"I'm at the front door. Going in."

Bolan pulled his gas mask over his head and checked the seal. He swung around the doorjamb and moved into the house. Two women were sitting on the floor of the hallway choking, crying and clutching each other. One looked up at Bolan's masked face and screamed.

Bolan roared through his mask. "Where's the woman?"

The women kept screaming. Bolan pointed his rifle and their screaming stopped.

Bolan repeated the demand in French. *"Ou est la femme?"*

One of the two women flinched away from the rifle. "Downstairs! She downstairs!"

Bolan jerked the muzzle of his rifle at the front door. "Run!"

The women jumped up and ran. Bolan swept into the living room.

"Striker, I have you in sight. I'm in the hallway to your left. Hold your fire."

Bolan and Manning linked up. "Gary, according to the maids your friend is downstairs. We—"

Bolan and Manning leveled their rifles. A man ran into the room and lurched to a halt. He wore a police uniform, and was carrying a machete in his free hand. His other hand was occupied holding a white woman in bra and panties over his shoulders while she tried to knee him in the face with her bound legs and pounded on his back with her manacled hands. He stood staring at Bolan and Manning with streaming, horrified eyes.

"You are both…under arrest," he stated weakly.

Manning stepped forward and pointed his rifle a foot from the man's forehead. "Talk."

The man dropped his machete to the tile floor with a clatter. He threw the woman on the couch and put up his hands. He tried to smile as he hacked and coughed. "I have information. Very important—"

The man staggered as he was stitched from behind with automatic fire. Bolan's rifle roared in his hands on full auto. The blond man had appeared down the hallway. His pistol snarled back. Bolan took hits on his armor and fired back. Sparks flashed in the man's hand as he leaped back out of sight down the hall. Bolan lunged to the door and sprayed his weapon around the doorframe. A door slammed shut at the end of the hall.

Manning knelt beside the woman and pulled the gag out of her mouth. "Heather!"

He pulled up his mask. His eyes and teeth gleamed out of the green, gray and black camouflage paint concealing his features.

The woman choked and gasped. Her reddened eyes flew wide. "Gary?"

Manning glanced around. He scooped her up and took her to the bathroom off of the foyer. "Stay in here, lock the door and turn on the shower to run water into your eyes. We have to clear the house!"

Manning sat her on the edge of the tub and left, slamming the door behind him. He joined Bolan in the hallway. Bolan peered around the corner. There was blood on the floor. There was also a CZ-97 machine pistol with blood on the grips. Bolan's eyes narrowed behind his mask. Only two kinds of people used machine pistols. Idiots and experts. Bolan glanced back over to the couch and the ex-Nigerian policeman lolling across it in bloody ruin.

Blondie kept adding up to trouble.

Manning read Bolan's mind as he glanced at the gun and the blood on the floor of the hallway. "Well, now, he's one-handed trouble."

Bolan emptied his magazine into the doorway down the hall. Manning did the same as Bolan reloaded and moved forward in a crouch. Manning came up alongside as Bolan kicked in the door.

The door opened into a spacious study. The gas had not reached this part of the house, and Bolan pulled up his mask. A massive portrait of Uwaifor dominated the wall behind a gigantic desk. Traditional Nigerian shields with spears crossed behind them were mounted on each wall along with hunting trophies and numerous awards and government citations. A pair of double glass doors opened out onto the side yard. Floor-to-ceiling windows looked out onto the back. The double doors were open, and their curtains blew in the morning breeze. Blood stained the glass panels by the double brass knobs.

"Looks like Blondie beat it for the bush," Manning observed.

Bolan kept his rifle shouldered as he scanned the room. There was another interior door off to the left. "Maybe." He indicated the closed door.

Manning moved off to one side and kept his rifle aimed at the door. Bolan scanned the room again. There was something wrong. Every hard-won battle instinct in Bolan's body tingled. The Executioner looked at the massive oak desk laden with papers. Uwaifor might actually have done legitimate government business from this room. Bolan gazed hard at the closed door. There were no bloodstains on the knob.

Manning stood motionless. "I don't think he's in there."

"I don't, either." Bolan looked around the room again. His eyes locked on to the wall behind them. There was a tribal shield mounted on it, as well. The shield was askew and there was a bloody handprint on the wall next to it.

The two spears were missing.

"Gary!"

Manning spun. Bolan brought his rifle around bucking on full auto. The glass windows shattered as the iron elephant spear flew like a lightning bolt. Manning staggered as the weapon sank into his chest and slammed him against the wall. His knees buckled, and he slid down the wall into a sitting position. The blond man dodged away from the windows as Bolan tracked him.

Bolan tossed his rifle away as it clacked open on an empty chamber. He pulled a frag grenade from his web gear. The safety lever pinged away as Bolan lobbed the bomb out the shattered window. Bolan dropped behind the massive desk as the grenade detonated outside with a crack.

Bolan rose with his Beretta 93-R in both hands and looked at Manning.

"I'm okay." Manning waved his hand feebly. "Go!"

Bolan swung his pistol in an arc before him as he went out the double doors. There was more blood on the landing. Steps led down to the yard. A heavy iron spear lay abandoned in the manicured grass. The lawn ended fifty yards away. White-washed clay walls separated the colonial villa from the verdant tropical forest surrounding it. Bolan noted the bloodstain at the top of the wall. The wall was ten feet high and topped with strings of barbed wire.

Blondie had done the fifty-yard dash and cleared the wall and wire in about seven seconds.

Bolan went back into the study. Manning groaned and pushed himself up. The immense spear lay at his feet. The body armor over his heart was cut open in a wide, ragged slit.

Tufts of Kevlar fibers stuck out, and the dark gray of the underlying solid trauma plate was exposed.

Manning winced as he pushed on the plate with his fingertips. He shook his head in wonder. "The bastard cracked it! Jesus! Can you believe that?"

Bolan stared at the spear. It was made almost entirely of iron. The thirty-inch leaf-shaped blade was designed to penetrate an elephant's hide and the mass of muscle beneath to reach its vitals. Woven Kevlar armor was not up to the task. Only the boron-carbide trauma plate beneath had saved Manning from being skewered from front to back.

Manning scooped up his rifle. "You get him?"

"No." Bolan shook his head. "The guy had six, maybe seven seconds. He took the open ground like a fullback and then pulled a Superman over the wall."

Manning nudged the spear at his feet. "You know something else?"

Bolan was pretty sure he didn't want to know. "No, what?"

"You shot that machine pistol out of his right hand."

"Yeah."

"He threw that spear with his left."

Bolan gauged the distance. The iron spear had been thrown through a plate glass window, traveled twenty feet and nearly pinned Manning to the wall like a bug. The math on the guy kept turning up ugly. "You know, he was wounded, and he could have escaped, but he stuck around to try and kill us."

Manning rubbed his chest. "Yeah, I kinda sense he wanted us dead."

"There was something he didn't want us to find."

Manning shrugged. "Yeah, or maybe it's because we saw his face."

"Maybe." Bolan holstered the Beretta and reloaded his rifle. "We clear the house, clean up and extract. Five minutes."

Bolan and Manning swept the house room by room. The basement was every bit the dungeon of horror of local rumor.

They also found forty kilos of heroin and about a million plus change in Euros, English pounds and U.S. dollars.

They emerged from the bloodstained chamber below. The fetid air still resonated with the unimaginable atrocities that had been committed there. Manning was tight-lipped. "We leave the money and the drugs for the authorities to find?"

Bolan sighed. Much of western Africa was wide open as far as crime was concerned. "The money they'd keep. The drugs they'll shoot up themselves or sell." Bolan pulled a white-phosphorus grenade from his belt. "We burn it. Burn it all down."

The Executioner pulled the pin and tossed the grenade down the cellar stairs. Manning retrieved Heather West from the bathroom and took her outside away from the gas. They had found handcuff keys downstairs, and Manning unshackled her. She stared at the Canadian in wonder. "What the hell are you doing here?"

"My job." Manning grinned. "You all right?"

West maintained the composure that had kept her cool in crisis spots on every continent in the world save Antarctica. "I've been kidnapped, beaten and fondled inappropriately, but I'm glad you showed up before the real fun started." She wasn't able to suppress the shudder that shook her shoulders. She covered with an arched eyebrow. "You know, I didn't believe you when you told me you were a journalist in Sarajevo. I checked with Reuters. They've never heard of you."

Manning changed the subject. "We've got a boat to catch."

Bolan went back to the veranda. "One more thing," he said.

Bolan reached into his webgear. The face of the blond man's friend was hamburger, but Bolan believed he could give a sketch artist a decent description. Bolan pulled out a kit and quickly fingerprinted the corpse. He looked around the gore-spattered tiles and then stooped to reach under the table.

His hands closed around the wooden case the blond man had given to Uwaifor. Bolan flicked the latches and opened

the case. The Executioner stared at the contents. Nestled in red velvet was a knife. The sheath and the handle were of matching silver. Raised scrolling of vines and flowers covered the hilt and the sheath.

Bolan drew the knife.

It came out of the silver sheath with an ugly rasp. Its six-inch length was roughly shaped like a chef's knife, and there was scalloping along the back spine. Bolan held it up. "Mean anything to either one of you?"

Manning shrugged. West's eyes were still red and swollen as she blinked at the blade. "Nigeria has hundreds of tribes. All of them seem to have their own regional cutlery variations." She matched Manning's shrug. "I don't know what it means, if that's what you mean."

Bolan snapped the case shut and thrust it into his bag. Heather West had been rescued unharmed. Ransome Uwaifor and Tunde Addo were terminated and their operation smashed. The mission was a complete success.

Bolan had a very bad feeling the mission had only begun.

Stony Man Farm

"We got lucky on this one." Aaron "the Bear" Kurtzman shook his head in wonder. "We got real lucky. We got a match on the set of prints you brought back. I don't know how you pulled this guy out of your hat in Lagos, but you hit the jackpot."

"He was strictly sideshow." Bolan examined the computer composite sketch. It matched the blond man's associate on the terrace to a tee. The fingerprints were inset along the bottom of the composite. Bolan looked at Kurtzman. "So who is he?"

"He's not a sideshow. He's a genuine bonus attraction."

"Okay, so who is he?"

Kurtzman paused for drama. "Razi Thamud."

Bolan had heard the name before. "He's Tunisian, isn't he?"

"By birth," Kurtzman agreed. He handed Bolan a thick file. "He's a child of the jihad by profession. Kind of shadowy. One of those guys we can't prove anything about. But the CIA has photographic evidence that he was friendly with Saddam Hussein and Khadaffi, and there is pretty good evidence he's been in contact with leaders of Islamic Jihad and shares some connections with al-Qaeda. He comes from a very wealthy North African shipping family. The Agency believes that most of his activities have been financing and facilitation. However, rumor has it he doesn't mind getting his hands dirty. No one's been able to link him to anything directly, though. He's also been spotted hanging around Indonesia and the Philippines."

Kurtzman sat back in his wheelchair. "Anyway, your little adventure in Nigeria has made him a nonissue."

"Yeah, but what was he doing there?" Bolan swiftly scanned Thamud's CIA file. It was interesting, but it told him nothing.

"Bear, Uwaifor was a heroin dealer. He had a nice setup, his own personal little feudal kingdom, but he was strictly small potatoes. If he hadn't personally irked Gary by kidnapping Heather West, he would never have shown up on our radar."

"Well, Uwaifor was a heroin dealer, and an elected magistrate. So there's money and political influence."

"So what?" Bolan shook his head. "Thamud could find heroin, money, guns, anything he wanted or needed in the Mediterranean and the Middle East and one hell of a lot easier and safer. According to his file he was a very cagey guy. Why would he deal with a Nigerian heroin cowboy, much less one who's abusing controlled substances, himself? Uwaifor was a mess waiting to happen."

"Okay, I'll bite." Kurtzman smiled. "What are you implying?"

Bolan frowned. "I don't think Thamud was in Lagos to see Ransome Uwaifor."

The Stony Man computer expert raised an intrigued eyebrow. "You think he was there to see Blondie."

Bolan's frown deepened. "It's just a hunch."

Kurtzman had learned profound respect for Bolan's hunches. "Okay, again, why?"

"I don't know." Bolan looked up from Thamud's file hopefully. "We get anything on Blondie's prints?"

"Nope, and we got a complete right-hand set from the knife case. His fingerprints don't exist in any database I have. Nor anything Akira's broken into in the last six hours." Both of Kurtzman's eyebrows rose. "An elephant spear, left-handed, from thirty feet. That's pretty impressive."

"Yeah, he was a pretty impressive specimen."

"Well, I don't want to sound like a broken record, but what was Blondie doing in Lagos hanging out with a pissant drug lord like Uwaifor? And what was he meeting with Thamud about?" the Bear asked.

"You said it yourself," Bolan replied. "Thamud was a facilitator. He was facilitating something. Uwaifor was at least nominally Muslim, and he supplied guns and money to some of the Islamic militants in northern Nigeria. Mostly so they could kill his political opponents. But he was dabbling and put his finger in the pie, nonetheless. Thamud would have heard of him. I think either Thamud introduced Blondie to Uwaifor, or Uwaifor introduced Blondie to Thamud." Bolan straightened in his chair. "Blondie gave Uwaifor a knife. Anything on that?"

Kurtzman punched a key on his computer and brought up the file on the knife. A digital photograph of the filigreed sheath and the knife appeared on the huge flat screen. "Cowboy didn't recognize it. I've given Akira a secondary task cross-referencing the knife design with everything he can find on West African knives. It's a pretty Byzantine task, to say the least." Kurtzman sighed and sank back into his seat. "What are you thinking? You think it was some kind of a thank-you gift?"

"I don't know." Bolan mentally reviewed the set of gold teeth Ransome Uwaifor had exposed at the gift. "It seemed to have more significance than just thanks."

"What do you mean?"

"I mean Uwaifor was giddy like a schoolgirl when Blondie presented it to him." Bolan stared hard at the image of the silver-handled knife in its silver sheath. "Unless a knife like that means something locally, I think…" Bolan's voice trailed off as he ran Uwaifor's giddy, gold-toothed smile through his mind again and again.

"You think what?" Kurtzman prompted.

"I don't know. It was his reaction when he received it. Either Uwaifor was a rabid knife collector and Blondie had just completed his collection—"

"Which you aren't buying." Kurtzman knew Bolan's thought processes better than most people. "Or?"

Bolan's eyes narrowed. "I think it was like a pledge pin."

Kurtzman's eyes widened. "You mean like a welcome to the club."

Bolan rose. "I need that knife identified, Bear. Something bigger is going on here."

Kurtzman chewed his lip. "Striker, don't you think we ought to give Hal or possibly the President some kind of mission statement or—"

"I've got some things to arrange, and then I have to catch a plane. Tell Hal I've got a bad feeling. Tell him I'll call him when I touch down."

"Touch down where?" Kurtzman already knew the answer to the question as he asked it.

"Back to Lagos." Bolan paused in the doorway. "Then probably Tunisia."

The council chamber

"WHAT HAPPENED, Fredi?" The three men at the table waited for Fredi to answer. Fredi let them wait while he took a chair and sat down heavily at the council table. It had been an ugly run through the jungle and an even uglier ride upriver. It had taken several ugly hopper flights to get him to an airport he felt was secure enough to risk a flight on a real airline. He was exhausted and jet-lagged. Fredi flexed his wounded right hand and grimaced at the dazzling spray of pain that shot up his arm. During his twelve-hour run through the jungle, his hand had gone septic. It had taken another eighteen hours to get home. The antibiotics and the emergency surgery required to save his hand had not done anything to elevate his mood, either.

He glanced over at Robi through red-rimmed eyes. "We were attacked."

Robi's brother, Gusi, shifted his immense frame in his chair. "What is the status of our transaction with Uwaifor?"

Fredi shook his head wearily. "Someone blew his head off."

"What about Tunde?" Gusi's massive skull tilted slightly. "Can we still do business with him? He seemed like the smarter of the two anyway."

"Someone blew his head off," Fredi replied.

The third man steepled his fingers and leaned forward. His thick, black hair fell about his shoulders. His flat black eyes were interested rather than alarmed or disturbed about the news. "And Thamud?"

Fredi leaned his head back and closed his eyes. "Someone blew his head off, too."

Gusi stared, puzzled. "Someone was doing a great deal of head shooting."

"Indeed." The dark one leaned his frame back into his chair. "Brains, brains everywhere, and not a thought to think."

Fredi blinked, Gusi scowled, Robi shook his head. All three men wondered, and not for the first time, whether or not Wilbur was genuinely insane. Wilbur ignored their stares. He had personally considered doing business with Uwaifor a brainless idea in the first place. The cranial fireworks that had gone down in Lagos only confirmed his opinion. However, he diplomatically changed the subject. "Tell me, Fredi, do you think the sniper was specifically trying to kill you, too?"

Everyone around the table pondered the unthinkable.

"No." Fredi shook his head. "Uwaifor was the primary target. Then the shooter took out Tunde. I do not believe Thamud and I were targets at all. Thamud was shot when he pulled out that carbine with the grenade launcher he keeps in his suitcase. It made him a threat to the sniper up on the hill. Two men assaulted the villa. They scattered the remnants of Uwaifor's men and effected the rescue of the woman. I heard them shouting in English. I suspect that they were English or Canadian special forces, and extracting the woman was their primary mission. However, they had seen me and Thamud, so I decided they needed to be killed."

Gusi spread his huge hands on the tabletop. Wilbur, Fredi and Robi were all six feet or taller with the physiques of Greek gods. Gusi was about five foot nine and about five feet wide. His limbs were like huge rounds of lumber. His craggy skull appeared to be carved out of stone. He peered at Fredi beneath the thick shelf of his brow. "And did you kill them?"

Fredi sighed. "They had body armor, automatic weapons and assaulted the villa with gas. We exchanged fire, and I was wounded. I was driven back and could not lay hands upon a firearm, so I extracted over the wall."

Gusi frowned with obvious displeasure.

Robi was more conciliatory. Every man at the table had an ego the size of a mountain. They all knew they could not allow those immense egos to interfere with their plan as it was about to go into operation. "That was probably the smartest course. We could not afford to have you captured."

"They would not have recognized Fredi." Wilbur glanced out from beneath coal-black brows. "But Thamud's face is known. They may well have recognized it before they blew it off."

Gusi shrugged his Herculean shoulders. "So what? There is nothing to tie him to us. He is just a face."

"Well, I am intrigued," mused Wilbur, whom they called "El Negro" behind his back. "I do not believe the Canadians have the logistic wherewithal to put a special forces operation into Lagos, particularly on such short notice as the woman's kidnapping. The whole situation stinks of Americans."

Robi nodded. "I would agree. What is it that you are thinking?"

"I am thinking they will try to investigate. However, I believe their assets in Lagos will be extremely limited. I believe they will have to expose themselves to do any real fact-finding. I find myself vaguely curious to find out what sort of men could give our dear Fredi such difficulty."

Fredi's fist clenched despite his stitches.

Gusi smiled very slowly. He recognized the look in Wilbur's eyes.

El Negro continued. "As you have mentioned, they have no idea who Fredi is or what he represents. All he is to them is a face that is in no database they have access to or would even think of trying." He suddenly rose from his chair with the lazy grace of a dangerous animal. "I am not even a face to them."

Robi arched an eyebrow in amusement. "And?"

El Negro's disturbing smile lit his eyes. "I think I am going to round up a few of my fellow faceless friends. Then I'm going to take a little trip to Lagos and see what develops." He paused before he left the room. "It is all very well to sit on a hill and blow off people's faces with a high-power rifle." His hand went to the knife at his side. Each man carried one just like it. "It is quite another to look in a man's eyes while you carve his face from his head."

3

U.S. Embassy, Lagos, Nigeria

The CIA station chief only had to look Bolan up and down once. "You're the one who rescued the journalist."

Bolan's smile neither confirmed nor denied. He held out his hand. "Cooper."

"Dudley." The chief took Bolan's hand. "Marc Dudley."

Bolan had done his research. The large black man in the impeccably tailored suit had been a highly decorated Ranger in the Gulf War and had risen through the ranks until recruited into the CIA paramilitary teams. During a mission in Bosnia he had gotten too close to some high explosives, and one of his eardrums had been perforated. It had left him with unacceptable hearing for the paramilitaries and prevented him from diving. However, Dudley's mind was by far his most valuable asset. He had become an agent and asked to be stationed in Africa. He had become chief of his own station in record time. Marc Dudley was a highly capable man.

The station chief knew absolutely nothing about Bolan save what his instincts told him. They told him the man he was shaking hands with was as stone cold an operator as he had ever met. Dudley grinned. "So what can I do for you, Cooper? I've been informed I should offer you every courtesy." He gestured at the pot of coffee and a silver tray on the sideboard of his office.

"Thanks." Bolan took a seat and opened his briefcase. He took out a file and handed it to the chief. "If you've got the time, I have some sketches I'd like to show you."

"Oh, good, I love sketches." Dudley opened the file and snorted at the sketch on top. "Ransome Uwaifor, dead." He glanced up at Bolan. "Nice work."

Bolan said nothing.

Dudley flipped to the next with a grin. "Tunde Addo, toast." He peered up at Bolan. "You gonna autograph these for me?"

"Keep going," Bolan urged.

Dudley flipped to the next sketch and stopped. "Razi Thamud?"

Bolan nodded. "You know him?"

"I know of him." Dudley's eyes narrowed again. "What's the connection?"

Bolan studied the man across the desk and his instincts spoke. He liked Dudley. He decided to put his cards on the table. "I was hoping you could tell me. The only connection I have is that Thamud was sitting at the same table as Uwaifor and Addo when they got whacked."

"You're joking."

Bolan smiled. "No."

Dudley peered at the sketch again. "You know, by the time some of my local contacts in the police force got there, the entire villa was burning out of control, and there were bodies everywhere. They had to identify Uwaifor and Addo from their dental records. You positive about Thamud?"

"One hundred percent."

Dudley snorted. "You know, I thought you might be." He nodded at the sketch of Thamud. "Well, now, this is a fascinating turn of events."

"Try the next sketch."

Dudley flipped to the next one and his brow furrowed.

Bolan leaned forward slightly. "You recognize him?"

"I don't know." Dudley's eyes seemed to be trying to stare through the sketch. "I can't put a name or a place to him, but I could swear I've seen him somewhere."

"Six foot two or three, built like a fullback..." Bolan prompted. "Expert shot with a machine pistol, ambidextrous, can hurl an elephant spear like an Olympic javelin."

"You know, you associate with the most fascinating people." Dudley glanced up from the sketch of the blond man. "White boy here was at the table that morning, too."

It was a statement, not a question.

Bolan nodded. "Oh yeah, he was there."

"Is he DOA, too?"

"No, he's MIA."

"Really?" Dudley examined the sketch the same way he had first examined Bolan. He did not like what he saw. "He looks like a real world-class asshole. Sounds like one, too, the way you describe him."

"He is. Death in both hands." Bolan met Dudley's gaze and held it. "And he's succeeded in piquing my curiosity."

Dudley didn't flinch before Bolan's eyes. "So, they were all having a little powwow that fateful morning?"

"Yeah, I'm real curious about that, too."

"So am I. I at least like to think I have a vague idea of what's going on around here. This makes me look bad."

Bolan nodded. "I was surprised, too."

Dudley fanned out the top three sketches with a sly smile. "Not as surprised as these three." Dudley finished his coffee and rose. "Let's go for a walk, Cooper."

Tin-Can Island, port district, Lagos

"YOU ARE SURE?"

The Nigerian glanced down fearfully. Few people were capable of looking El Negro in the eyes when he was smiling, save those who were his own kind, and even they sometimes felt a little nervous. The informant flinched as men seemed to appear in the alley like smoke and surround him. They were dark skinned like himself, but the way they held themselves told the Nigerian that they were far from local talent. The man facing him looked like no man he had ever seen. The predatory smile stayed on his face as he fanned out five hundred Euros in his left hand. He held up the sketch they had compiled from Fredi's description and gave the Nigerian a long look. "Be sure."

The Nigerian was a street criminal with a very nasty reputation. His hard-earned belief in his own toughness failed him before the man who stared at him unblinkingly, and the lanky, loose-limbed, grinning men he had with him. "Yes, mister. We watched the airport. The white man you described did come. He went to the United States Embassy. He is being watched. I have ten of my boys on it."

El Negro loomed over him. "Do you know who this man is?"

"N-no." The Nigerian pressed himself against the wall of the alley. "Who?"

"He is the man who murdered Ransome Uwaifor and Tunde Addo."

The Nigerian's jaw dropped. He had worked indirectly for Uwaifor. Most street criminals in this quarter of Lagos did. Uwaifor's power, the legitimacy he had achieved as a politician and his partying lifestyle had elevated him to god status among the up-and-coming criminals in Lagos. The killings of Uwaifor and Addo and the burning of his palatial villa by parties unknown had sent shock waves through the Nigerian underworld.

El Negro noted the man's reaction and continued. "The white man is a mercenary. He works for the CIA. I am given to understand that the CIA station chief, Dudley, has helped the FBI root out your American contacts for transactions across the ocean."

"Yes." Dudley had been at the forefront of the American effort to stop the flow of African drugs into the Americas. He had so far proved impossible to corrupt or kill. "Yes, he has—"

"He has done this because he is a lackey of the whites. The CIA intends to take over the heroin trade in Nigeria. Killing Ransome was simply the first step."

The Nigerian's eyes widened. West African heroin had recently been only a West African problem. Now that it had gone international, the Nigerian drug lords had suddenly begun running into unpleasant American acronyms like CIA, FBI and DEA. El Negro's words only confirmed his worst suspicions. The flat black eyes of the big man were hypnotic.

"They consider you and your people less than monkeys. Monkeys that have somehow stumbled upon a gold mine. The Americans, the white men, they intend to take your gold mine from you with their mercenaries and their tribeless Negro slave soldiers like Dudley. They will kill all your big men. They will kill young warriors like yourself so that you will not become big men who can threaten them. They will take the big money and let the weakest traitors among you scramble on their knees for the pennies they would toss you. They will take your heroin. They will take your finest women. They will reduce you to little more than slaves in your own trade. They will—" El Negro paused significantly "—colonize you again."

Anger kindled behind the Nigerian's eyes. He had no more than a third-grade education, but from the southernmost tip of South Africa to the northern shores of Morocco, there was one word that rang with bitterness and shame for every African.

Colonize.

White mercenary had a similarly ugly ring.

El Negro's words walked like spiders across the web of the young man's mind. He knew every button to press, and it amused him to kindle the flames of patriotism in a savage, codeless street criminal. Nationalism was a tremendous motivator of men. So were money, drugs, guns and power. Mixed together, they made quite a cocktail. "Ransome Uwaifor was a big man, and when the white men murdered Uwaifor and Addo, they also murdered friends of mine. I intend to see these white men dead. Will you help me?"

The man blinked with sudden nervousness at the idea. The man standing before him was certainly not African. His hair fell in loose blue-black waves to his shoulders. His skin was the color of saddle leather. "This white man is a mercenary, a soldier, as you say. Dudley is a spy. They will be hard to kill. I would need—"

"Money," El Negro suggested happily. "And guns. These things I have. You have friends, do you not? Many friends and associates? Friends who would help you kill the white man and his slave traitor? If they were given money and guns, and our enemies were delivered into their hands, at a time of our choosing?"

The criminal considered. He had tracked the big white man from the airport. He walked with the presence of a mountain, and the CIA man, Dudley, was rightly feared. "I do not know, I—"

"I will give you one million Euros." El Negro smiled at the shocked look in the petty criminal's eyes. "I will supply you with all the guns you need. Also, I would remind you that Uwaifor and Addo are dead. There must be new big men in Lagos to fill the hole their loss has left." He put a comradely arm around the young man's shoulder and led him to the back of the alley. Two limousines were parked behind a warehouse. "I would like to show you something."

One of El Negro's men opened the trunk of one limousine, and the street criminal stared in renewed wonder. The trunk was neatly stacked to bursting with a mix of shoebox-sized bales of stacked and bound one-hundred-Euro notes and kilos of heroin.

El Negro smiled as he watched the flames of pride and avarice twine on the Nigerian's face. He motioned to another man, who threw open the trunk of the other limousine. It was piled high with dozens of Russian submachine guns. He watched the slow smile suffuse the Nigerian's face. He put his hand on the man's shoulder again and leaned close as he threw the final piece of kindling onto the fire.

"My friend, who better to take the place of Ransome Uwaifor than the man who avenges him?"

Lagos, Nigeria

THE EXECUTIONER ATE goat stewed in peanut sauce. It was delicious. The walls of Mama Jacqueline's Jam House were lined with photos of Bob Marley, Fela Kuti, Muhammad Ali and Nelson Mandela. Strangely enough, one wall was devoted to Elvis Presley, who was currently blaring across the tinny-sounding stereo speakers. Bolan and Elvis were the only white presence in the thronged room. Elvis seemed fine.

Bolan was getting some strange looks.

Dudley grinned over his beer. "You nervous?"

"You want to eat good Yoruban, you go where the Yorubans go." Bolan grinned over a forkful of goat. "This is delicious."

"You got that right. Listen, I've been thinking about Thamud's presence and what you—"

Bolan spun in his seat as Dudley's eyes flared. People in the restaurant suddenly began screaming. Men with guns were bursting through the hanging beads that comprised the front door. One man brandished a submachine gun overhead while pointing a machete at Bolan like a judging finger of razor-edged steel.

"Colonizer!"

The Beretta 93-R was already in Bolan's hand. He brought the pistol up from under the table, and his 3-round burst walked up the man's sternum and toppled him across a pair of screaming patrons. A howitzer erupted behind Bolan and nearly blew out his right eardrum. The thunderclap flopped the second man through the door like a puppet with its strings cut. Bolan dropped to one knee while Dudley dropped to the other side of the table with an immense stainless-steel revolver held in both hands. The revolver boomed, and Bolan's machine pistol snarled. The next two men through the door bounced against each other and jammed the doorway for a split second before falling.

Hell erupted as the men outside began firing.

Bolan threw himself flat. The front window shattered inward in a cascade of razor-sharp shards as over two dozen men began opening up. Bolan grimaced at the crescendo of muzzle-blasts and the hundreds of supersonic booms whip-cracking overhead. The assassins were amateurs, and they were emptying entire magazines into the restaurant. But someone had equipped them with Russian Bison submachine guns, and they were each burning sixty-four high-velocity rounds per trigger pull.

"Jesus!" Dudley snarled, and his revolver boomed above the spiteful ripsawing of the submachine guns.

Nelson Mandela, Fela Kuti, Muhammad Ali and Elvis took the brunt of the barrage as the inexperienced killers emptied their weapons and their muzzles climbed and stitched the walls with hundreds of bullets. The crescendo faltered as the killers' weapons suddenly began racking open on smoking empty chambers. They fumbled fresh drums from their jackets.

The Beretta 93-R trip-hammered in 3-round bursts that stitched the reloading killers where they stood on the sidewalk. The men behind them ripped their weapons back into life and the sheer firepower forced Bolan to hit the floor.

"Christ on a crutch!" Three more men fell dead to Dudley's revolver, and the stainless-steel pistol clicked dry. Dudley rolled under the table and broke open the spent pistol. He produced a speedloader and shucked in six fresh shells. He snapped the cylinder shut and brought up the weapon as a torrent of bullets ripped into the tabletop and chair backs less than two feet above his and Bolan's heads. "Sooner or later these shitheads are going to get lucky!" Dudley shouted.

"You think?" Bolan had dropped the spent Beretta. Each of his hands came out of the pockets of his leather jacket holding a grenade.

"Damn!" Dudley grinned like a crazy man and began firing his revolver as fast as he could pull the trigger. Bolan pulled the safety pins with his thumbs and the cotter levers of both grenades pinged away as he opened his hands. He pushed himself up and lobbed both grenades toward the front of the shattered restaurant.

"Shut your eyes!" He warned Dudley.

The concussion wave of the flash-bang grenade rolled through the restaurant, and Bolan saw the veins of his eyelids as they lit up orange in the glare of the magnesium flash. After the deafening bang Bolan could not hear the hiss of the CS tear-gas grenade breaking into its individual bomblets and spreading irritant gas from multiple high-pressure nozzles. He snatched up his Beretta. "Kitchen! Go! Go! Go!"

Bolan threaded his way toward the kitchen. The floor between the tables was jammed with huddled patrons screaming and crying. Bullets flew like bee storms overhead. Bolan broke from his crouch and leaped for the kitchen doorway to cover Dudley. The big CIA chief was charging for the kitchen. One of the killers came choking and screaming through the expanding gas. He held a submachine gun in each hand like giant pistols. Both weapons waved out of control as he held his triggers down. Dudley's door-filling physique blocked Bolan's shot.

"Down!" Bolan flung himself aside as Dudley slid through the kitchen door. Brick and mortar flew like shrapnel into the kitchen as the shooter hosed down the landscape and screamed for Dudley.

"Slave traitor!" the man screamed.

Dudley ducked down beside an oven and reloaded his revolver. "Did he just call me a slave trader?"

Bolan slid a fresh magazine into the Beretta. "I think he called you a slave *traitor*."

Dudley's eyebrows drew down dangerously. "That's messed up."

Bolan agreed.

"Ransome and Tunde call for vengeance!" the man screamed. Multiple submachine guns firing on full auto ripped pans from hooks and smashed crockery as everything in the kitchen more than four feet off the floor was riddled. A pair of cooks crouched hugging each other by the refrigerator. They stared at Bolan and Dudley in terror. Bolan fired a 3-round burst back through the kitchen door. Nearly five hundred rounds answered back.

Dudley snapped his pistol shut. "The car's parked out back."

"They'll be waiting for us." Bolan stared meaningfully at the narrow scaffolding of stairs that led up from the kitchen. "Death from above?" he asked.

"Lead on," Dudley replied.

Bullets began tearing through the back door from the alley. Bolan hugged the floor as he moved and then scrambled up the steps. The boards creaked dangerously beneath his and Dudley's weight. Bolan pushed open the trapdoor. The second floor was a loft filled with sacks of rice, potatoes and charcoal. Bolan had to stoop. He moved to the window facing the alley. He pulled open the double panes and glanced out. Dudley's Renault was parked where he had left it, except that the hood was up and most of the engine's hoses and wires were ripped out. A Volkswagen van and a convertible Thing were parked blocking the Renault. Bolan counted a dozen heavily armed men filling the alley. The back door below smashed open under one of their boots, and the men in the alley began spraying their weapons into the kitchen.

Bolan and Dudley began firing down into the killers. Six men fell before the survivors managed to register surprise and look up. Four more fell as they raised their weapons. Bolan and Dudley exchanged fire with the remaining two men. The Russian submachine guns spewed bullets into the eaves of the restaurant. Bolan and Dudley aimed rounds at the body mass.

Dudley's voice dropped an octave as he shoved his last speedloader into his revolver's cylinder. "They messed with my ride."

"Yeah." Bolan nodded.

Bolan put a foot on the windowsill and jumped. The Volkswagen Thing bounced on its springs as he landed in the back seat. He stood up and vaulted over the driver's seat and slid behind the wheel. The chassis shrieked and scraped cobbles as Dudley nearly went through the floorboards.

"Go, man! Go!" Dudley urged.

Bolan didn't need encouragement. Gears ground on the ancient automobile. The tires spun on the wet cobbles, and the car suddenly lunged forward as they gained a grip. Shouts and gunshots echoed in the alley, but Bolan left them behind as he yanked the wheel and took the Thing down a side street at breakneck speed. "Friends of yours?"

Dudley shrugged as he kept his eye and the muzzle of his revolver trained behind them. "They called you a colonizer."

"They called you a slave traitor."

Dudley scowled.

"You recognize any of them?" Bolan asked him.

"I think, maybe." Dudley nodded grimly to himself. "That two-gun bastard. I know his face. I'll have to get in touch with a contact I have on the police force and check mug shots."

"They'll be watching the Embassy and your house." Bolan eyed the narrow back streets of Lagos as he whipped the car through them. "You got a convenient safehouse?"

"No. Hell no. Screw the safehouse. All we need is a little intel and some great big guns and we go rolling thunder on these assholes tonight."

Bolan glanced at Dudley's massive stainless-steel revolver as he crawled into the passenger seat. Bolan scrutinized the pistol's matching nickel-plated Tyler-T grip adapter, bobbed hammer and the cutaway trigger guard. Dudley wore his religious convictions in his shoulder holster. "A wheelman, huh."

Dudley nodded without taking his eyes off the street behind them. "Yup."

".44 Magnum?"

"Nope, .41. The .44 wastes too much time and energy." The big man shrugged. "A .357 is all right for women and men with weak hands."

Bolan smiled in recognition. "Elmer Keith, *Sixguns*."

Dudley's smile lit up his face. "I admire your taste in literature, Cooper. Head for the river."

4

Tin-Can Island, Lagos

"You failed."

Henry Abayomi squirmed under El Negro's unrelenting gaze. He had taken the stranger's guns, money and drugs, and the white man and Dudley had outshot him and thirty-five of his most dangerous and desperate associates. Abayomi had fled the scene in the van with five of his friends, all wheezing and choking from the gas. The police had met the rest of them, and one of the most horrific gun battles in the history of the streets of Lagos had ensued. Nearly all of them were dead or in jail. Abayomi had gone to his girlfriend's house on Tin-Can Island and hidden in her concealed cellar.

El Negro had shown up, unannounced, in the middle of the night and pulled Abayomi up like a turnip.

El Negro's frightening friends had come with him. The lanky, dark-skinned men spoke to one another in a language that wasn't any of a dozen dialects that Abayomi had a smattering of. All Abayomi could tell was that they were speaking about him with a mix of amused scorn and speculation. But the strange men were the least of the criminal's problems. His new Russian weapons had been taken from him before he was even fully awake.

Abayomi sat in a wooden chair in the kitchen. He did not know where his girlfriend was and was much too concerned about himself to ask. El Negro stood looking down at him. El Negro was not amused. "And you let them get away."

"But I—"

"Were there more than just two of them?" El Negro already knew the answer to his own questions. "Did they have reinforcements?"

"They had guns! Grenades! Gas!" Abayomi instantly regretted his outburst. He examined his shoes miserably. "You did not warn us."

El Negro was silent for a moment. That much was true. He had observed the battle from a restaurant several rooftops away. Fredi had been right. The American commando was indeed a very dangerous individual, and Dudley's reputation for toughness had been well proved. The two Americans had stood shoulder to shoulder and shot it out like no one El Negro had seen before.

Still, El Negro did not approve of failure. Henry Abayomi had failed. The enemy had seen his face. El Negro weighed life and death. Henry Abayomi had seen his face. He had come here to clean up Fredi's mess and instead the mess was spreading. He smiled to himself. Perhaps this particular aspect deserved to be a little bit messier still. He leaned in closely toward Abayomi and lowered his voice. "Listen, this is what I would like to do."

Abayomi's scream was cut off as El Negro's fingers seized his throat with horrible strength. Steel rasped out in El Negro's free hand.

His men smiled and reached under their shirts.

It was party time.

THE THING CRAWLED down the waterway. Dudley smiled smugly as they rode through the narrow watercourses. He had not been aware that the old slab-sided Volkswagens could float, nor that the ex-military versions could be driven in the water using the wheels for both propulsion and steering. Dudley had been a U.S. Army Ranger for a number of years, and was jump and scuba qualified.

This was his first amphibious assault.

He was doing it in a Volkswagen.

They had not gone back to the Embassy or Dudley's house or Bolan's hotel room but instead had driven to some very dark corners of Lagos. They had picked up some weapons and picked up a name. Dudley was a man who appreciated powerful, old-fashioned weapons. The Ithaca 10-gauge "Roadblocker" shotgun had its barrel cut down to the forestock. The magazine held only three rounds plus one in the chamber, and the recoil would be uncontrollable save in the hands of a very powerful and experienced man. For backup, he was carrying two .41 Magnum revolvers.

Bolan shook his head. God help the man who was on the wrong side of Marc Dudley this night.

Bolan's M-2 carbine lay on his lap as he drove. The CIA Special was a relic of the Vietnam war. The barrel had been cut down to the forestock, leaving just enough muzzle to bolt on the flash-hider. The stock was from an M-1 and had to be inletted for the full-auto selector lever of the M-2 action. The metal stock was folded. Bolan had taped together a pair of 30-round magazines for a quick reload. Each was stuffed with semijacketed lead softpoints, into each of which someone— Bolan assumed Dudley—had drilled an eighth-inch hole to produce some very ragged and ugly-looking hollowpoints.

Dudley shrugged. "I know what you're thinking, but if you load them with hollow points, there's hardly a better one-shot stopper than .30 carbine." Dudley looked over at Bolan and dared him to contradict. "It's a fact."

Bolan smiled. "Jim Cirillo, *Lessons of a Modern Gunfighter*."

Dudley grinned delightedly and shook his head. "Jesus,

Cooper. If *Jeopardy!* ever had a carnage-and-mayhem week, you'd be grand champion."

Bolan shrugged modestly. "I would." He aimed the car down a side canal.

Dudley suddenly pointed at a group of scattered shacks that rode a sandbar in a loose clump. "The one on the far left. That's one of his hideouts. Belongs to a girlfriend of his."

Dudley had indeed recognized one of the men who had assaulted the restaurant. The man's name was Henry Abayomi. The house was a shack with a tin roof, though it was larger and had more frontage than most of its neighbors. One window shone with light in the back facing the canal.

Dudley slid off the safety of his shotgun. "How do you want to play it?"

"You take the front, I'll take the back? We can—"

A muted scream cut off Bolan's words. It was the scream of a man in mortal agony. Bolan stepped on the gas. The Thing's engine snarled and the rear wheels threw up rooster tails of spume. The car nosed forward through the water and lurched as its wheels hit the mud and sand of the bank. Dudley kicked down the windshield. The gears shrieked and the engine roared as Bolan clawed for torque. The ancient Volkswagen suddenly plowed uphill as it found purchase.

Dudley slumped in his seat prudently. "Damn!"

The steel bumper of the Thing met the thin mud-and-straw wall and cracked it like an eggshell. The tin roof groaned and shrieked as its rivets popped. Plaster and straw rained in all directions. Like most of the local houses, the shack was basically a large central room with add-ons. In the corner dedicated to the kitchen, six men stood around a table with knives in their hands. A naked, bloody, squirming man lay on the table. The men surrounding him were in the process of stuffing his gag back in his mouth as the car crashed into their midst. One of the torturer's hands was between the bleeding man's legs. His other hand was momentarily frozen in surprise, poised to cut something off.

Bolan stepped on the accelerator and aimed at the two men by the victim's feet. They surprised Bolan by hurling themselves into graceful cartwheels in opposite directions. One of the torturer's acrobatics was cut short as Dudley's shotgun detonated like dynamite going off. The killer ruptured in midflight like a water balloon and collapsed into a buckshot-riddled heap.

The other man's cartwheel spiked to a halt with an Olympic-quality flourish. In the same motion the man hurled his knife. The knife flew over the hood unerringly and unimpeded.

Bolan felt the burn of steel as the knife sank into his left shoulder.

The killer was already drawing a pistol from his waistband as Bolan raised his carbine. The man staggered backward as the 5-round burst of hollowpoints blossomed into bloody wounds along his torso and blew out his throat.

Two more men fell before Dudley's shotgun.

The remaining two killers were nearly blurs as they moved. Bolan barely caught a glimpse of the big man who man dived straight through the glass of the kitchen window. The other ran for the front door while simultaneously firing behind himself with a pistol.

Bolan and Dudley shot him at the same time, and the burst of carbine fire and the hornet swarm of buckshot bounced the man face first into the door he sought and left him in a bloody heap on the mat.

The VW ground to a halt inches from where Henry Abayomi lay bound and naked on the table, screaming beneath his gag. Bolan leaped from the car and kept it between him and the kitchen window. Dudley shucked fresh shells into his shotgun. He ran back to the hole in the wall and quickly glanced out. Bolan came forward as he motioned. People in the adjacent shacks were shouting in alarm.

There was no sign of the escaped man.

Dudley spoke low. "If he ran, he'd hit the water. That's

what I'd do. There are a million places to lose himself. If he did, we won't find him." Dudley let out a long breath. "Not without help, and that's going to come way too late, if at all, and require a great deal of explaining."

"Yeah." Bolan's eyes searched the dark. He remembered how the blond man had doubled back and made a very real attempt to take Manning and himself with one hand and an elephant spear. "Maybe."

"You think he's still out there?" The tritium dot of Dudley's front sight was a ghostly green eye against the darkness over the water. Both men's heads snapped up as the sound of an outboard motor ripped to life. They trained their weapons into the darkness and simultaneously wished for night-vision goggles in vain.

Bolan shook his head. "Not anymore."

"You got a knife in you, you know that," Dudley pointed out.

"Yeah, I know." Bolan motioned at the naked man on the table. It was the same man who had led the attack at the restaurant. "Why don't you see to our buddy, Henry. He looks cold."

"Why don't you sit down." Dudley eyed Bolan with concern. "You're leaking like a sieve."

"No time." Bolan walked over to the man on the table. Abayomi stared wide-eyed and trembling over his gag. Whoever his captors were, they had only begun to work on him. They had given him a few messy, painful knife cuts on his face and his hands to make him scream and warm him up for the real fun. He still had a full set of everything he had been born with.

Henry Abayomi had been very lucky.

Bolan's blue eyes burned down on the bound man. "Remember us?"

The gagged man's eyes went impossibly wide.

Bolan pointed at the silver-handled knife in his shoulder. "You see this?"

Abayomi shuddered and tried to press himself through the table. He made a horrified squeak as Bolan pulled the knife free. The squeak rose to a muted scream as Bolan shoved the knife in front of Abayomi's face. He held it there as if he were showing a dog that had messed in the house what it had done wrong. "This is yours. It was meant for you. Your balls were beneath it. You owe me."

Bolan's eyes blazed. His voice was as quiet as the grave. "You owe me your life, Henry. You owe me your balls. You owe me your unborn children. There is nothing that you don't owe me. Do you understand?"

His head bounced up and down on the table as he nodded spastically.

Bolan ripped the gag from his mouth. "Tell me you understand."

Abayomi began babbling a rich stream of English, pidgin and Hausa. It was very clear he understood and was pathetically grateful. He snapped silent and went rigid as Bolan stabbed the knife into the table beside his head.

Bolan sat on the hood of the car. "Cut him loose and tie him up, would you?" he asked Dudley as he examined his wound.

Dudley got the man off the table and neatly hog-tied him and piled him into the back of the VW. Abayomi lay in the back seat shuddering and mumbling. Bolan pulled a bandanna from his pocket and packed it against his wound.

"You look kind of pale," the CIA man said.

Bolan opened his eyes again and glanced at the knife spiked into the table. "You ever seen a knife like that?"

"No, can't say that I have. Why?"

"The blond guy I showed you the sketch of was giving one to Ransome Uwaifor right before I blew his head off."

"No shit." Dudley looked at the knife again and then at the dead men strewed around the room. "You know, these boys don't look local."

"I was thinking the same thing." Bolan looked back at the shaking, mumbling heap in the back seat. "What's he babbling about?"

"You, me." Dudley frowned. "And some guy named El Negro."

Bolan raised a fatigued eyebrow. "Who's El Negro?"

"I don't know. Not me." Dudley snorted. "The locals have some colorful nicknames for me, but none of them are that nice."

"What else is he saying?"

Dudley smiled slightly. "Henry's telling himself that you're an obeah."

"A witch doctor?" Bolan closed his eyes again. "I'm a white guy."

"Yeah." Dudley nodded. "They're the worst kind."

5

CIA safehouse, Lagos

"So why is a black man in Africa calling himself El Negro?" Dudley took another pull from his beer. "I ain't buying it."

Bolan slowly made a fist as the IV refilled his blood volume. It had taken fifteen stitches to close the wound in his shoulder, and his brachial artery had been nicked. He was definitely a few pints low, and the nurse Dudley had routed out of bed from the Embassy had demanded at least two days' downtime, preferably a week. Dudley looked perfectly prepared to sit on Bolan for at least forty-eight hours.

Bolan and Dudley had grilled Henry Abayomi for four hours and then dropped him off naked and trussed in front of the main Lagos police station. What little information he had given them was confusing in the extreme. Bolan shrugged and drank bottled water. "No, 'El Negro' doesn't sound very Nigerian, but I think for the first time in his life Henry was on the level."

"Henry said that this guy El Negro wasn't like any African he'd ever seen." Dudley polished off his beer. "And like we agreed, El Negro's boys may have been brothers, but they didn't look local, either."

Bolan stared again at the silver-handled knife in its silver sheath. He was starting to build a collection of the damn things. "So you say you've never seen a knife like that around here?"

"No, I haven't, and that's something else I've been thinking about. You know, no one in West Africa carries a knife like that." He waved his hand at the wall. The safehouse contained many objects of West African art. Dudley waved at a two-foot-long, wildly curved knife on the wall with a blade as wide as a man's hand. "People in West Africa carry knives like that. That's a panga, and would fall loosely under the category of chopper. It's your basic machete. There are about a billion regional differences in shape and materials, but all of them are basically the same. It's your West African wonder tool. The jungle is always encroaching. People who live out in the sticks use them as lawnmowers, agricultural implements—hell, a good man can build a hut, build a fire, catch, kill and clean his dinner all in one day with that alone and what he can manufacture with it."

Dudley folded his massive arms across his chest and gazed long and hard at the knife that had skewered Bolan. "You couldn't cut cane or blaze a trail through jungle with that. It looks more like a ceremonial or presentation knife. Like I said, this is West Africa, and if the brothers around here want to make something ceremonial, the brothers make it out of gold."

"It is anomalous," Bolan agreed.

"Looks more European to me," Dudley opined.

"Me, too." The wheels in Bolan's mind turned as he considered the knife. He felt a little light-headed and wished he had more blood for his brain to work with. A thought occurred to him. "European might explain the name, too."

"What do you mean?"

"Well, we're pretty sure El Negro isn't local, and we're thinking these knives that keep showing up aren't, either."

"Yeah. And?"

"Maybe our friend's name is from the Spanish."

"Well, that would explain a thing or two." Dudley

shrugged. "Actually, it doesn't explain anything. But it's an interesting idea."

"A guy calling himself El Negro in Africa is pretty stupid, I admit, but in Spain, the brothers are a little harder to come by. It's an actual nickname there."

Dudley's brow furrowed. "But what's the connection between Nigeria and Spain? Spain has some influence in Morocco and other parts of North Africa, but you got the Sahara between us and them."

"Razi Thamud is from Tunisia," Bolan stated.

One corner of Dudley's mouth twitched. "You're right. Still, for the last fifty years Tunisia has had much closer ties to France than Spain. I don't see it.

"Neither do I. Not yet." Bolan raised an eyebrow at Dudley. "How's your French?"

"Two years in high school. I get to flex it a little bit here in Africa now and again, but not much."

"How about your Spanish?"

"*Dos cervezas, por favor,* and *¿Dónde esta el baño?*" Dudley shrugged. "That's about it."

"How about your Arabic?"

Dudley gave the Black Power salute. "*Asalaam aleikum,* my brother." He opened his fist and grinned. "I learned that in high school, too."

Bolan leaned back on the couch and closed his eyes. "You're hired."

Porto-Novo, Benin

"I TOLD YOU he was trouble."

El Negro rolled his eyes. He kept his phone crooked against his shoulder while he sewed up the cuts his arms had taken when he dived out the kitchen window. He pushed the needle through his flesh. The pain didn't register on his face. Fredi was what registered on his face. Fredi was the king of

"I told you so." To his credit, he was also one of the few humans whom El Negro was not completely sure he could kill with his hands.

The other was Gusi.

El Negro bit off the end of the thread and wrapped his arm with gauze. "I think we should kill this man."

"I think we have exposed ourselves sufficiently," Fredi replied.

El Negro seethed silently.

"Robi will agree with me."

El Negro snorted. "Gusi will agree with me."

"Gusi always agrees when it comes to murder." It was Fredi's turn to snort derisively. "Gusi likes killing people."

"It is how he has advanced so far in his trade. It is how we will all advance toward our objective."

Fredi paused. The logic was hard to argue. "This man means nothing to us."

"He has destroyed our operation in West Africa. Our connections in the Middle East will have to be rebuilt. This will take a great deal of time and money."

"He has wounded your pride. It is that of which we speak."

El Negro raised his bandaged arm. He had unconsciously made a fist. His knuckles had whitened with the pressure. The corded muscle of his forearm could break beer bottles simply by squeezing. Fresh blood stained the gauze where his stitches pulled through the flesh. "And yours, Fredi." El Negro smiled at the blood oozing down his arm. "It is a wound I cannot bear. Nor can you."

"Pride kills."

"We kill," El Negro countered. "You have faced this man, as have I. He is no normal opponent. He is like no obstacle we have crushed before. He will not stop. You have sensed this."

From thousands of miles away, Fredi considered the remark. Fredi didn't personally believe in the psychic powers that some of El Negro's associates attributed to him. However,

El Negro's instincts were indeed supernaturally keen, and this man—the commando—had completely smashed the Nigerian operation.

El Negro whispered like a snake, "Blood is owed."

Fredi scowled. El Negro also had the disturbing habit of reading minds, but Fredi attributed this to the fact that they had known each other since birth. Fredi held up his bandaged hand and his scowl deepened. Blood *was* owed. Robi would say it was bad business, but they had all prospered specifically because of certain principles they had all sworn to. One of the high commandments was that no blood debt was left unpaid. The highest was to leave no enemies behind. "We will have to put it before the council—"

"Gusi will agree. If you and I and Gusi agree, Robi will agree."

"We have not consulted Nano," Fredi retorted.

"Nano will want to come and do it himself."

Fredi rolled his eyes in amusement. That was certainly true. Nano's and Gusi's public status often kept their hands out of the wet work, and both of them regretted it bitterly. "What is it that you propose?"

"I don't believe the man has gotten a good look at me. It will be a simple matter to change my appearance to differ from any description he may have gotten from Henry Abayomi. They have few if any leads left here in Nigeria. If they succeeded in identifying Razi Thamud, and I believe they have, he is the only real clue they have left and their only chance at all of compromising us. We must manipulate this lead, lure this American to a place of our choosing and kill him."

"That was what you just tried, and I believe you are all out of men."

El Negro ignored the rebuke. "So bring more with you."

Fredi laughed. "You would like me to bring you more men?"

"Yes, get a hold of some of my boys. You know where to

find them. Bring some of your own that you trust. We will not rely on intermediaries. We will do this ourselves."

"We must do more than kill him." Fredi looked at his bandaged hand again. "We must find out exactly who this man is and just what he represents. We must carve forth every bit of information from him. The information he gives us must then be confirmed."

A feral smile crossed Fredi's face as his eyes turned to the silver-handled knife on the table in front of him. "Then we shall discuss with him, at length, the blood debt he owes us."

El Negro simultaneously considered his own bloody arm and the knife he carried that was a twin of Fredi's. "Now we are thinking alike."

Fredi's smile thinned. "I would dearly love to come." He shook his head. "But I am not sure if it is wise."

"I would dearly love for you to come, Fredi. It is surely the wisest choice, and we work so well together in these sorts of situations."

Fredi considered his knife with longing. "They have my description. My face is known. They have probably distributed it to every intelligence asset they have."

"Exactly." El Negro grinned from ear to ear. "That is why you will be the perfect bait."

Fredi threw back his head. Harsh laughter echoed across thousands of miles of airspace between the two killers.

6

Tunis, Tunisia

The Executioner took a seat in the shade of the café and gazed out across the shimmering heat mirages rising from the brown cobblestones of the bazaar.

"Jesus, it's hot." Dudley mopped his brow and peered through the crowds.

"Yeah, but at least it's a dry heat."

Dudley turned and regarded Bolan unblinkingly. "You're a sick man."

Bolan nodded. It had been forty-eight hours since the fight in Nigeria, and he still felt a quart low. The ovenlike North African heat sucked the strength from his weakened body and left him feeling slightly dizzy.

Dudley watched, mildly appalled, as a string of camels heavily laden with dates lurched, groaned and drooled as they passed by. "God, get me back to the jungle." He finished his mint tea and poured himself and Bolan another round. "You think this Gassim guy is going to show?"

Bolan sipped his tea. It was a good question. American intelligence assets in North Africa were thin. American assets in Tunisia were downright anorexic. Tunisia was a small country and geopolitically not of great strategic importance. While she had some oil and phosphates, Tunisia was not a petroleum giant like some of her neighbors. The greater part of the Tunisian economy was still based on agriculture. Bolan had given the description and the sketch of the blond man to the local CIA station, but he hadn't hoped for much.

However, he had gotten a bite.

The local CIA man had called in a favor with the much more substantial French intelligence presence. They had produced Gassim ibn Khalil. U.S. intelligence knew nothing about the man. The French had been unwilling to give up Gassim for interrogation. They apparently considered him an important asset, but they had been willing to set up a meet. Gassim knew of both the blond man and Razi Thamud. He was willing to give up some information as long as he was not implicated.

And for a price.

Bolan squinted into the mob in the bazaar. "This has to be our boy."

A man came sauntering out of the crowd past sellers of melons and copper kettles. He was large, and people made way for him. He wore the burnoose and striped brown shawl of the men who lived in the deep desert. He had a short black beard and mustache, and a huge *jambiya* dagger was thrust through his sash. He looked like a movie caricature of a North African nomad, save that he walked like a man who had spent long years in the saddle. His skin was burned mahogany by the desert sun, and thin lines radiated out from the corners of his dark eyes from squinting against it. He walked up to the table and looked at Bolan and Dudley for a long moment. A startling white smile broke out across his face. His English was thick, but articulate. Bolan noticed he spoke with an English accent. "You are the Americans."

Bolan smiled. "Have a seat."

"Ah." The man sat and looked at the two men hopefully. "Can you speak French?"

"A little." Bolan nodded at Dudley. "Him less."

"Ah, we shall struggle with English, then." He sighed and took some tea. "You are looking for the German."

Bolan and Dudley glanced at one another.

"The German. Fredricht." Gassim's dark brows drew together slightly. He took a piece of paper from inside his tunic and unfolded it onto the table. It was a copy of the sketch Bolan had relayed to French intelligence. Gassim tapped the blond man between the eyes with his finger. "Him."

Dudley shot Bolan a glance. Bolan kept his eyes locked with Gassim's. Gassim didn't blink. Bolan asked, "How did you recognize us?"

"How could I not?"

Bolan raised an amused eyebrow.

"Very well." Gassim shrugged elegantly. "I shall tell you something for nothing."

"What's that?"

"Fredricht is interested in you." Gassim took two more sheets of paper from his tunic. The sketches were much cruder than the one Kurtzman had generated at the Farm, but they were clearly Dudley and Bolan. Gassim sighed. "In certain places, your descriptions have been circulated. There is a price upon both of your heads."

Bolan measured the big man from the desert. The nomad's face was unreadable. Bolan had dealt with North African nomads before. Normally such men were very subtle in their dealings. Getting information and making deals was a game of chess; beating around the bush was considered an art form. This guy was coming right out and throwing all the cards on the table in the opening round. Bolan didn't like it, but he kept his face pleasant.

Dudley sipped some tea. "You ever heard of a guy named El Negro?" Dudley emphasized the Spanish vowels.

The man pondered the name for a long moment. "'The dark one?' From the Spanish?"

"Yeah, mean anything to you?"

Gassim gave Dudley a confused look. "Well, there are many with dark skin in Tunisia, but it would be a strange name. Few here speak Spanish." He shrugged in defeat. "I am considered to have dark skin by many, but I am a Berber. You mean one who is dark, like you."

"Yeah, that's what I'm thinking."

"Fredricht has a number such as those who work for him, but I have never heard that name."

Bolan set down his tea. "Tell me about Fredricht."

Gassim looked squarely at Bolan. "Fredricht is a very bad man."

"Tell me about his hands," Bolan continued.

Gassim smiled and stared at Bolan very pointedly. "One of them is injured."

Bolan and Dudley glanced at each other. They were on to Blondie; the question was how did Gassim fit into the equation? "Tell me more about him."

"You seek him, so you know of him." Gassim's poker face remained set. "I cannot tell you more."

Dudley smiled in an unfriendly fashion. "Why not?"

"It is in my power, perhaps, to help you find him. Then, whatever business you have between you…will occur. However, should you fail, and if it is obvious to him that you knew of his activities here in Tunisia, one of his prime suspects as to how you came by such information shall be myself. As I have said, Fredricht is a very bad man. Any aid I give you must be—" Gassim sought a word "—oblique. Whatever the outcome, my hands must remain clean if I am to remain safe, and to stay in business."

Dudley shook his head. "I don't like it."

"I think you will like meeting Fredricht even less." The Berber sat back and waved a dismissive hand. "I have been told that the United States is very nice. Perhaps you should go back there. While you still can."

Dudley glowered. Gassim seemed unmoved. Bolan poured

the Berber some more mint tea. "Tell me, why would you betray Fredricht to us?"

"Why, for money." Gassim looked upon Bolan as if he were simple. "I am told you are willing to pay a considerable sum in American dollars to he who can cause you and Fredricht's paths to coincide. I like American dollars." Gassim smiled. "Men of the desert love that which is cool and green."

"But you do business with Fredricht." Bolan smiled back. "Do the men of the desert betray their business partners so easily?"

Gassim scowled. "I do not *do* business with Fredricht. I have *done* business with Fredricht, and I will tell you something else for nothing. I did not enjoy the experience. Fredricht is a very bad man, and I am not his partner. Fredricht does not have partners. Those who do business with Fredricht end up one of two ways. Working for Fredricht, or dead. It has been my personal observation that that which Fredricht puts his fingers in, he soon closes his fist around. I do not wish to be enclosed by the fist of Fredricht. It confines, it squeezes and it strangles. I have seen it. I have felt it, and by the will of Allah it was my great good fortune to escape it."

Gassim leaned forward and extended a finger at Bolan. "I will tell you another thing. I do not believe you wish to do business with Fredricht. I believe blood shall be spilled in the streets of Tunis. In such a situation, one must choose sides. I have traveled to Libya. I have friends in Iraq, and other places, and I have learned that when blood must be spilled it is best not to bet against Americans. In the desert, I can do business unmolested and unseen. However, if I attract the wrath of your United States by being on the wrong side in this matter or by betraying you, I know that I cannot remain unseen from your satellites. I have heard of the black helicopters. I do not wish to wake in the night to find a platoon of your Special Forces friends outside of my tent. I have many reasons to wish Fredricht joined with the bones of his fathers. Many of them are highly personal. That I would do it for American dollars, for freedom from Fredricht and for the indifference, if not the goodwill, of the United States, are all the reasons that you should require of me. If they are not…"

Gassim gave his elegant shrug and reclined in his chair again.

Bolan sat back in his chair. "Two million."

Gassim's eyes flared only for a moment, and he regained his poker face. "Five."

"Four. Two when you give us the information that leads us to him." Bolan patted the black suitcase that rested by his knee. "Two more when I have his head."

Gassim cleared his throat. It was clear they were talking about sums of money larger than he was used to. "And what if it is Fredricht who separates your head from your shoulders?"

Bolan's eyes were tombstones in his head. "Then light a candle for me, take your two million and ride deep into the desert as fast as you can."

Gassim's eyes seemed to remeasure Bolan. "I am right." He nodded to himself. "If blood is to be spilled, never bet against the Americans."

Tunis Carthage International Airport

BOLAN COCKED his submachine gun. The French MAT-49 was slab sided, and except for its bolt and barrel it was made entirely of stampings and welded sheet metal. Its telescoping wire stock looked as if it might have been made out of a coat hanger. Nearly all of its blue finish was worn off, and as a whole the weapon was a diseased, phosphate-gray color.

It looked like a piece of junk.

However, it was a dependable weapon. The MAT-49 had performed in Algeria and Southeast Asia and was beloved of French soldiers everywhere. Bolan examined the top round in one of his spare magazines and noted the splash of red paint on the base and the black tip with satisfaction. France had been one of the last countries in the twentieth century to adopt an assault rifle. Their submachine guns had soldiered on long after other nations had gone to gas-operated rifles. As a stop-gap measure they had beefed up the 9 mm ammunition they issued for their submachine guns. The French-made armor-piercing incendiary rounds would fly at sixteen hundred feet per second and were for submachine guns only. They would blow up most any handgun that attempted to fire them.

Dudley was appalled. The weapon looked like a toy in his huge hands. He held it as if it were a dead rat. "Man takes me into harm's way and gives me a squirt gun."

Bolan smiled. "It's the best your local boys could do on short notice."

Dudley grumbled to himself as he shoved a Manhurin .357 Magnum revolver unhappily into his belt.

Bolan shrugged as he holstered his own .357 and put a silenced PPK in the holster at the small of his back. He checked his watch. The plan was to meet Gassim, who would personally take them to the place where they could catch up with Fredricht and have a little talk. Bolan hunched his shoulders into the straps of his parachutes.

Bolan had changed the plan.

They had a good satellite photo of the meet point. Like most North African cities, once you got past the more modern edifices, the local neighborhoods were a bewildering maze of flat-roofed clay buildings. Few, if any, had street signs. If you didn't know how to negotiate the spiraling alleys, then it was clear you didn't belong there. They were also perfect places for ambushes.

Bolan didn't trust Gassim. He didn't intend to drive up with two million dollars in a four-cylinder Citroën sedan. Bolan looked over at their plane. The single-prop French Criquet looked about as old as their weapons.

"Great little plane. I love it." Jack Grimaldi grinned as he ran a hand over the worn wooden prop. "Love it, love it, love it."

"Then let's do it." Bolan and Dudley checked each other's

chutes and clambered into the Criquet's cramped interior. "Jack, you have the coordinates?" Bolan asked.

Grimaldi waved a satellite map. "*X* marks the spot. Listen, this was the best plane we could arrange on a timetable as short as you're running."

Bolan nodded. "It's a nice plane."

"Yeah, but it's 1950s technology. It's about a billion degrees outside, and between me, your fat asses and all your gear, we're pushing well over seven hundred pounds. This bird is going to max out its altitude somewhere in the low teens, and it's going to take an hour of shallow climbing to get there. I don't have any oxygen, and you boys don't have the time."

Dudley looked up. He had earned his jump wings the hard way. "So no HALO."

"No, no high-altitude low-opener out of this bird. Not tonight." Grimaldi looked to Bolan. "Low-altitude low-opening, or do you want something in the middle?"

"Low, real low." Bolan checked his watch. "The meet is set for dusk. There's no way we fly the plane high enough not to be noticed, and we don't have the time to waste. So I say we buzz them and hit them at the same time. I want to go real low. Like base-jumping low."

Dudley raised a leery eyebrow. "I've never done a LALO."

"It's a gas. You'll love it." Grimaldi pushed his starter button and the Criquet's little four-cylinder engine fired. "Here we go!"

"APPROACHING TARGET! I'm taking her down to five hundred feet!"

It was nearly dusk, but heat still shimmered up from the twisting, compact, brown sprawl of Tunis. Bolan held his pilot chute in his hand. There would be no time for rip cords or standard deployment. An average base jump was seven hundred feet. They were jumping from five hundred. Their chutes were packed without bags and were free inside their rigs.

Dudley looked distinctly unhappy with the situation.

Bolan shouted over the wind of the open doors. "Listen! This is going to be a matter of seconds! There's going to be some significant line stretch and probably no time for a decent flare and a stand-up landing. We're going to have to—"

"Do a parachute landing fall!" Dudley shook his head in disbelief. "I know!"

"Five hundred feet! Twenty seconds to target!" Grimaldi shouted.

The wind whipped at Bolan as he stepped out the door. He grabbed the Criquet's wing strut and put his foot on the landing gear. Dudley did the same on the other side.

"Ten seconds!"

Bolan looked through the cramped cabin. Dudley's eyes were wide as dinner plates beneath his goggles as he watched Tunis whip by beneath his feet. Bolan shouted as the wind tried to tear them from their perches. "You all right?"

Dudley nodded.

"Go! Go! Go!" Grimaldi roared.

Dudley went. Bolan jumped a split second later and threw his pilot chute. The chute caught wind and snaked up behind him. The city flew up at Bolan as if he had been shot from a catapult. They'd caught a break on the target. Nearly every house in the old section of Tunis was identical. The target house had a swimming pool that formed a blue oasis in the unrelieved sea of brown blocks and courtyards and gave them a reference.

Dudley's chute deployed.

Bolan grimaced as his own chute deployed and line stretch cinched his harness around his torso like a boa constrictor and squeezed the air from his lungs. Bolan took his one available second to survey the target.

They were supposed to meet Gassim out on the street. Gassim was there standing beside a parked van. From his vantage, Bolan also saw there were men with guns in the alley behind the meeting point. In each of the two adjoining streets there was a pickup truck with more armed men.

It was a trap.

Bolan roared into his radio to Dudley. "We have company!"

"No shit!"

There was no more time. Bolan aimed himself at the roof. His eyes flared as he realized they were screwed. Most roofs in Tunis were flat. The satellite photo had not shown them the pitch of the roof. The clay tiles of the house were at a distinct slope pointing downward.

"Dudley! The roof is—"

Dudley flared for all he was worth and hit. A parachute-landing fall was a desperate attempt to spread the hit over your entire body and hopefully not break any bones. Tiles shattered beneath Dudley's boots as he hit. He torqued his body over and then hit with his knees, hips, side and shoulder and then rolled. Dudley's parachute landing fall was textbook. A professional jump master would have wept with joy had he seen it. The fact that the roof was sloped assisted him. It also assisted his momentum. Dudley continued to roll. In fact Dudley was tumbling.

And he couldn't stop.

Dudley flailed his limbs to no avail as he rolled. The CIA man got his feet under himself but he had way too much forward velocity. Dudley pushed off with both feet and windmilled his arms through the air as he ran out of roof.

Dudley went into free fall over the courtyard and disappeared.

"Christ!" was the last thing Bolan heard.

Bolan hit.

Tiles exploded beneath his feet as he plunged straight through the roof.

Timbers tore. Splinters ripped at Bolan's hands and face as clay shattered and broke around him in a shower. Screams greeted him as he dropped into empty space. Bolan suddenly yanked up short as his lines caught on something. He hung suspended seven feet from the floor.

Two men with AK-47s sat on a low sofa smoking cigarettes. They stared up at Bolan in utter disbelief as he swung in the air. Bolan unclipped the MAT-49 from his webbing and yanked the magazine down and in place with one swift movement. The submachine gun began hammering in his hands as the men started to stand. The two 5-round bursts sent the two men down gurgling and slumping.

Bolan drew his knife and slashed at the cords holding him aloft. He swung to one side as the lines parted and then dropped as he cut the last. The jolt went up his ankles as he hit the tile floor. Bolan did an about-face and moved for the courtyard.

Outside, people were shouting.

Bolan came to a blue wooden door and cracked it open.

Dudley was in the swimming pool. Three more men with rifles had the drop on him. Dudley held his submachine gun over his head gingerly and tossed it away into the deep end of the pool as one of the men jerked his weapon in that direction.

Bolan stepped through the doorway firing.

Two of the three men were cut down before they knew what was happening. Dudley's .357 appeared with sleight-of-hand suddenness, and the third man jerked backward and toppled as the CIA man put three rounds into his chest.

Dudley slogged up out of the pool trailing his sodden chute behind him. He shook his head wearily. "Some jump." He clicked out of his straps and threw away his MAT-49's spare magazines as he scooped up one of the fallen rifles. They moved swiftly to an outer door. Dudley cracked it and leaped back as bullets tore through the blue wood.

The ex-Ranger shook his head as his combat drop went from bad to worse. "What are they shouting?"

"That we're in here." Bolan's eyes flared as he heard a sizzling whoosh from outside. "Down!" he yelled.

Bolan and Dudley hugged tiles as the grenade hit the door and blew it into smoking blue splinters. Bolan rolled and sprayed his weapon through the smoldering doorway. Dudley fired a burst from his captured rifle and kicked himself clear of the line of fire. Bullets were streaming through from dozens of guns.

Bolan pulled the pin on a white-phosphorus grenade and tossed it through the door. The gunfire outside died down slightly as streamers of burning, molten metal spewed out of a cloud of white-hot gas.

Bolan rose and ran back across the courtyard and Dudley followed.

"I didn't see anyone on the eastern corner as we dropped!"

"Let's do it!" the CIA man agreed.

Bolan and Dudley swept through the house. Dudley paused only to loot spare magazines from the fallen on the couch. They burst into the kitchen and found a man with a rifle yelling into a phone. As the man turned, Dudley nearly lifted him out of his shoes with a buttstroke from his weapon.

Bolan snatched the phone out of the air before it could fall. Dudley grabbed the man and pinned him to the counter before he could crumple. Bolan raised the receiver to his ear and listened to the shouting voice.

Bolan recognized the voice.

It was Gassim.

Gassim was shouting in Spanish, and he wanted to know what the hell was going on.

A hard smile froze on Bolan's face as he spoke into the phone. *"Buenos dias, El Negro. ¿Como estas?"*

There was a long silence on the other end of the line. *"Muy bien. ¿Y tu?"*

Bolan perked an ear as the house shook. It sounded as if someone had just rammed a car into the front gate he and Dudley had abandoned. Bolan switched to English. "I'm a little busy."

El Negro continued in English. "Tell you what, friend.

Surrender immediately, and I won't let the Tunisians slice off your nuts."

"I'll take a pass, *amigo*. I saw the little party you were about to have with poor old Henry in Lagos. I think you're saving that gig for yourself."

Bolan could almost hear the man smiling on the other end of the phone line. "You have not been in contact with your intelligence source in Nigeria, probably because he is with you in the house. Had you checked within the last four hours, you would have found that Henry Abayomi is currently in the Lagos morgue, and he is without his nuts."

"Thanks for the info. Gotta run." Bolan hung up the phone.

The problem with most older North African houses was that they were shaped like hollow blocks and had few if any outer windows. Everything faced inward toward the courtyard.

Bolan informed Dudley, "Henry Abayomi is dead."

Dudley was unfazed. "Couldn't have happened to a nicer guy."

"And I'm pretty certain El Negro is from South America."

"Now that is interesting." Dudley cocked his head at the sound of running feet outside. "Sets me to thinking."

"Oh?" Bolan slipped a fresh clip into his weapon.

"Yeah, I'm suddenly having the hunch that El Negro's buddies, the ones who were brothers but we didn't think were African? I'm betting they were Brazilians."

"Well, that's an interesting observation." Bolan listened to the gathering noise outside. "I think they have the house surrounded."

"I think you're right."

"How much C-4 do you have?" Bolan asked.

"About a pound. You?"

"The same. Listen, here's what I'm thinking. They've got the house surrounded and the doors covered. There are no doors on the eastern side."

"So we make a door." Dudley smiled.

The man Dudley was holding was shaking his head and beginning to spit teeth. "What about Lucky, here?"

Bolan leaned forward and asked the man in Arabic where Fredricht was. The man's eyes narrowed with lucidity, and a stream of profanity spewed forth from between his bloody lips.

Dudley yanked the man forward by the front of his shirt and crashed his forehead into the bridge of his nose. Cartilage cracked and blood spurted as the man's eyes rolled back in his head. Dudley let the man fall unconscious to the floor. "Let's go make a door."

Bolan took out a block of C-4 and stripped off the adhesive backing. They stopped midway down the hall. Bolan reviewed his mental map. "I make it middle of the street, east side."

Dudley nodded in agreement. "I believe you."

Bolan pressed the block against the wall and pushed in a detonator pin. They both moved down to the opposite doorways at the ends of the hallway. Bolan raised his tiny remote. "Fire in the hole!"

They ducked around the doorways as Bolan pushed the button. There was a loud thump, and heat and powdered clay blasted in all directions. Bolan immediately moved through the dust and stench. A three-foot smoking hole let in the diffused orange light of the North African dusk.

Bolan leaped through.

Bolan looked up and down a narrow alley and saw nothing. Dudley came through the hole. They only had seconds before they were caught in the open.

"Which way?" Dudley asked.

Bolan looked up and down the alley again. The gutter at his feet caught his eye. It was one of the nice things about the French. Whatever their other social failings, for the past hundred years any city they colonized had a beautiful sewer system.

"We go down!" Bolan pointed at the ancient-looking iron grating. "Blow it!"

Dudley knelt and pressed his block of explosive up under the clay behind the grate. He and Bolan ducked and covered as Dudley hit the detonator. The sewer grating leaped, twisting and spinning into the air on a plume of vaporized clay.

Bolan looked up at the buzz of small engines.

A pair of unarmed men came around the corner on motorcycles. They were looking behind in wide-eyed horror, probably at the gunmen filling the streets. Their heads snapped around at the sudden sound of the explosion. Bolan gave them no time to examine their options. He leaped up and swung his right arm around like an iron bar and clotheslined one of them beneath the collarbone. The man went buttocks up and fell to the road in a stunned heap. Dudley raised his rifle to his shoulder, and the other man dropped his bike and hit the ground running. Dudley fired a few shots over his head to keep him honest and on his way.

Bolan righted his fallen motorcycle and rolled it into the gaping hole in the alley.

Dudley suddenly dropped his own vehicle and went for his gun. "Shit!"

Men came around the corner with rifles.

Bolan brought up his weapon and stitched the first man with a burst in the chest. Bolan and Dudley stood and exchanged fire with the other three. The men shuddered and fell as bullets tore through their torsos.

"Move!" Bolan whipped back around. "We've—"

Bolan cut short. Dudley was sitting on the ground. He'd been shot through both legs. He looked up at Bolan and shook his head in bemused outrage. "Goddamn!"

Bolan seized Dudley's arm and heaved him up. "Can you walk?"

"I can walk out of he— Shit!" Dudley's legs collapsed beneath him.

"Then you're driving!" Bolan grabbed Dudley by his web harness and dragged him to the open sewer. He jumped down and heaved the big man down after him. The drop was six feet, and Dudley's weight spilled them both to the floor.

Bolan righted the fallen bike and yanked it back onto its kickstand. He heaved Dudley out of the muck and set him on the seat. He flopped the big man's bleeding legs onto the foot rests and pressed the starter button. The little engine sputtered and buzzed into life. The feeble headlight came on and illuminated the long dark passage ahead. The bike creaked on its springs as Bolan climbed on the back. "Go!"

Dudley cranked the throttle, and they lurched ahead through the sewage.

"Take the first bend you can find!" Bolan suggested.

Dudley nodded. "Roger that!"

Bolan and Dudley drove through the sewer, both waiting for the torrent of bullets to come ripping through their backs. Suddenly they came upon a branch and Dudley nearly dropped the bike as he took the turn.

"You tell me if you start getting sleepy on me," Bolan prodded.

"This whole thing was your goddamn idea. You just figure out which way to go and where we should come up."

"Look at my right wrist. What does the compass say?"

Dudley peered down at the illuminated dial. "We're heading north."

Bolan considered. "Keep going. This is a sewer, and Tunis is a coastal town. North will take us to the sea."

The little motor howled beneath their combined weight as Dudley leaned on the accelerator. "The sea it is."

7

Secure communications room, U.S. Embassy, Tunis

"We got hammered." Bolan shook his head bitterly at the computer screen. Despite his best efforts it had taken an hour to get Dudley back to the Embassy, and the big man had bled just about bone-white before they could get IVs in him and start pumping blood packs. Dudley had volunteered and had known the risks, but that didn't change the fact that a good man had nearly died on Bolan's watch. "Fredricht's friends were armed to the teeth. They were expecting Armageddon."

"They were expecting you," Kurtzman responded. "Going through the roof was a semibrilliant maneuver. If you had shown up in a frontal or flanking assault with anything less than all of Able Team in armored vehicles, you'd have gotten slaughtered."

"We got mauled."

"You got some good intel." The cybernetics expert brought up the composite of El Negro. They had combined the descriptions they got in Lagos with the image of the bearded and burnoosed man calling himself Gassim. "El Negro is South American. His henchmen are Brazilian. He's in cahoots with Fredricht."

Bolan let out a long breath. "It's all supposition."

"Yeah, but I'm buying it." Kurtzman's fingers hit keys on his computer back in Virginia. "It makes a strange kind of sense."

"Okay, so how does the German, Fredricht, enter into it?"

Kurtzman frowned. "I don't know. That one is an anomaly. I've been checking with Interpol. They have no ongoing cases or even any mention by informants of any German guy named Fredricht operating in Tunis."

Bolan stared long and hard at the two composites.

Kurtzman recognized Bolan's expression. "What are you thinking?"

"I'm thinking Gassim wasn't Gassim. Gassim was El Negro."

Kurtzman smiled. "And you don't think Fredricht is Fredricht."

"At this point, I'm thinking his real name is much more likely to be Frederico." Bolan switched screens and brought up a photograph of the silver-handled blade. "What have we got on the knife?"

"I couldn't find anything in any West African or European sources." Kurtzman smiled when he said it.

Bolan frowned. "So, what are you grinning about?"

"I got smart. I sent it to Calvin, and sent it to him blind, just asking him to tell us what he made of it without any preconceived notions of yours or mine."

Calvin James, the Phoenix Force commando, was just about the best knife fighter Bolan had ever met. His knowledge of blades and blade techniques from around the world was encyclopedic.

Bolan smiled. "What did Calvin have to say?"

"Let's ask him." Kurtzman hit a button to achieve a three-way satellite link between North Africa, Virginia, and Chicago's South Side. Within moments Calvin James's face appeared on a split screen with Kurtzman's.

"Hello, boys."

"You got the knife Aaron sent you?"

James held the knife up for the camera. It glittered in his dark hand. "Got it right here. What about it?"

"Quick question. I've picked up two of those in Nigeria, in two separate fights. One bet is they're West African, and maybe have some kind of tribal or ceremonial significance. There's also an outside chance they're Spanish or Portuguese, or even possibly North African. Any ideas?"

James snorted at the suggestions. "Where'd you say you found them, again?"

"Lagos, Nigeria."

James's eyes narrowed slightly. "Really."

"Really. Why?" Bolan was very curious.

James shrugged. "Well, this knife isn't West or North African, and it ain't from the Iberian peninsula, either, at least not directly."

Bolan allowed the Phoenix Force pro his moment of drama and then took the bait. "Okay, so what is it?"

James grinned happily. He enjoyed his rare moments of trumping the big guy. "It's a *facon*, a gaucho knife. And every cowboy riding the pampas in Argentina carries one."

U.S. Embassy infirmary

"ARGENTINA?" Dudley sipped fruit juice from a straw. His massive frame took up nearly every inch of the hospital bed. "You're kidding me."

"I have it on pretty good authority." Bolan handed the man some lilacs he bought from a street peddler. "Here. Get better soon."

"Jesus." Dudley took the flowers with a roll of his eyes. "First he gives me a wussy 9 mm, then he puts me in a wussy French plane, then he takes me for a ride on a wussy little motorbike. Now he brings me flowers." Dudley raised an eyebrow. "I worry about you, Cooper."

"I suppose a hug is out of the question." Bolan was relieved to be joking with Dudley.

Dudley ignored the comment. "Well, if the lead really goes to Argentina, you may be in luck."

"How's that?"

"I happen to have a friend down there. He was in the Rangers with me before he went on to Delta Force. He was recruited by the CIA about the same time I was." Dudley smiled back in memory. "Smarter than your average white man, and a hell of a lot more trustworthy than most paramilitary spooks. He was in Colombia for a while. I have no idea what the government has had him doing in Argentina for the last two years other than getting drunk and chasing tail. Name's Doug Kubrik. You use my name. Tell him Dudley sent you. He owes me a favor or two."

"I'll do that, thanks."

"You just let me know how this all turns out. I want to know when you put El Negro in the ground. He knows my name and he knows where I live. I don't want to go back to Lagos with him still breathing."

Bolan held out his hand. "I'll give him your regards."

Dudley took Bolan's hand and shook it. "And kill that goddamn white boy Fredricht's ass, as well. I've never met him, and I already don't like him."

"They're all going down," Bolan said. "And I'm telling them all Dudley sent me."

Carthage, Tunisia

"You boys really screwed up." Gusi's gravel-like voice sounded almost jovial over the secure phone line.

El Negro and Fredi sat in a warehouse they controlled glaring and sipping tea.

"They're just two stupid *yanqui* cowboys, out of their element," Gusi continued. "In North Africa, for God's sake. How difficult could it be?"

"Three," El Negro corrected. "Someone flew their plane, and he was not local."

"I see." Gusi snorted over the phone in derision. "So now you are claiming they had air support."

Fredi snarled. "You try killing them!"

"I don't *try* to kill anything." There was a dangerous edge to Gusi's voice. "I have killed every man, woman, child and beast I ever set out to. Were it not for the risk of exposure, I would fly over there and kill the two stupid *yanquis* myself, and then beat the shit out of the both of you. Nano is so angry he is ready to fly out right now. You know how Nano is."

Fredi and El Negro bristled but said nothing. They knew all too well how Nano was. Gusi lectured on.

"I do not know who he wants to kill more, the Americans or you. I am tempted to tell him to go ahead and do both. Instead, I have spent the last hour talking him down." Gusi paused for a moment, then made his tone more conciliatory.

"Listen, I am not telling you anything new. But some of us have at least the semblance of respectability to maintain—and covers—which, at least for the moment, must be able to withstand scrutiny. We have a plan, or don't you remember? You two are the 'secret agents,' our shadow warriors, who are supposed to be able to take care of little problems like this while the rest of us prepare the way."

El Negro restrained his anger. "Dudley is a very dangerous man. That we already knew. This unknown commando, he is something else again. He operates outside of any rules. I believe he is making up his mission as he goes along. It makes him unpredictable, which is the most dangerous thing in the world."

"Yes," Gusi agreed. "I do understand. He does seem to operate outside the usual framework of CIA agents and Special Forces troops, yet he still seems to be able to call upon the full resources of the United States intelligence services. He is something of a conundrum."

Fredi flexed his wounded hand. "Perhaps we should call a meeting of the full council."

"We are all in attendance."

Fredi and El Negro sat up, startled. They could hear the amusement in Gusi's voice. "We have all been listening to your report with our undivided attention."

Fredi and El Negro shot each other a look. They had been ambushed, and if there was a vote right now, they were both already in the doghouse and they were outnumbered. It was very possible that this was a power play on Gusi's part.

Gusi seemed to read their minds. "Do not be stupid. We are a democracy, the last real democracy left. The question is what is to be done about our little problem."

Nano's voice came clear and cold across the line. "We leave no enemy behind us."

"Indeed, no enemy behind us. As we all agreed long ago." Gusi sighed. "The question, then, is how."

"Dudley is wounded through the legs and in the U.S. Embassy here in Tunis," Fredi suggested.

"I am not sure how I feel about assaulting a United States Embassy just yet," Gusi rumbled. "It could raise more problems than it might solve."

Robi spoke for the first time. "He cannot stay there forever. Sooner or later he will return to his posting in Nigeria, and then he is ours. If we kill him, I believe his friend will try to avenge him."

"What if he does not go back to Nigeria?" Nano snarled. He was still clearly angry about the situation.

Robi's tone was mollifying. "Where, then, the United States? In many ways that might be easier. You know, I suspect he has family there, and a man's family is always the best way to reach out and touch him."

Nano audibly brightened at the idea of arranging something unique and interesting for Dudley's immediate family.

"That is an excellent idea. I will begin researching it immediately," he said.

There was relief on both sides of the line. Nano was always more manageable when he had a project. He was truly a case of the Devil finding work for idle hands.

"Where is the commando now?" asked Robi.

Fredi glared at his hand again. "Probably still here in Tunis. It was where he had his last leads. I have had the Frenchmen we paid to feed information to the Americans killed. Tunisia and Nigeria are the last leads they have, and they are dry unless we choose to feed them new ones. Though, if we do, they will suspect a trap."

El Negro spoke with great reluctance. Leaving no enemies behind was one of their most important rules. The other was that there were no secrets between them. "There is one other thing."

There was a moment of great quiet on both sides of the ocean.

"Oh?" Gusi inquired.

"Yes, I had a short conversation with the commando, in Spanish."

Gusi's voice went flat. "Really."

"We have been working with our contacts in North Africa and the Middle East for some time. Almost everyone here speaks Arabic, then a local dialect, and French. I have found speaking with my local operatives in Spanish to be a quick and suitable method for giving orders I do not want generally heard or understood. The American broke across a line of communication during the assault in the house. He speaks Spanish."

"And what kind of conversation did he break into?" Nano's voice dripped venom. "I suppose you were giving out all our names and addresses?"

El Negro restrained himself. "I was demanding a situation report on what was going on inside the house. Then the American spoke. He learned nothing, other than I spoke Spanish. I believe his breaking onto the line was an attempt at intimidation."

"I do not see how this hurts us." Robi was undisputedly the

most intelligent of all of them, and all of them were sub genius at least. "So you spoke Spanish. You could have spoken in French or Arabic. What lead does it give them? Will it lead them to Mexico? Spain? Colombia? The Galapagos Islands? It was a small breach of security, but I approve of having a command language with our operatives."

"I agree with Robi," Gusi rumbled. "There has been no breach. The *yanquis* have nothing. If they show their faces in Tunisia, we have them. If they show their faces in Nigeria, we have them. We shall simply wait for them to raise their heads and then twist them off. One is wounded, and the other without leads."

Gusi's voice was ugly with satisfaction. "Where can the *yanqui* go? And what can he do?"

8

Buenos Aires, Argentina

The Executioner stared at the huge man sitting across from him.

The CIA had to be putting something in their operatives' kibble. The man across the table was six inches shorter than Dudley but about a foot thicker through the arms and chest. His hair was buzz cut barely a millimeter from a size-ten skull.

Doug Kubrik was the kind of spook who made things happen.

"So, Cooper." Kubrik was staring at Bolan with the frankness of a horse-trader examining a breed he wasn't familiar with. He didn't look up as the waitress brought them their coffee. "Dudley sent you?"

Bolan smiled. "He said I would most likely get my ass beaten, but I could try dropping his name anyway."

Kubrik snorted in amusement. "Yeah, Dudley sent you. How is the militant bastard?"

"He's in Tunisia, about two quarts low and with holes through both legs."

"Really." Kubrik's face went ugly. "Well, let's go back to Africa and kill some people."

"The trail leads here."

"Really?" Wheels turned behind Kubrik's eyes as he tried to see the connection. "How?"

Bolan took out one of the knives. "You know what this is?"

Kubrik answered without hesitation. "It's a *facon*, why?"

"Because I've got people in Africa being carved like Thanksgiving turkeys with them and other people handing them out like party favors. I also had at least one guy in Tunisia giving orders in Spanish. His nickname over in Africa was El Negro. Mean anything to you?"

"Well, just about anyone can have that name. Most Argentines are of European descent, so it could mean you're black. It could also mean you're part Indio, or it could mean most all of your family are blondies of English descent and you're the one who takes after the Andalusian uncle and has dark hair. El Negro is a fairly common nickname throughout Latin America, and it just means 'dark one.' It could have about a million different meanings."

Kubrik's words clicked in Bolan's mind. Bolan's instincts spoke to him as he thought of El Negro and Fredricht. Bolan handed Kubrik the sketches of the two men. "That's Fredricht and that's El Negro. Somehow they're in cahoots, and I'm going with your theory that El Negro is the dark one in the organization. Fredricht was supposedly German, but I'm betting that's bullshit."

"There are a lot of people of German descent in Argentina. It's a nation of immigrants. So he may have a German last name, but I'll bet you anything his first name is Frederico." Kubrik looked up from the sketches.

"Okay, so Frederico and El Negro are handing out *facons* in West Africa. Any ideas?" Bolan asked.

Kubrik shook his head. "It's odd. I don't recognize these boys, but that doesn't mean anything. I'll run their descriptions through contacts I have in the Argentine police."

"I'd appreciate that."

"What else you got?"

Bolan shrugged. "Nothing."

"Nothing." Kubrik's blue eyes widened slightly. "You just came on down here with nothing but a couple of knives and the will to succeed."

"Yeah, pretty much."

Kubrik grinned from ear to ear. "Screw this coffee crap. Let's get a beer."

Buenos Aires

NANO WAS LIVID. "Do you know who these are pictures of?"

Fredi and El Negro each stared at very reasonable facsimiles of themselves done by a computer sketch program. Fredi shrugged. He was getting very tired of being yelled at. "I don't know, Nano, us?"

"Yes, you!" Wineglasses jumped as Nano slammed both hands down on the tabletop. Nano was so incredibly handsome it was almost evil. Women swooned when he turned on his movie-star smile and sparkling eyes. With his sculpted eyebrows pointing down in rage and the light of insanity gleaming from deep within his gaze, that same smile made Nano look like Satan himself. Nano could turn each on and off like a light, and even those who had known him since childhood could not tell what was truly behind either one.

El Negro responded but the answer was clear to everyone at the table. "They are being circulated by the Americans."

"You are damn right, Negro!" Nano screamed. "The man neither of you can seem to kill is here! Looking for the both of you, which means us!"

Fredi began to rise from his chair. "I have had just about enough of—"

The table jumped again as a knife stabbed down into the ancient wood. The knife was enclosed in Gusi's huge hand. Everyone at the table stared at it, and remembered what it meant. Gusi's face had darkened, but he spoke reasonably. "We have all had enough of this American. He needs killing."

Robi pushed his gold-rimmed glasses up the bridge of his nose. He didn't need them. They were an affectation of his profession. "If he is here, he will be consulting with CIA counterparts, just as he did in Nigeria and Tunisia."

Fredi nodded. "That has been his method of operation. Who would he consult with here?"

"I have done some research." Robi produced a file and passed it around.

Nano scowled at the photo of the massive bullet-headed individual depicted. "Another cowboy."

"Another Army Ranger," corrected Gusi. He peered more closely at Doug Kubrik's file. He'd had experience with U.S. Army Rangers. Army Rangers had trained many of Gusi's men. They impressed the hell out of him. Gusi frowned. Much of the man's file had been redacted and blacked out. "But this man is not the CIA station chief, or even part of the Embassy staff," he said.

"No." Robi shook his head. "The CIA has very little in the way of ongoing operations here in Argentina. The Americans are more concerned about the Argentine economy and what Argentina is going to do with her next IMF loan. From what little my sources have been able to gather, this Kubrik is a CIA paramilitary operator. I cannot yet confirm it, but I believe he engaged in multiple operations in Colombia against the drug cartels for the U.S. government. I will have more from our Colombian contacts soon. I personally suspect he is cooling his heels here in Argentina either as a rebuke for some indiscretion or his government is giving him downtime after numerous combat missions."

"Either way he will be extremely dangerous. If he is indeed a paramilitary operator for the CIA, then he will be more than a Ranger. He will probably have gone on to join the ranks of Delta Force before the CIA hired him." Gusi shook his head. "Our mysterious American seems to have a way with picking up very lethal allies."

"They are two men with very limited options." Robi shrugged. "And they will undoubtedly still go to the United States Embassy for intelligence-gathering purposes."

El Negro scanned Kubrik's file. "These men are operators. They will surely see the Embassy as the Achilles' heel that we do. They will know that our agents will detect them and from that point we will strike out at them. They will be staging the opportunity to try and flush us out or find clues."

"Good." Nano's eyes glinted dangerously. "We wish to find them and kill them. They wish to find and kill us. Everything is as it should be, and I think it is time some of our friends whom we have shown our hospitality returned us a small favor."

Gusi's eyes widened slightly. "I believe I know what you are thinking, Nano."

"Of course you do." Nano's toothpaste-selling smile slid back onto his face.

U.S. Embassy, Buenos Aires

"STICK OUR NECKS OUT and see who swings the ax, that's our plan?" Kubrik smiled as he said it. It appeared the CIA paramilitary man did not have a problem with the idea.

"Yeah." Bolan nodded. "That's about it."

The embassy staff made way for the two very dangerous men who moved in their midst. Bolan and Kubrik moved down the hall and stopped at a cubicle. The nameplate on the outside said Kari Morgan: Cultural Attaché. Bolan smiled. "Cultural Attaché" was standard jargon the world over for a CIA spook.

It appeared that they were expected. Kari Morgan smiled at Kubrik as he and Bolan rounded her cubicle partition. "You owe me Kubrik," were her words of greeting.

"What have you got?" he responded.

"I—"

Bolan caught himself as the Embassy building shook to its foundations with a roar. Windows shattered and screams and shouts rang out throughout the building. Bolan reached for his Desert Eagle. "We just got hit."

Sudden bursts of gunfire erupted. Bolan recognized the firing signature of FN assault rifles.

Kubrik produced a nickel-plated, .45 Colt New Service revolver with a one-inch barrel, a bobbed hammer and the front of the trigger guard cut away. It looked like nothing so much as a chrome-plated, hand-crank meat grinder. Kubrik broke open the action and checked his loads.

Morgan racked the slide on a .22-caliber Beretta semiautomatic as she rapidly spoke into her cell phone.

The two men broke into a run down the hallway toward the sound of the explosion. They had to swim upstream against the flood of Embassy staff running away from it.

Bolan roared, "Down!"

Embassy staff flung themselves to the floor. Without the thicket of fleeing humans Bolan could see all the way down the hall. A man in a business suit burst through a doorway. He wore mirrored sunglasses and bandanna across his face beneath them. A rifle smoked in his hands. He whipped his muzzle around as he saw Bolan.

The Desert Eagle reacted in Bolan's hands. The gunman was slammed back against the doorjamb by the impact of the .50-caliber hollowpoint. Kubrik's gun blasted beside Bolan. The shot blew the killer's rifle out of his hands and crumpled him forward in a heap.

Smoke and dust choked the lobby of the Embassy. A pickup truck loaded with explosives had blown a ten-foot hole in the outer wall. Armed men surged around the twisted wreckage and swept toward the hall. Bolan and Kubrik took positions on either side of the door to the lobby and began firing.

The gunmen began falling in the sudden cross fire. Muzzles swung around blossoming flame, and Bolan and Kubrik put the marble of the door frame between themselves and the answering maelstrom of lead.

Kubrik broke open the action of his brutally chopped revolver and began furiously jacking in fresh shells. "We're outnumbered!"

Bolan slid his spare magazine into the Desert Eagle and racked the slide home on a fresh round. "And about to be outgunned!" Bolan dropped low and whipped his muzzle around the doorframe. The big pistol recoiled in his hand, and one of the crouching killers stood up as if he'd taken an uppercut to the jaw and then fell down again.

"Here!" A voice shouted behind them. Bolan glanced back to see Kari Morgan approaching in a crouch. She was burdened by three M-16 rifles and web belts loaded with spare magazines she had obviously looted from the Embassy guard armory.

Bolan fired a double tap through the doorway. "Kubrik!"

Bolan took a rifle and threw a belt of ammo over his shoulder. "We need one alive!"

"Can't guarantee it." Kubrik clicked the bayonet over the muzzle of his rifle. "Severely damaged, maybe. How do you want to play this?"

Bolan snapped his own bayonet into place. "Just be yourself."

Morgan brought a rifle to her shoulder. "I'll cover you."

Bolan and Kubrik went through the door.

Bolan sprayed his M-16 on full auto as he dived into the lobby. Bullets tracked him as he rolled past a desk, and wood splinters flew. The muzzle-blasts of three big rifles seemed to point straight at him as he came up. The whipcracks snapped all around Bolan, and tracers drew smoking lines as they charged him. The men shooting at him were not marksmen. The folding stocks of their rifles were still folded from concealment, and they hadn't snapped them back into place to aid their shooting. Their rifles climbed off target as they held their triggers down on full auto. These men were suicide assassins. Fanatical bravery and surprise were their technique of choice.

It wouldn't be enough against the Executioner.

Bolan flipped his selector lever to semiauto as he brought his M-16 to his shoulder. The rifle bucked against his shoulder three times in the space of a second. In that same time the heads of the three killers suddenly rubbernecked in clouds of splintered bone and gore. The three men fell forward in unison. Bolan continued firing past them as two more men leaped up and charged.

"Look out!" Kubrik screamed as he threw himself down.

Bolan did the same as another truck plowed into the wall next to the first. Orange fire expanded into the lobby and swept over the heavy wooden desk and filing cabinets Bolan lay behind. The glass partition shattered and a lethal cloud of shards flew overhead. Bolan distended his jaw to clear his ringing ears and blinked at the pulsing afterimages of the blast.

Kubrik's weapon began hammering on full auto a few feet away. Kari Morgan's rifle fired from the doorway in rapid, methodical shots. Another fifteen feet of hole had been blown into the wall of the Embassy. Part of the adjoining roof had collapsed. Gunmen were crawling across the rubble and firing their weapons. They were coming straight at Bolan. Smoke and dust filtered the sunlight streaming in from outside, turning the Embassy lobby into a choking gray-gold twilight lit by rifle fire.

The killers charged in.

Bolan shot them as they came. Two men came howling out of the smoke on Bolan's flank. Bolan shot one and his rifle clacked open on empty. Bolan dropped and clawed for a spare magazine. The other killer had sprayed his rifle empty. There was no time to reload as the assassin took his rifle by the barrel and wielded it overhead like an iron club.

Bolan rose and lunged.

The bayonet sank into the man's midriff up to the muzzle.

The killer gasped and folded as Bolan yanked the blade free. The stock of the M-16 shattered as Bolan whipped it into the side of the man's skull.

M-16s erupted from the upstairs gallery as responding Embassy guards began firing down into the warzone in the lobby.

Kari Morgan shouted from the doorway, "Rifle!"

Bolan turned to take the rifle she threw. The lobby elevator pinged and instinct made Bolan turn and draw his Desert Eagle. A man ran out into the smoking lobby. He wore a long coat and his eyes were pinholes of hatred as they fixed on Bolan. His hands came out of his pockets. The Desert Eagle rolled twice in Bolan's hands and racked open empty. The man halted as if he had run into a wall, then fell backward. Bolan charged forward at the second man who came out of the elevator.

The killer's coat flew like wings behind him as he ran at Bolan. His open coat revealed the sticks of dynamite belted to his body. Bolan ignored the searing heat as his hand closed around the barrel of his pistol. The assassin's hands came out of his pockets holding a pair of small cylinders trailing wires into his pockets. Bolan flung the Desert Eagle like a tomahawk.

The assassin leaped over his fallen companion and nearly fell as he took the four-pound pistol in the face. He faltered just a moment and Bolan closed in. Bolan seized both of the killer's wrists. The man cringed as Bolan's thumbs viciously dug into his ulnar nerves and paralyzed both of his hands. He grunted in shock as Bolan yanked him forward by the wrists, then broke his nose with his forehead. The killer screamed as Bolan crossed both of his wrists, spun and broke the man's elbows across his shoulder.

Bolan grabbed both of the man's hands. They were sweat slick and spasming.

Time was suddenly compressed. Despite his best effort Bolan could only watch as one of the thin black cylinders squirted out between their entwined fingers. The assassin's thumb came off the detonator button and it fell from his hand trailing its connecting wire.

Bolan was dead.

Bolan still retained hold of the man's wrists. He turned and rammed his hip and shoulder into the suicide bomber and threw him cartwheeling through the air into the elevator. Bolan leaped to one side. He blinked in surprise as no blast came. His eyes flew wide as he heard the twin clicks and hisses of fuses lighting.

The crippled man in the elevator and the dead man on the floor were detonating simultaneously.

There was no time for any technique. Bolan seized the dead man on the floor. His joints cracked with strain and his muscles screamed in protest as he heaved the corpse into the elevator. Bolan hit the button as he spun away to one side and hugged the wall. The elevator pinged and the doors started to close.

Orange flame rocketed between the closing metal doors. Chunks of wall ripped free and flew through the air, borne on the blast wave of smoke and heat. A great hot hand slapped Bolan across the lobby. He rolled and tumbled out of control until he was brutally stopped by solid marble.

Bolan lay in a heap against the wall and wheezed. He could see nothing but flashing yellow-and-white lights. He couldn't hear anything except a muted roar deep within his ears. Breathing was his biggest problem. He couldn't seem to get any air into his lungs and what little he could consisted of choking dust and burning smoke.

Bolan lay in what was a pretty decent approximation of Hell.

The Executioner blinked as an immense shadow suddenly loomed over him.

Kubrik was shouting something, but it sounded as if he were shouting underwater. Bolan closed his eyes. The flashing lights were much more intense, but it felt much more peaceful.

Bolan wasn't aware of Kubrik hurling him over his shoulder in a fireman's carry and hauling him out of the devastation.

9

CIA safehouse, Buenos Aires

"Mister, you dance about as close to the edge as anybody I've ever seen."

Bolan lay back on the bed and yawned against the ringing in his ears. Coming from a former Delta Force man, that was either very high praise or a very stern reprimand. The yawning didn't help, and the effort made his headache nearly blinding. Bolan glanced up at Kubrik. The CIA man's face was streaked red and blistered by flash burns. Bolan smiled sympathetically, and it hurt his face. He had no desire to look in a mirror. "We manage to capture anyone?"

Kubrik's eyebrows were gone. However, a pair of angry red muscular ridges smeared with salve bunched unhappily as he shook his head. "The ones we shot were pretty much all kills. The elevator channeled most of the bomb blast into a fireball that expanded into the lobby like a fan. The hostiles were directly opposite the elevator when their two little pals went kablooie. The ones that weren't blown to bits were turned into Tater Tots."

"How's Kari?"

"She's pissed." Kubrik smiled. "She says I owe her dinner and a night of tango on the town."

Bolan stared at the CIA man. "You tango?"

Kubrik feigned hurt. "I dance like Fred Astaire." He waved a hand at his burned face. "I like them short, dark and spicy, and with a mug like this, you have to get by on smooth moves and loutish charm."

Bolan smiled. Dudley was right. Kubrik was good people.

Kubrik shook his head. "I don't know if we're going to be able to get any meaningful data from what's left of the bodies."

"We've already got a lot of meaningful data," Bolan stated.

"Well, other than the fact that the worldwide jihad has come to South America, I don't see what we got other than our asses kicked."

Bolan shook his head and then grimaced at the effect it had on his throbbing brain. "That wasn't a terrorist attack, at least not directly."

Kubrik frowned and peered into Bolan's eyes as if looking for signs of concussion. "Uh…you lost me, big guy."

"If they wanted to blow up the Embassy and kill as many Americans as possible they would have gone about it completely differently. Like one big truck bomb. The truck bombs they used weren't bombs. They were breaching charges on wheels. Their purpose was to stun the people inside and make a door for the gunmen that Embassy guards weren't watching or could easily defend."

Kubrik considered. "Yeah, well, that was kind of strange."

"More importantly, our two suicide bombers came out of the elevator. How did they get in the elevator in the first place?"

Kubrik grimaced as it hit him. "They were already inside the Embassy."

"That's right," said Bolan, "and if they were already inside the Embassy, why the trucks and the gunmen? Why didn't they just blow it up?"

Kubrik paused. "Because that wasn't their objective."

"It was the suicide bombers who let the cat out of the bag."

Bolan ran the scenario in his mind again for the hundredth time. "I tried to stop them, but one of them still managed to let go of one of his detonators."

"Yeah, I saw that." Kubrik looked at Bolan with wary respect. "And I'll tell you something. I've never seen anyone move that fast."

"Yeah, thanks, but I still didn't stop him, and that's the rub. He didn't go off."

"So, you and I both know terrorists tend not to be the sharpest knives in the kitchen." Kubrik frowned. "And homemade bombs are uncertain subjects. Half the time they don't go off, or else they go off at the wrong time."

"No, that's not it. It was the design. Suicide bombers almost always use dead man's switches. They're holding the plungers down. All they have to do is let go. That way, even if they're shot, their bombs still go off. I was trying to keep him from letting go of his detonators, but he did anyway. But he and his friend weren't using dead man's switches. They were using proactive switches they had to detonate by pushing down rather than letting go. He didn't fail to detonate because I kept him from releasing. He didn't go off because my first move paralyzed his hands and he couldn't push down."

"Well, yeah, that's fascinating." Kubrik rubbed his massive head in thought. "But what does it mean?"

"It means our boys weren't supposed to blow up no matter what. They were supposed to blow up only when they got close enough to their objective for a confirmed kill."

"Okay, I'll bite. What was their objective?"

Bolan let his head sink back into his pillow. It was blissfully soft and cool. "Their objective was you and me."

"You and me?" Kubrik was surprised.

"Yeah."

The CIA man's face went flat. "You're saying Middle Eastern terrorists staged a suicide attack against the United States

Embassy in Buenos Aires and their objective was to kill you and one Douglas Adam Kubrik?"

"Well, killing lots of bystanders and striking a blow against the Great Satan was probably a side benefit of the job, but you and I were definitely the targets. I saw the guy's eyes when he saw me. It was recognition. There's another thing, too. Our two bombers still went bang even after they had both been disabled. Neither one punched his buttons. I'm thinking someone radio detonated them remotely when it was clear that they hadn't achieved their objective."

Kubrik raised one angry red ridge of an eyebrow. "Like who?"

Bolan challenged. "You tell me."

The eyebrow fell. "Our buddy El Negro, and his blond friend, Frederico."

Bolan smiled wearily. "You think?"

"So the guys who hit us aren't terrorists, then?"

"Oh, they're terrorists, all right. Full-on martyrs with God on their side."

Kubrik folded arms the size of fire hoses across his chest. "So what kind of leverage could Blondie and El Negro have to make terrorists do hits for them, much less suicide hits, and on a couple of jokers like you and me?"

"That's a good question." Bolan sat up in bed and ignored the room as it swam. "We're just going to have to go and ask them ourselves."

EL NEGRO SMASHED his fists mercilessly into the striking post. Sweat sheened his dark skin and his lungs worked like bellows. His hips torqued to throw every ounce of his power into every blow. That power was considerable. The straw matting padding the post was shredded and hung in bloodstained tatters. El Negro's heavily callused knuckles had split. His fists pistoned into the post like tandem steam hammers. His bloody hands met bare hardwood. They smashed away great splinters with every blow as El Negro fixated his depthless rage on the target in front of him.

Every blow smashed the life from the commando.

The *yanqui*'s bones shattered. His internal organs ruptured within the cracked cage of his ribs. His tendons tore. Muscles pulverized and blackened into paste. His face buckled into bleeding, misshapen meat capable only of screaming.

And all of that was only a prelude to the knife.

With the one thousandth blow El Negro let out a roar. His fist opened into a blunt spear. The striking post cracked like a gunshot as El Negro's hand passed through it. Shards of wood flew, and the post split down the middle as if it had been struck by lightning. El Negro stood trembling, his chest heaving. Sweat ran down his bare torso in rivers. Blood dripped from his fists onto the floor. One half of the shattered post listed like a drunk in its mooring. The last splinters holding up the other half broke, and the five-foot length of wood fell to the floor with a hollow clunk.

There was a moment of deafening silence. It was broken by the sound of solitary applause.

El Negro turned to face his cousin.

Gusi stood to one side slowly clapping his hands. He shook his head as he surveyed the blood. "You know, Wilbur, a man should take care of his weapons."

"Because a man's weapons take care of him." El Negro smiled slightly as he normalized his breathing. "I remember the words of our fathers, Gusi. I remember well."

Gusi spoke again. "Kubrik is alive."

El Negro nodded. "As is the commando."

"That is unconfirmed."

"By your agents, Gusi." El Negro threw a towel around his neck. "But nevertheless, it is so."

Gusi shifted uncomfortably as he looked into the dark eyes of his cousin. "Your black magic, Wilbur?"

"Call it what you will." El Negro examined the lines of blood running down the back of his hand as if there were things there he could read. "But I know that he is alive."

Gusi shook his head slightly. "You spend too much time in Brazil."

"You do not know enough to scoff so lightly."

The two men stared at one another.

Despite the ties of blood, El Negro had almost been denied membership in the inner cabal. It was unsaid, but throughout his life his blood had been thought too impure. The original olive complexion of his skin and the darkness of his eyes and features had always branded him an outsider. When their plan had come together, he had been unwilling to accept any position outside that of the inner circle. He had turned his back on them all, without a word, and gone off on his own.

El Negro had gone into the jungle.

He had walked into the rain forests of Brazil with nothing but his knife and disappeared. A decade later he returned from the very heart of darkness, scarred, tattooed and the phantom head of his own jungle empire of drugs, guns and gold. He brought with him millions in liquid assets, and he came with a reputation befitting his nickname. His face was unknown to the Brazilian, Argentine or any other police organization.

From campfires in the Amazon Basin to the barrios of Rio de Janeiro, it was said no one knew El Negro's face because he was a sorcerer and he could kill a man by looking in his eyes.

Gusi didn't believe that. He had known El Negro since they were children. But he knew one thing. Ten years ago, El Negro had gone into the jungle. And he had come back a changed man.

CIA safehouse, Buenos Aires

"WHAT HAVE YOU GOT on our friends, Bear?" The conversation was taking place over a borrowed CIA satellite rig. It was a generation behind what Bolan was used to.

"One confirmation." Kurtzman punched keys in blurry, not quite real time back in Virginia. "We were able to match one of the tissue samples you sent with DNA in the Pentagon terrorist database."

"Who did we get?"

"Abderahmane Khalidi."

Bolan watched information begin to scroll out on his printer. "I've read the name in a report someplace."

"He's Algerian, and on our list of wanted terrorists. He's a relatively minor player, but highly dangerous. He hung with the crowds that call for the violent expulsion of all Israelis from the Holy Land. He's a real charmer and is thought to be an organizer and recruiter of suicide bombers."

Bolan glanced at the blisters on the back of his hands. "Looks like he did his job."

"At this point my best theory is that the other men in the attack were men he recruited." Kurtzman sighed. "We need more DNA samples. Dental records would be helpful. However, I understand most of the bodies were in pretty bad shape."

Bolan shook his head as he read Khalidi's file. "It's worse than that. Kubrik took the samples, and they were quick and dirty ones before the Argentine police arrived. The police took possession of the bodies, and according to Kubrik he is getting zero cooperation. The whole thing is being played as if America had brought its dirty laundry to Argentina. The papers and the politicians here are having a field day with it."

"Well, in a way, we have. You were the target, you know."

"No, the dirty laundry was already here, and whoever soiled the sheets is trying to clean up the mess." Bolan stared hard at the file. "Their choice of weapons and how they got access to them is what interests me."

"You mean the guns and explosives?" Kurtzman frowned quizzically. "The explosives they used were standard—"

"No, the guns and explosives were the implements. The terrorists were the weapons, and last time I checked, suicide squads based on religious fanaticism usually aren't for hire."

Kurtzman saw where this was going. "They did it because they owed somebody."

"They owed Blondie and El Negro. And they owed them for a lot more than Nigerian heroin, French guns in North Africa or sets of fancy Argentine steak knives."

"I got a call from Hal." Kurtzman didn't look happy. "The President isn't exactly sure what you're up to or what's going on."

"If it makes him feel any better, neither am I."

Kurtzman rolled his eyes. "You know, Hal just loves telling him that."

"I know," Bolan agreed, "but something is going on down here in Argentina, Bear. It's ugly, and it's a lot bigger than we can imagine at the moment."

"Well, other than a dead lead with the DNA, I don't know what else to do from my end."

Bolan smiled. "Well, that's good, because I have a job for you."

Kurtzman perked up. "Oh?"

"Yeah, you mentioned the guns." Kubrik had been a busy man running in and out of the flames while Bolan had been unconscious. Bolan looked at the two FN-FAL rifles lying on the bed. The black plastic furniture was further blackened and bubbled by fire, and much of the finish had been scratched or burned off by the blast. "I'm almost dead certain these are Argentine military issue."

"That's almost a given." Kurtzman peered at the beat-up

weapons across the link. "It's almost certain they were stolen from the Argentine military, as well."

"At least reported stolen. I'm going to give you the serial numbers. Grab Cowboy, and have him and Akira hack into Argentine army, navy, marine, and air force records. Find out what lot these weapons came from and who they were issued to. Find out if they were rotated, re-issued or transferred to someone else. Look for anything that looks funny in their service life. If it turns out they were reported stolen, find out where they were stolen from, who the officer in charge at the time was and, for that matter, find out who was ultimately in command of the base or the region. I need a total breakdown. I need it yesterday."

"Jesus, it'll take time to—"

"Grab Encizo. I don't care where he is, but yank him and get him to the Farm. The records Akira is going to hack will all be in Argentine Spanish, and Rafe knows the local idioms. I don't want to lose any pertinent details to some translator program of Akira's."

"Okay, what are you going to do, meantime?"

Bolan grinned wearily. "I'm going to sleep for about eighteen hours. Then I'm going to enjoy reading what you got for me."

10

San Telmo District, Buenos Aires

El Negro examined his strike teams.

One team was made up of Muslims. They were men from all over the world—Arabs, North Africans, Filipinos and Indonesians—as well as from Eastern Europe and the vast southern expanses of post-Soviet Asia. Some were wanted men. Others were faceless to the Western intelligence machine. All were wedded to a common purpose. In the Southern Hemisphere, with new names and the cabal's protection, they were officially legitimate businessmen in Buenos Aires. They were inflamed with zeal by what their comrades had done against the American Embassy already. They yearned to make an even bigger mark, to strike a larger blow and impress themselves, the world and God with how they would make the Great Satan pay for his crimes.

They were men totally prepared to die.

El Negro examined his other team.

Some were men from the lowest strata of the Argentine and Brazilian streets. Others hailed from the darkest bends in the Amazon River or the dust, heat and mountains of Patagonia. They were faceless men, chosen for their ruthlessness and ambition. El Negro had taken them from their sinkholes and lives of petty crime and molded them in his own image.

These were men totally prepared to kill.

Gusi stared at them blandly.

El Negro spoke low. "What do you think?"

Gusi shrugged. "They failed before. I know they are pleased to have blown up part of the American Embassy, and are eager, but they are not professionals." Gusi let out a long breath. "They have never dealt with someone like this commando. He is a professional. A gunfighter, who appears and disappears at will. They will not survive an encounter with him save by luck."

There was a moment of contemplative silence. El Negro broke it. "This *yanqui*, I have a sense of him."

"Oh?"

"Yes. He is here to destroy us, but he does not know who we are. He may well suspect the terrorist attack on the Embassy was aimed at him."

Gusi nodded slowly. "And?"

"And so, what we need is another terrorist attack."

"Really."

"Yes. We will initiate the attack. The commando will respond. My men will be waiting. While the commando is killing the attackers, my men will kill him." El Negro smiled slowly. "I think it might be best if you had some of your own men present to make sure of things."

Gusi scowled. He had his own men, but until the plan was in full effect, they could only be used in places where their presence could be justified, or in situations Gusi had complete control over.

"You are thinking if they are discovered their presence could not be justified."

Gusi's scowl deepened. Sometimes El Negro's reputation as a mind reader was a little too uncomfortably close to the truth. "Yes, I am."

El Negro shrugged. "Well, has there not been a terrorist attack within the capital just this very week?"

Gusi laughed despite himself. "Indeed. There has, hasn't there?"

CIA safehouse, Buenos Aires

MACK BOLAN WATCHED CNN in Spanish. Governor Mariano Lopez Del Valken stood before the cameras in front of the American Embassy. He passionately decried the outrage of a terrorist act on Argentine soil. Bolan smiled. Even as he expressed his horror, beneath his sentiment there was a very subtle undercurrent of allusions to the United States bringing the heretofore-unknown blight of terrorism to Argentina's shores.

Kubrik pointed at the screen. "They say that asshole will be the next president."

Del Valken stood before the blackened holes in the U.S. Embassy while workmen cleared rubble behind him. He was intensely charismatic. Bolan had to give the man credit. He was a brilliant speaker, and the camera loved him.

Bolan turned to Kubrik. "So who is this guy?"

"He's the governor of Cordoba, and one of the young lions of Argentine politics. Some people say he's a reformer. Others say that he's a demagogue and that he's dangerous. He's not part of the establishment. For the people that in itself is almost enough. The people here consider the government a Mafia. Most people don't have any hope. For that matter, most people here don— What is it?"

Bolan stared intensely at the screen.

Del Valken's eyes had flown wide and his speech trailed off on his lips. He was staring past the camera. The camera wobbled and suddenly swung to see what he was looking at. The image of a Mercedes truck barreling straight on nearly filled the television screen. The grill of the truck filled the camera lens and the screen suddenly went black.

The safehouse was two blocks from the American Embassy. The windows shuddered in their frames with the sound of the blast.

Kubrik jumped. "Shit."

Bolan rose and shrugged into his body armor. "We're moving."

"You know it's a trap."

Bolan nodded. "We're going in."

Kubrik grinned from ear to ear. "Then let's go in hard." He slapped the Velcro tabs of his own armor and went to the closet. He came out with a weapon in each hand. His grin grew to insufferable proportions. "You familiar with these?"

Bolan perked an eyebrow.

Kubrik held a pair of FN-2000s.

The Belgian weapons were all ergonomic humps and curves of black metal and plastic. On the social end protruded a few scant inches of 5.56 mm rifle barrel, and beneath it the maw of a 40 mm grenade launcher. The launcher was pump action with a 3-round magazine. On top of the rifle a housing like a rounded shark fin enclosed a 1.6-power optical sight with a built-in laser range finder and onboard fire-control computer for grenade launching. The FN was the absolute state of the art in individual combat weapons. The FN-Herstal company had produced an individual weapon system of a kind that even the United States barely had in prototype stage. The FN weapons were available for military testing by individual governments. None had been issued to troops yet.

Back at Stony Man Farm, Kissinger was testing them extensively. How Doug Kubrik had gotten hold of a pair of them for his personal use was a mystery.

Bolan took the offered weapon and the belts of magazines and grenades. "How?"

Kubrik smiled inscrutably. "I'm well liked in Belgium."

Bolan racked the action of his weapon and powered up the integrated fire-control system. "Let's do it."

Kubrik handed Bolan a gas mask. "The first round is CS,

the next two are canister. You've got more of each plus willie petes and antiarmor in the bandoliers."

"Got it." The two of them charged out onto the street. Hundreds of people were screaming, running and clutching one another. Smoke billowed over the rooftops in the direction of the Embassy. Rifle shots rang out. People running in the opposite direction gave a wide berth to the two grim-faced men. With their armor, masks and weapons they looked like invaders from Mars.

The site of the Embassy was a war zone. The frontage of the building was a blackened, smoking hole. Fire glowed hellishly from the interior. Once more, men with guns were swarming the building. This time they were shooting anything that moved. It was a trap. They were daring Bolan to strike. The terrorists would be trouble enough. It was the hidden assassins among the victims, dressed as responding police officers or people on the street who would come in for the kill while he and Kubrik were engaged.

Bolan raised his assault rifle and his finger slid around the trigger of the grenade launcher. He spoke into the radio in the mask. "Fumigate them! Fumigate everything!"

The weapon in Bolan's hand thumped and vomited pale yellow flame. Kubrik's thudded a second later. Bolan was loading three more CS grenades. The weapon boomed in his hand as he pumped the action and sent the grenades through the holes into the Embassy and the grounds surrounding it. Kubrik's weapon hammered as quickly as he could work it. The skip-chaser grenades broke into individual bomblets that bounced along the ground, spewing gas from their nozzles.

Bolan and Kubrik plunged into the swirling fog of war.

Every man with an AK-47 went down.

None of the attackers were wearing gas masks. Most were overcome by the combination of smoke, dust and gas. They wiped at their streaming eyes, firing their guns in the air, at each other and at anything they could see with their smeared vision. Bolan fired burst after burst. His rifle barrel went hot as he fired and changed magazines. It was the second time the Embassy had been attacked. More innocent lives had been taken. It was no place for mercy, and there was no time to take prisoners.

The jaws of the trap were closing.

Every burst from the FN-2000 was a headshot.

The Embassy had been broken open like a melon. It looked like the hungry mouth of Hell. Lost souls staggered weeping and screaming out of the gaping hole and what was left of the doors. Bolan shoved Embassy workers to the ground as he sought out gunmen.

A Marine tottered out of the smoke. The bayonet of his M-16 was fixed and he shook his head against the gas and dust. He trained his weapon on a chattering AK-47 and shot the terrorist down. Bolan and Kubrik were barely shapes in the fog, but the muzzle flashes of their weapons flickered and marked them.

Bolan tackled the Marine as he trained his weapon on Kubrik. The Marine struggled violently as Bolan yelled to make himself heard through his mask. He rammed his respirator against the Marine's ear and shouted the one thing that might calm him.

"Navy SEAL! Navy SEAL! How many injured inside?"

The Marine wheezed and choked. Bolan released him as he stopped struggling. "Don't…don't know!"

"Regroup! Get your men out of the building! Help the victims! Put up a cordon if you can! No one gets in or out!" Bolan leaped up. Men with automatic rifles were plunging into the smoke. Bolan racked the action of his grenade launcher and chambered a personal-defense round.

The governor of Cordoba blundered in front of him and his targets.

Bolan lunged forward and bodychecked the governor, knocking him to the broken pavement. Bolan fell on top of him and through his mask roared in Spanish to stay down. He couldn't tell if Del Valken had heard him or simply had all the air smashed out of his lungs but he didn't move. Bolan used the governor as a benchrest and brought up his weapon.

He caught the first three men coming in. They staggered and jerked as they took multiple hits and fell. Men at the perimeter of the gas cloud slowed as they saw their comrades fall. Bolan fired another round at knee level. The range was long at fifty meters, but two of the assassins were swept off of their feet. Their comrades seized them and began pulling them back. Sirens wailed close by.

Bolan yanked the governor. "Move!"

The governor moved, choking, trying to get out of the cloud. Bolan grabbed him and dragged him toward the Embassy. A terrorist stumbled out of the smoke firing his weapon blindly. Bolan shielded the governor behind him. Bolan's finger was still on the grenade launcher. The weapon tried to wrench itself out of Bolan's grip as he fired it one-handed.

The range was less than seven meters. The terrorist took all thirty buckshot in a dinner-plate-sized pattern in the chest. The killer flew back over the wreckage he had crawled from.

Bolan moved into the shattered Embassy. The lobby was gone, and a section of the second floor had collapsed. The building was beginning to burn out of control. If the assassins were clever, they would have sharpshooters covering the exits. Marines and workers helped pull their injured fellow Americans out of the building.

Bolan saw the Marine he had tackled ushering a pair of screaming women toward the back. Bolan yanked up his mask. "Hey, Marine!"

The private looked over.

"This is the governor of Cordoba! Get him out of here!"

The governor blinked at Bolan with streaming eyes. *"Gra-*

cias. Muchos gracias." He switched to wheezing English. "Thank you, my friend. You saved my life."

"Glad to help." Bolan scanned about for Kubrik. "Stay with the Marines. They'll take care of you."

Bolan moved on. He pulled his mask down and spoke into the mike. "Kubrik! Kubrik, where are you?"

Instinct made Bolan turn to the hallway where the previous day's firefight had taken place. The hallway led to where Kari Morgan's office had been. Kubrik emerged from the smoke and flames.

Kari Morgan hung limp in his arms.

Bolan ran forward as Kubrik knelt and laid his woman down. Her face was a mask of blood, and her legs were severely burned. Bolan checked her pupils. One was larger than the other. Her eyes were unfocussed and unresponsive to the gas and smoke. "We've got to get her out of here, and you and I are sniper bait dressed like this."

Bolan stripped away his mask and armor. He turned his U.S. Embassy baseball cap around and pulled it low over his eyes.

Kubrik stripped off his mask. More than dust and smoke and irritant gas reddened his eyes. "These bastards go down. Blondie, El Negro, every last one of them goes down."

"They go down," Bolan agreed. "Every last one of them."

11

CIA safehouse, Buenos Aires

"There is no way you are taking me off of this one." Kubrik's ham-size fists were white-knuckled with fury. His burning eyes weren't taking no for an answer.

Bolan regarded the CIA man calmly. "You still frosty?"

"No." Kubrik glared and consciously unclenched his fists. "But I will be."

Kari Morgan was in the Buenos Aires General Hospital burn unit. The combination of burns and blunt trauma she had suffered when the roof had fallen on her put her on the critical list. Bolan knew all too well what Kubrik was feeling.

"You haven't lost Kari. Not yet." Bolan was stone cold. "I need you frosty or not at all."

Kubrik squared his shoulders. "I'm cool."

"Good." Bolan nodded. "I knew I could count on you."

"So when does the word come down?"

"I sent the intelligence that's been gathered from the second attack to a friend of mine. I'm going to drop a dime on him and see if he's come up with anything." Bolan shrugged. "From there we're probably going to have to make up the words as we go along."

Stony Man Farm

AARON KURTZMAN EXAMINED Bolan across the link. Other than being filthy and covered with smoke stains he seemed all right. "Mack, this is bad. Our Embassy has been hit twice in the same week. Everyone from the President down to the man in the street is going apefire on this."

"What did you get on the weapons?" Bolan asked.

Kurtzman typed keys and transmitted information. "Well, working backward, the weapons the terrorists used in the second attack were Chinese AK-47s. There are millions of them in circulation worldwide. I doubt whether we'll uncover anything significant. Cowboy's still on it. Now, you said you had some shooters who came in on your flank during the firefight. I ran the info the CIA team got on several of the dropped rifles. They were Imbel MD2 assault rifles. Standard Brazilian army issue. We ran the numbers; they came from a lot of one hundred rifles that were reported lost in transit a year ago."

Bolan raised a speculative eyebrow.

Kurtzman leaned forward. "What?"

"They switched weapons."

Kurtzman considered. "Okay, but terrorists and criminals tend to take whatever weapons they can get. So they ran out of FALs."

"No." Bolan peered intently into space as his instincts spoke to him. "I was supposed to die in the first attack. We're betting that El Negro and Blondie are locals. I'm getting the feeling these guys think they own Argentina and can do anything they want. When the first attack on the Embassy failed, I think they suddenly felt a little vulnerable and had to tie up loose ends. They didn't want to issue out of the same batch of weapons as before." Bolan's stare intensified. "What did you get on the weapons from the first attack?"

"FN-FAL rifles, Argentine Industria Militaria manufacture. Akira and Encizo broke into the Argentine army's ordnance database like you asked. According to Akira it was a pretty crude setup. It took him all of thirty seconds to break in. Then Encizo let his fingers do the walking and translated the data from the Spanish. The two weapons Kubrik secured came from two different lots manufactured in the 1970s." Kurtzman smiled slyly. "They had two things in common."

Bolan knew the look well. "Yeah, and?"

"And for one, a year ago, both rifles failed to pass inspection and had been declared unfit for service. According to records they were stripped and cannibalized for usable parts. The rest was melted down or trashed."

"They seemed to be working just fine two days ago."

"Funny, that."

Bolan nodded. "And these nonfunctional weapons no longer officially exist, either."

"That's correct."

"What else did they have in common?"

"Well, it may not mean much, but both weapons were issued to army bases in the province of Cordoba."

"Really." Bolan nodded. "Tell me about Cordoba."

Kurtzman punched keys and brought up a map inset on both of their screens. "Argentina is a huge country, Striker, but it's still a virtual city-state. You've been there. A third of the population lives in the greater province of Buenos Aires, and everybody who's anybody lives in the city of Buenos Aires itself. You have a few major cities on the coast, the wine country, ski resorts in the Andes to the west, and then a vast small-town and village farming and ranching interior. Cordoba is pretty much smack-dab in the middle of the country. Other than being landlocked, it's a microcosm of the country itself. It has marshes, forests, mountains and plains. It isn't in the Stone Age, or light-years from the capital, but if you live there, you are living in the sticks."

Bolan's smile grew. "Really."

"Really." Kurtzman knew Bolan's look, as well. "Why?"

"Because I know someone from Cordoba who happens to owe me a favor."

"Really?" Kurtzman's brows drew down quizzically. "Who?"

Bolan's smile was feral. "The governor."

Casa Rosado, Buenos Aires

GOVERNOR DEL VALKEN grinned from ear to ear as he opened the door. "Come in! Come in!"

The governor led Bolan to a hugely overstuffed chair. Del Valken was wearing several thousand dollars' worth of impeccably tailored Italian silk. The Casa Rosada was Argentina's equivalent of the White House. As a governor, the fact that Del Valken had his own office within it attested to his importance.

Del Valken laughed. "I would kiss you, but I know how you *yanquis* feel about that."

Bolan smiled. "I'm used to it."

Del Valken took a seat behind a massive teak desk and reached into a humidor. *"Cubano?"*

"No, thanks." Bolan glanced around the office while the governor selected a Monte Cristo Especial cigar for himself. A vast portrait of Che Guevara dominated the wall behind the desk. Bolan leaned back in his chair as Del Valken lit his cigar and savored the smooth and powerful Cuban tobacco.

"So, my friend, how may I be of help to you?"

"Well, as you know, the United States Embassy has been attacked twice in Buenos Aires."

"Yes." Del Valken nodded thoughtfully. "And today I would most likely be burning the American flag outside of it for the cameras, but now that you have saved my life, I am afraid I must retract many of the statements I have made to the press. Is that what you wish?"

"No, Argentina is a free country, just like the United States. You're entitled to your opinions about us."

Del Valken smiled. "That is very North American of you."

"Thank you." Bolan smiled in return. "However."

"Ah, yes." The governor shook his head ruefully. "The however."

"I would like to ask you a few questions," Bolan stated.

Del Valken shrugged. "As I have already said, I owe you my life. But I will not assist you in espionage against my country."

"I wouldn't ask it."

"You would be the first CIA agent I have ever met who didn't."

Bolan shook his head slightly. "I don't work for the CIA."

Del Valken opened his mouth and then closed it. "Strangely enough, I believe you."

Bolan opened the file he'd brought with him and put a photograph on the desk. "The weapons the terrorists were using in the first attack were FAL rifles, Industria Argentina manufacture."

Del Valken frowned at the photo. "You think they were stolen?"

"No, both rifles were officially classified as worn out, stripped for parts and the rest melted down." Bolan tapped the photo. "Those rifles and the others used were not stolen. They were issued to the terrorists, and it was an inside job."

"You believe there are cells of foreign terrorists operating in Argentina?"

"I'm not totally sure of it yet, but I believe foreign terrorists are being armed, equipped and possibly trained and given sanctuary in your country."

Del Valken scowled. "Impossible."

Bolan looked at the governor pointedly. "Further, I believe the situation is going on in the province of Cordoba. That is why I have come to you."

Del Valken's eyes flew wide for a moment and then vised back down into a scowl. He took a deep breath and let it out. "Listen, I will tell you something you already know. My country's political and economic system is corrupt, from top to bottom, and we are spiraling out of control. People call me a reformer, others a pretty boy and a demagogue. But since you have saved my life and we are sitting here talking together as men, I will tell you something else. To get to where I am, to be a possible candidate for the presidency, to put myself in position where I can have the power to fight for the genuine reforms I give speeches about, I have made compromises. My hands are not clean. Many say that my stance as a reformer is a sham, that I am a wolf in sheep's clothing and that I am as dirty as any of the old men here in the Casa Rosada. Some mornings I look in the mirror and truly cannot say whether they are right or wrong. I walk a tightrope, my friend, and I have fallen. Many, many times."

"I appreciate your candor."

"Thank you. Since you do, I will also tell you this. I am the governor of Cordoba. The highest power in the province. I have many friends in the military. Many of them are not very nice men. So what I am saying is this, if what you say were going on, I would know about it. Not only would I know about it, but I would be a part of it and I would be getting my cut. If not, they would kill me and find some more tractable puppet to take my place."

"Funny how that truck bomb went barreling into the Embassy right about the time you happened to be standing outside making a speech to the press." Bolan paused. "How many people knew about your speaking schedule yesterday?"

Del Valken's cigar drooped in his mouth.

Bolan took out the composites of El Negro from Nigeria and in his alias as Gassim in Tunisia. "Do you recognize this man?"

"No." The governor was still clearly dealing with the shock of Bolan's previous statement. "Who is he?"

"He is heavily involved, but all we have is an alias, El Negro. Does that mean anything to you?"

"No, but if he is a criminal and operating out of Cordoba, I can find out."

Bolan took out another photocopy. "How about him?"

Del Valken's jaw dropped. He looked as if he might be ill. He slowly looked up from the photocopy of the blond man from Nigeria.

"I know this man."

12

Rio Lujan

The Executioner swam through the darkness. The Lujan was
a tributary of the Rio Del Plata, which separated Argentina
and Uruguay. It was one of a maze of rivers in the great delta
at the river mouth. The Lujan didn't run particularly swift, but
the current was steady and Bolan was swimming against it.
His wet suit and tanks were commercial rentals from a Buenos Aires dive shop. They weren't rebreathers, and he would
be leaving a bubble trail, but Bolan doubted anyone would notice it at four o'clock in the morning. Bolan navigated with
the luminous dial of his swimboard. It gave him distance,
depth and compass direction. He had inserted from a rented
boat a mile downriver, and he was closing in on his target.

Governor Del Valken had gone from disbelieving to appalled, and the sight of the blond man in the sketch had sealed
the bargain. The governor knew the blond man. He was scared
shitless of him. It seemed everyone from Nigeria to North Africa to Argentina was scared of him.

It seemed Frederico "Fredi" Vikkers was not a very nice man.

U.S. Intelligence had nothing on him. Argentine crime
lords weren't the number-one concern of the CIA, and in a
country where nearly every government official was on the

take, Vikkers was just one more drop in the morass that Argentina had become.

Locally, however, Frederico Vikkers was known, very well known, and he was feared. What little Kurtzman had been able to dig up in the past twelve hours was almost stereotypical crime king. Vikkers ran an outwardly legitimate string of very successful import-export businesses. Bolan smiled around his mask. In his experience import-export was synonymous with smuggling.

Del Valken had walked a political minefield during his rise to power to keep himself at arm's length from Vikkers. Vikkers was the kind of crazy where you didn't dare ignore the man, but at the same time God help you if you made eye contact. Del Valken had told Bolan that Vikkers was the kind who made offers one didn't refuse.

Bolan glanced to his left. He could see the dim glow of Kubrik's instruments a few feet away. Bolan spoke into his communicator. "One hundred meters to target. Surfacing."

The device turned his voice into a series of short-range sonic pulses that would be picked up by the tiny sonar ear in Kubrik's rig and translated back into words. There was a slight time lag between transmission and translation. Bolan heard the incoming pulses before they turned into words.

"Affirmative, Cooper. Surfacing."

Bolan kicked upward and broke the surface of the Lujan.

The stretch of river was fairly dark. The Lujan was part of the resort area of El Tigre. In the deltas the mansions of the rich nestled haphazardly side by side with the huts of fishermen and bohemians, as well as the summer homes of the middle class. Vikkers had paid for some privacy, and his was the only house for several hundred feet along this stretch of river. The mansion was old Tuscany in style with wide paneled windows and double doors with fountains and prevailing gray stonework.

It was the kind of house any Mafia don would be proud to call home.

The Gold Eagle Reader Service™ — Here's how it works:

Accepting your 2 free books and mystery gift places you under no obligation to buy anything. You may keep the books and gift and return the shipping statement marked "cancel." If you do not cancel, about a month later we'll send you 6 additional books and bill you just $29.94* — that's a saving of over 10% off the cover price of all 6 books! And there's no extra charge for shipping! You may cancel at any time, but if you choose to continue, every other month we'll send you 6 more books, which you may either purchase at the discount price or return to us and cancel your subscription. *Terms and prices subject to change without notice. Sales tax applicable in N.Y. Canadian residents will be charged applicable provincial taxes and GST. Credit or debit balances in a customer's account(s) may be offset by any other outstanding balance owed by or to the customer.

If offer card is missing write to: Gold Eagle Reader Service, 3010 Walden Ave., P.O. Box 1867, Buffalo, NY 14240-1867

NO POSTAGE
NECESSARY
IF MAILED
IN THE
UNITED STATES

BUSINESS REPLY MAIL

FIRST-CLASS MAIL   PERMIT NO. 717-003   BUFFALO, NY

POSTAGE WILL BE PAID BY ADDRESSEE

GOLD EAGLE READER SERVICE
3010 WALDEN AVE
PO BOX 1867
BUFFALO NY 14240-9952

GET FREE BOOKS and a FREE GIFT WHEN YOU PLAY THE...

Lucky 7

SLOT MACHINE GAME!

Just scratch off the silver box with a coin. Then check below to see the gifts you get!

YES! I have scratched off the silver box. Please send me the 2 free Gold Eagle® books and gift for which I qualify. I understand I am under no obligation to purchase any books, as explained on the back of this card.

366 ADL D34F   **166 ADL D34E**

FIRST NAME

LAST NAME

ADDRESS

APT.#

CITY

STATE/PROV.

ZIP/POSTAL CODE

7 7 7	**Worth TWO FREE BOOKS** plus a **BONUS Mystery Gift!**
🍒 🍒 🍒	**Worth TWO FREE BOOKS!**
♣ ♣ ♣	**Worth ONE FREE BOOK!**
🔔 🔔 🍒	**TRY AGAIN!**

(MB-04-R)

DETACH AND MAIL CARD TODAY!

Bolan kicked toward the pier. A pair of speedboats bobbed in their moorings at a lower landing. A hedge of flowering shrubbery ran the perimeter of the mansion's embankment. Bolan avoided the pier and pushed his swimboard onto the embankment. He kicked out of his fins and tanks. He and Kubrik broke the plastic wrapping from around their FN-2000 weapon systems.

They began crawling up the embankment.

They stopped at the hedge. Bolan pulled his night-vision goggles over his head and scanned the river frontage of the mansion. He found the strategically located video monitors and the ghostly beams of the infrared laser net that spread out across the grounds at calf level.

Bolan spent long moments judging the angles and then picked his path.

He and Kubrik dropped below the edge of the embankment and crawled toward the tree line girding the eastern edge of the mansion. They rose up among the trees and scanned for more cameras and lasers. Bolan took the tree line and estimated the angle of the video camera watching the eastern edge of the house. Kubrik covered him as he stepped over the pale line of an infrared laser. Time froze into agonizing stillness as Bolan crept his way to a fountain that formed one part of a decorative stonework wall. Bolan squatted on his heels and covered the grounds with his weapon. He listened while a stone cherub urinated in a remarkable arc from the top of the fountain.

Kubrik hunkered down beside him. "What do you think?"

"I'm thinking about running across the lawn and blowing the door."

Kubrik's lips twisted into a grin beneath his night-vision goggles. "I like it."

"I thought you might."

"You want to use flexible charge?"

"The second the cameras pick us up, we're made. So I was

thinking we'd just run up, throw the satchel charge and walk on in."

Kubrik's grin redoubled. "I like it."

Bolan picked his line of attack and moved swiftly to the next fountain. Peering over the edge, he could see through the tiled courtyard that led to immense glass-paned double doors. The inside was lit.

Within he could see Fredi Vikkers and El Negro.

They were surrounded by some of their men, and they were peering intently at a computer screen. Bolan rose and powered up the laser range-finding module of the FN-2000. Vikkers and El Negro looked up simultaneously from the screen. They looked directly at Bolan and smiled.

"We're screwed." Bolan flicked his selector lever to full auto and fired.

Sparks bounced off the bulletproof glass of the doors.

Bolan's and Kubrik's night-vision goggles solarized and went whiteout as hidden floodlights threw the grounds into an incandescent glare. Bolan ripped off his goggles and fired his grenade launcher. The barricade-breaching round smashed through the bulletproof pane and split apart, spewing CS gas.

Vikkers and his men were already pulling on gas masks.

The enemy had adapted to his previous tactics.

Armed men were spilling out onto the grounds

"Break contact!" Bolan snarled. "Head for the water!"

Bolan pumped the action of his grenade launcher and fired frags onto the patio. He and Kubrik sprinted across the lawn. Bolan's lips split into a grimace as diesel engines roared out on the darkness of the river.

"Jesus!" panted Kubrik. "You have a plan?"

"Head for the water! Escape and evade!" Bolan pumped his arms and worked for every ounce of speed. It wasn't the best of plans, and to have any chance at all they had to reach the water before the searchlights on the boats hit them. Bolan skidded to a halt as multiple searchlights played their harsh beams atop the hedge walling off the embankment.

"Goddamn it! We—" Kubrik's voice trailed off as the engines on the river roared and shifted gears. Squealing, grinding and clanking followed the roar. Bolan's eyes flared as he recognized the sound.

It was the sound of armor.

The decorative hedge erupted as the nose of an M-113 armored personnel carrier with its swim vane deployed plunged up and through like a breaching whale and then slammed down. The searchlight traversed seeking targets. The .50-caliber machine gun and flanking M-60s atop the armored vehicle swept the grounds for targets, as well.

The great armored box clanked forward on its tank treads.

Bolan ripped the satchel charge from his shoulder. "The river! Don't stop for anything!" Bolan pulled the pin on the satchel charge as he headed straight into the teeth of the armored beast. He heard the hiss of the fuse igniting as the vehicle's spotlight lit him up. Bolan's vision went orange behind his eyelids as he hurled the ten pounds of high explosive between the tracks of the M-113. He threw himself to one side as the three machine guns ripped into life.

The searchlight tracked him and the lethal lines of machine gun fire converged. Great divots of lawn went skyward as the streams of bullets flowed toward him with sickening speed.

A cushion of orange fire lifted the nose of the armored vehicle and washed out to the sides. Heat singed Bolan's eyebrows and shards of metal whizzed overhead. The screams of the gunner were lost as the flame and blast ripped through the floor of the Carrier and erupted out of the hatches in great plumes where the gunners had been standing.

Bolan was yanked to his feet by his web gear. Kubrik roared in his ringing ears. "Go! Go! Go!"

Bolan and Kubrik charged past the burning hulk and

plunged headlong for the embankment. Bolan hauled up short and threw himself backward.

Three more armored personnel carriers were clawing their way up the embankment.

Their machine guns raked what was left of the hedge. Kubrik fired a grenade backward as he spun and ran after Bolan. "The trees! Head for—"

Bolan fired a grenade into the eastern tree line. Armed men were coming out of it, and coming out firing. Bolan ran straight into the lights of the central grounds. He dropped his rifle on its sling and pulled his only two smoke grenades and hurled them behind him to cover both flanks. Tracers streaked past. Bolan made for the side of the house. Vikkers's mansion was actually on a small island in the vast network of delta. Bolan headed for the westward side of the island. He stumbled as a bullet struck his armor but Kubrik yanked him straight. Both of them fired grenades at the side of the house. They kept running and vaulted a low wall. The supersonic crack of bullets whipped the air all around. Bolan skirted the pool and pointed at the sheltering dark line of trees beyond. "There!"

The tennis court lay between them and cover.

Chain link vibrated as they hit the fence. Bolan waited for the bullet in his back as he took the fence like a spider and fell to his feet to the other side. Red clay was ripped up as bullets sought them.

Kubrik fell hard. Bolan yanked him up and there was blood on his hands. They charged to the other side of the courts and hit the fence again. The bullet Bolan had been waiting for hit him between the shoulders like a sledgehammer. The air was crushed out of his lungs and his fingers weakened in their grip on the links.

Kubrik grabbed him and heaved him over the top. Bolan couldn't tell whether his armor had held or not. Kubrik popped smoke and the two of them stumbled panting into the darkness of the trees.

"You…all right?" Kubrik gasped.

"You?"

Kubrik was breathing too hard to speak

The two men held each other up as they backed farther into the trees. The M-113s clanked and roared around the side of the house in an armored wedge. The stone wall they had vaulted disintegrated beneath the nose of one. The chain link of the tennis court was ripped off of its posts and the red clay of the court cracked and shattered beneath the treads of the second. Half of the water in the pool flew up in the air in a great wave as the third vehicle ran right over it as if it weren't there. It swam across until its treads ripped into the steps of the shallow end and clawed up and out.

The armored juggernauts came on. Faceless men in gas masks with rifles were deploying outward in a skirmish line behind them.

"Jesus H. Christ…" Kubrik wheezed. "Jesus H. Christ…"

Bolan was more than ready to accept divine intervention, but he had learned long ago that God mostly helped those who helped themselves.

"Tell me…" Kubrik sagged. "Tell me you have a plan."

Bolan nodded as he tried to pull air into his own burning lungs. "I do."

Kubrik's left arm hung uselessly at his side with blood dripping from his limp fingers. He grimaced as Bolan packed a field dressing against the wound. "I'm listening."

Bolan wound the dressing tight and shoved Kubrik's arm through his webgear as a makeshift sling. Kubrik was bleeding like a stuck pig. Bolan suspected the radial artery was cut. "Make a fist. Keep squeezing the dressing between your arm and your chest."

"What's your plan?"

"This island is only a couple of acres. We can't play hide-and-seek for very long, and you aren't up to a swim."

"So you want to double back and steal one of the boats."

"No." Bolan shook his head. The idea was tempting. "Even if we can get to one of the boats, the M-113s will chop it to pieces before we can hot-wire it and get it moving. I'm also thinking since this is an ambush the boats are deactivated, or even rigged to blow."

"Great," coughed Kubrik. "So?"

"So we steal one of the M-113s and fight our way out."

Kubrik blinked. "We don't have any antiarmor munitions."

"I know. But their armor is welded aluminum. Good up to rifle fire and shell splinters."

"Like I said." Kubrik shook his head. "We don't have any antiarmor munitions."

"I'm going to wait for one of them to clank past, and then I'm going to cut a small hole in it with the flexible charge. Then you're going to toss a frag inside." Bolan smiled wearily. "With any luck you'll take out the crew in one shot." Bolan watched the behemoths come on. "We take the vehicle, button it down and sail it downriver. At least it will even the odds."

Kubrik stared. "Mister, you are nuts."

"Fine." Bolan sighed. "You cut the hole. I'll pop the grenade."

"No, no, that's okay. You go right ahead." Kubrik shook his head in utter disbelief as he pulled a fragmentation grenade from his bandolier. He held it up in his functioning hand. "Pull the pin for me."

Bolan pulled the pin and then took the hoop of flexible charge from Kubrik's pack. He cut a foot-long length with his knife as they continued to back away from the oncoming armor. Bolan mashed the ends together and pulled away the adhesive strip of the charge. He pushed in the detonator pin. "You ready?"

"You are nuts," reiterated Kubrik.

They crouched in the bushes as the spotlights swept the trees. They crouched lower as tracers streaked overhead. The trees shuddered with bullet strikes and rained down showers of brown leaves. The enemy was firing for effect. The ground beneath Bolan's boot heels was soft and wet. The water was somewhere close behind them. He and Kubrik were just about out of room.

Saplings cracked and shattered and shrubs were ground beneath the tracks as the M-113s mauled the marshy scrub forest. The vehicle on the left flank was coming straight for them. Bolan hunched as the spotlight crashed blindingly over their cover. As soon as it passed he faded left through the bushes. Bolan dropped beside the bole of a dead oak and waited as the clank and whine of the tracks shuddered the earth beneath him.

The armored box was two feet from Bolan's face. He slapped the hoop of flexible linear charge against the top edge of the hull. The port-side machine gunner shouted in alarm from behind his shield as he spotted Bolan and traversed his machine gun even as the vehicle lumbered past. Bolan threw himself back behind the bole. The top edge of the dead trunk ripped to splinters as the machine gun roared into life.

The machine gun stuttered silent as the gunner shouted again in alarm. The big, bloody CIA man had appeared like a ghost beside the vehicle. He shoved his grenade through the smoking hole and was nearly ground beneath the treads as he sprinted across the vehicle's path to draw fire away from Bolan.

All three machine guns followed the limping man.

A hollow whipcrack echoed from within the armored belly of the beast. All three gunners screamed simultaneously. The lethal radius of a U.S. fragmentation grenade was ten meters. The troop compartment of the M-113 was a four-meter-by-two-meter hollow box. There was no cover to be had. Any steel fragments that missed human flesh ricocheted off the armored walls, floor and roof and tried again. For a split second M-113's interior became a meat grinder. The only men with any kind of cover were the machine gunners standing in the hatches. They took the buzzsaw effect of the flying shrapnel from the groin down.

The engine powered down as the dead driver no longer pressed down on the accelerator. The M-113 crashed into a tree and half-uprooted it before its forward momentum stopped. Bolan was already up. He prayed the controls were not too badly chewed up as he grabbed equipment cleats welded to the side and vaulted himself up. The machine gunner manning the .50-caliber MG had slid back down inside the troop compartment. The two men manning the M-60s floundered and flailed in the gun hatches, screaming. Bolan hauled up one of the howling men clogging the hatch. "Kubrik! Come on!"

Kubrik grabbed the side of the vehicle and tried to pull himself up. He gasped and fell backward into the dirt.

Bolan flung the wounded man in his arms over the side. "Kubrik! Use the tree!"

Kubrik staggered to the front of the vehicle and put his foot on the half-uprooted tree. "Get in! Get this bastard moving! I'm all—"

A searchlight lit them up. The other M-113 had a straight line of sight through the trees on its stalled brother. Bolan whipped up his rifle and put a burst into the blinding eye of the searchlight. The man behind it jerked backward. Bolan's second burst smashed out the light itself. It would not be enough. As the searchlight winked out Bolan could see the enemy vehicle was slightly different from the rest. The leading vehicles carried three machine guns on top. This one carried only two.

The .50-caliber MG had been replaced with a 106 mm recoilless rifle.

Bolan turned to leap as fore and backblast of the recoilless weapon lit up the treeline.

Time seemed to slow. The M-113 rocked beneath Bolan's feet. Orange fire geysered out of the open hatches. The armor plate beneath Bolan's boots lifted upward with unstoppable force. Bolan's knees almost buckled as if he were in a rocket-assisted elevator. Bolan rose into the night. For one incredibly lucid moment he seemed to be surfing over the trees on a flaming plate of aluminum armor. Bolan's platform revolved out from under his feet. Bolan continued to soar across the scrub forest in a spectacular arc.

The Executioner didn't see the tree that rose in his path. He felt the limbs smashing into him like clubs as he pinwheeled into them. He only felt them for a moment.

Bolan was totally unaware of the dark waters of the Lujan as they closed over him.

13

Cordoba

Governor Mariano Lopez Del Valken's movie-star looks twisted in demonic anger. "I handed him to you! On a fucking silver platter I handed him to you! At a time and place of your own choosing! If I had known you were this incompetent I would have killed him myself! In my office! It would have saved us all a lot of time and trouble!"

"Now, Nano." Gusi spoke soothingly. "We—"

"How could you screw this up? You had your own precious jack-booted prima donnas for the job! Trained by the goddamn *yanquis* themselves!" Del Valken's voice rose towards a scream. "You had tanks!"

What he'd had was armored personnel carriers, but Gusi didn't bother to press the point. "The point is, the commando is dead."

"Dead? Dead?" The governor waved his arms. "Do you have his body? Do you have his head?"

Gusi strained to keep his own simmering anger in check. "We blew him up, Nano."

"A finger? His dick? Anything?" Del Valken whirled on El Negro. "You! Witch boy! Look into your damn power and tell me! Is the commando dead?"

El Negro stared grimly into the middle distance. "I don't know."

"The witch boy doesn't know." Del Valken shook his head in disgust. He glared at Gusi. "But you, you know."

Gusi's lips split into a snarl. He'd lost good men, and he was tired of the governor's tirades. He was tired of being the only one who could keep Del Valken on his leash.

What Del Valken needed was a shock collar.

Gusi's voice dropped dangerously low. "He was standing on top of the APC, Nano. One of my men shot it with a cannon. The APC blew up like a firecracker. I have seen the photos." Gusi's voice dropped another octave. "There are burned and blown-up bodies, heads, fingers and dicks all over the place."

"I want his head!"

"You are welcome to go to the mansion and assist Fredi in putting all the pieces back together if you wish."

Del Valken's fist crashed down on the table. "He knows who I am! He knows I am the one who set him up! If he still has his head, his dick and his trigger finger, he will come!" He pointed a condemning finger at Gusi. "And tell me, Gusi, how long do you think it will take him to find out who it was who ordered in tanks?"

The governor had a point. Robi might have had the most astronomical IQ at the table, but Del Valken was a brilliant second place. The fact that he was nuts only made him more dangerous.

And Del Valken would soon be the president of the most powerful nation south of the Rio Grande.

Gusi controlled himself. "Listen, Nano, it is almost dawn. My men have been combing the river in an official capacity. Terrorists are in the Lujan, and martial law has been declared. Come light we will start dredging for the body and Fredi and El Negro will have their men visit every house on the river within a ten-kilometer radius in a much more…private capacity. The *yanqui*'s description is being circulated. A price is already on his head, dead or alive. We will also let it be known that the price of sheltering the commando will be catastrophic for anyone involved, as well as their families and descendants. As a matter of fact, anyone caught assisting him will not have any descendants. Their line will end."

Robi spoke for the first time. "What about the CIA agent, Kubrik?"

"He is alive," Gusi said. "But not by much. He was already shot and had lost a great deal of blood. He took more injuries from the cannon blast. Fredi has him. We have medics keeping him alive, and hopefully getting him into some kind of shape to survive an interrogation, at least long enough to tell us something useful."

"I want to see the commando's head," Del Valken repeated. However, the insane light had receded from his eyes back to the deep, dark place it festered within him.

"He is dead, Nano. We shot him with a cannon. He blew up. My men saw it." Gusi settled his bulk back in his chair. "He is being eaten by fish."

Rio Caraguata

BOLAN AWOKE being mauled by beasts.

Something was biting his shoulder and yanking him along and slobbering on him. Bolan swatted at it feebly until something smacked him in the back of the head again and he saw stars. A voice shouted once, sharply.

"Bambu!"

Bolan reached for his rifle but found he no longer had it. His wet suit was shredded and most of his webgear was gone. Bolan only had vague images of half-consciously trying to shuck out of his gear as he was drowning. He peered down groggily. His feet were still in the water. One of his boots was missing. He was lying at a slant on something extremely uncomfortable. Bolan focused his eyes and realized he had been dragged up the wooden steps of a very rickety-looking pier. Bolan turned his head and again had to refocus his aching eyes. The massive, droopy-eyed head of some immense New-foundland-chocolate Labrador mix loomed over his right shoulder, wagging its tail and drooling on him happily.

Pain shot down Bolan's spine as he craned his head upward. A bare-chested man squatted at the top of the steps. He regarded Bolan with a somewhat sleepy though inquisitive stare. He had the lean physique of a man who made his living doing very hard work. He took a bite out of a baked potato and chewed it meditatively. He smiled around his food.

"Hola."

Bolan opened his mouth and was racked by a fit of coughing. The coughing reached down into the pit of his stomach, which spasmed. Bolan rolled over and retched up what seemed like gallons of river water. He sagged for long, exhausted moments on the rough wooden steps. Bolan wiped his chin and looked up. *"Hola."*

The man raised a speculative eyebrow. *"¿Americano?"*

Bolan smiled weakly. *"Norte americano."*

"Ah." Most United States citizens were unaware of the fact that the citizens of Mexico, Central and South America considered themselves Americans. Most, at least at some level, found the habit of *yanquis* calling themselves Americans, rather than North Americans, somewhat objectionable. The man smiled at Bolan's cultural sensitivity.

"You look like shit," opined the man in English. He held out what appeared to be his breakfast. "Potato?"

"Maybe later." Bolan groaned as his stomach lurched. "Where am I?"

The man cocked his head at the strangeness of the question. "This is my house. You are on the Rio Caraguata." He waved his potato at the dog. "Bambu pulled you out."

Bolan looked at the massive mutt. It thumped its tail on the steps. "Nice dog."

"Thank you." The man seemed pleased. "My name is Diego."

"Mine's Matt." Bolan tried to do geography in his pounding skull. "Where is the Rio Lujan, from here?"

"Ah." The man pointed with his potato. "Over there."

It hurt too much to sit up, but Bolan got the idea it wasn't far at all. Bolan did notice there was a short-bladed machete sunk into the wood of the pier by the man's right hand. The man noticed Bolan noticing. "Are you a terrorist?" he asked.

"No." Bolan began to push himself up. His knife was still in his remaining boot.

"Bambu," the man said.

At the man's word, Bambu's demeanor changed. The sleepy brown eyes glared malevolently. The black lips wrinkled back from massive jaws and hackles rose as he exposed his teeth. "Mister, maybe you had better lay there and rest for a moment."

Bolan rested on the steps. "I'm not one of the terrorists."

The man nodded noncommittally. "Ah."

"Frederico Vikkers is working with the terrorists." Bolan gambled. He waved a hand vaguely at himself and his shredded and bloody wet suit. "Fredi and I came to a disagreement about it last night."

The man's brow furrowed. He nodded again very slowly. "Ah."

Bolan was either saved or dead. He smiled hopefully. "You know Fredi?"

"Fredi Vikkers is a very bad man," Diego stated flatly.

"He is," Bolan agreed. It seemed to be a worldwide consensus of opinion.

"Yes." Diego seemed to have come to a decision. "Well, perhaps we should get you inside where you can rest. If you do not wake up dead, I will fix you something to eat. So…"

Diego's voice trailed off. The sound of motors was coming from upriver. Speedboats, and more than one. He looked down at the bloody, bruised and burned side of beef in a shredded wet suit on his steps.

The side of beef had passed out again.

BOLAN AWOKE in a hammock.

He cracked his eyes open. It was cool and dark, and smelled damp. He glanced up and could see light coming through cracks in the wooden ceiling above him. He was in a cellar. His wounds had been bandaged, and some rank-smelling salve had been applied to them. His nose told him the burns on his lower body had been smeared with honey. It appeared the honey jar had run dry and the burns on his arms and face had been smeared in butter. Bolan smelled soup.

He also smelled a woman in the room.

"You are awake." The woman spoke English haltingly and with a heavy Argentine accent.

"What's your name?" Bolan asked.

"Debi," the woman said. "Eat some soup."

"Thank you." Bolan took a wooden bowl and spoon in his bandaged hands. His hands shook but he got the food into his mouth. It was fish and rice with tomatoes. It was delicious. Bolan found he was starving and took it as a good sign as he dug in. "Where is Diego?"

Bolan's eyes had adjusted to the gloom. Debi's voice was calm. Her face was clearly upset. "He is resting."

Bolan's eyes narrowed. Something was wrong. "What happened?"

"Fredi. Fredi's men. They came, looking for you. Diego does not like Fredi. He yelled at Fredi's men and called them *putos*. He said he would not tell them anything even if he did know something. They tore our house apart. They beat him very badly. They shot Bambu." Tears spilled down her cheeks. "The neighbor and I took you through the woods to the neighbor's house when Fredi's men came here. Then we brought you back here when they moved to the neighbor's house. His wife and I brought you back."

Bolan laid the empty bowl on his stomach and rested. It appeared he had done a great deal of traveling while he had been unconscious. "I am sorry. This is my fault."

"It is not your fault that Fredi Vikkers is a son of a bitch." Debi's voice was absolute stone as she said it.

"How far are we from Fredi's house?"

"A little less than a kilometer upriver." She struck a match and lit a kerosene storm lantern. "Diego asked me to bring you a paper."

Bolan winced and shoved himself up slightly. His Spanish literacy wasn't perfect, but he could more than get the gist of it. Terrorists had attacked the home of respected businessman and well-known humanitarian Frederico Vikkers. An anonymous tip had allowed elements of the Argentine army's Third Corps and the Fourth Airborne Brigade to intercept and destroy the terrorists in a desperate predawn firefight. According to the paper, police and government sources believed the attack was but one in a possible series of terrorist attempts to kidnap leading Argentine businessmen, industrialists and politicians.

Mariano Lopez Del Valken, governor of Cordoba and possible future presidential candidate, swore that any and all attacks by foreign terrorists on Argentine soil would be dealt with ruthlessly. There was a sidebar reiterating Del Valken's own brush with death at the hands of terrorists outside the American Embassy. A poll question beside the story asked Would You Vote Del Valken For President If He Ran?

A thin smile ghosted across Bolan's battered face.

Sixty-two percent of those polled in the capital said yes.

In his home province of Cordoba, Governor Del Valken's approval ratings had gone through the roof.

"Do you have any of my things?" Bolan asked Debi.

"I buried them."

"Did I still have my belt?" Bolan switched to Spanish as Debi looked at him, perplexed. *"Mi cinturón...militaria."*

"Ah." Debi rose. "I will fetch it."

Bolan rose as she walked up the stairs and went outside. His head swam and he had to grab the wall to steady himself. He tottered up the steps and found himself outside in the early evening. Debi had disappeared. Bolan walked up a second set of steps that led to the house and walked in. Most of the few furnishings in the house seemed to be handmade. There was no television and no kitchen to be seen. Diego was lying on a sofa. His face was a misshapen lump of bruising. Both of his eyes were swollen nearly closed. His pupils seemed to swim in a red sea of broken blood vessels. They tracked Bolan as he reeled in and propped himself up against a wall.

Bolan nodded. "You look terrible."

"Yes. Thank you." Diego sighed. "They are looking for you. They are offering a great deal of money."

"I know. Thank you for the paper."

"You are welcome."

Debi came back in and handed Bolan a coiled web belt. Bolan examined the sum total of what was left of his gear. His grenades were gone, as were his rifle and pistols. He had some spare magazines but nothing to stick them in.

"Do you have a gun?" he asked Diego.

Debi looked shocked. Diego shook his head minutely. "No."

"Can you get one?"

"It takes a—" Debi looked for a word "—permit."

"Can you get one anyway?"

Diego groaned and shifted in his sickbed. "It might be possible."

"You have a phone?"

"No."

"Can you get one?"

"My boat threw its propeller last month. I have not been

able to afford a new one yet." Diego looked away in embarrassment. "Debi would have to row to town."

Bolan uncoiled the belt. He ripped open a Velcro seam on the inside.

Diego's and Debi's eyes bugged as Bolan began producing U.S. hundred-dollar bills. "Debi, will you row to town? Get me a phone. Get me a gun." Bolan counted out five thousand dollars.

Debi stared in shock as Bolan put the small fortune in her hand.

"Oh, and buy yourself a new propeller." Bolan sat down creakily on the couch beside Diego. He put on the most winning smile he could manage. *"Por favor."*

14

Stony Man Farm, Virginia

"Jesus Christ!" Aaron Kurtzman nearly shot out of his wheelchair. "Striker! Where the hell are you!"

The connection was horrible. Bolan's words came through static and were slightly delayed. "Well, that's an interesting question, Bear. I'm not exactly sure. I'm on the Caraguata River, around a mile away from Fredi's house and one river over."

"You had us scared! Are you all right?"

"I'm pretty banged up. Is there any word on Kubrik?"

Kurtzman frowned at the warning light blinking on his phone. "This doesn't sound like a secure line."

"Randomly bought cell phone, best I can do. Any word on Kubrik?"

Kurtzman settled unhappily in his chair. "No word at all. He's MIA. What do you know on your end?"

"We got lit up by a 106 mm recoilless rifle. I pulled a Peter Pan and went into the drink. Some good people pulled me out of the water this morning. I didn't see what happened to Kubrik." Bolan was quiet for a moment. "What's the word in Washington?"

"Not good. The Argentine ambassador is accusing the

United States of playing spy games and using Argentina as a playing field in its war against terrorism. The Argentine government says it's not going to stand for it. The minute the President finds out you're alive, I suspect you're going to have some explaining to do." Kurtzman peered at the map of Argentina on his computer screen and began dialing it down to the area of El Tigre. "Listen, Striker, none of that matters at the moment. I need your coordinates. You sit tight and I will arrange for extraction."

"That's a negative, Bear. I don't know exactly where I am. People here get their mail from a central depository in town. Most of the houses on the river don't have numbers. Also, some real nice folks fished me out of the river, and every second I stay puts their life in further jeopardy. The enemy is combing the river, searching houses, offering rewards and making threats. Police and military units are dredging for bodies. If any strange gringos show up within a hundred miles looking for me, they'll be spotted."

"Then get to the town of El Tigre. I'll have Rafe set something up through the locals."

"My description has been circulated. It's an hour by boat, and most boats are being stopped and searched. If I show my face in town, I'm dead."

"I'm going to insert Rafe into Buenos Aires. Jack is already there. I'll have them link up and wait for you to contact them. Rafe should be in place in twenty-four hours."

"Good enough."

"So what do you want me to do?"

"First off, do me a favor. I want you to find out where the Argentine army's Third Corps and the Fourth Airborne Brigade are stationed and who would be in authority to deploy them on the Lujan River."

Kurtzman's hands were already flying across his keyboard. "I'm on it."

"Then find out where Fredi Vikkers was born."

Kurtzman looked up from his typing and smiled. He'd already tracked that one down. "Cordoba."

"Figures."

The Stony Man cybernetics whiz punched more keys and then sat back as information began to scroll across his screen. "Third Corps, headquarters, Cordoba. Fourth Airborne Brigade, headquarters, Cordoba."

"You know, Bear, I'm starting to think something is rotten in the province of Cordoba."

Kurtzman grinned. "You think?"

"Who would be in command?"

Kurtzman frowned and began punching keys again. "That's going to take a little longer."

"Take all the time you need, but do it quickly."

"What else can I do you for?"

"Five minutes after we hit solid ground at Vikkers's, they hit us with an amphibious assault. M113's fitted with heavy weapons came up right out of the river behind us. Where would Third Corps or airborne get that kind of equipment?"

Kurtzman scrolled backward through his listing on the Argentine armed forces. "The First 'Patricios' Motorized Infantry Regiment is headquartered in the province of Buenos Aires. That's roughly an hour or so by train, and then another forty-five minutes to an hour by boat from where you hit Fredi. If we count back from the moment you left Governor Del Valken's office, they would've had about forty-eight hours to get in position."

"They had armor and special forces troops in position and concealed on the Lujan. They must have buried magnetometers in the grounds and put motion sensors in the trees before we showed up, as well. This was a crackerjack operation, Bear, and someone with clout ramrodded it through. I don't think Del Valken could have simply used his influence as governor of Cordoba to get a military operation under way in under forty-eight hours, particularly in a neighboring province. He doesn't have that kind of influence yet, and Argentina doesn't run that efficiently. Whoever masterminded the military side of this was already in the know. I'm thinking they're actually part of whatever is going on down here, and had the power to stretch out their hand and make it happen. Find him."

"Well, that can't be a very big list."

"See if you can get a CIA tail on Vikkers and Del Valken."

The computer expert shook his head as he typed. "Now that could be tough. The U.S. has never had a very big intelligence presence in Argentina. What little we have usually operates out of the Embassy, and that got hit twice last week. Things are a mess, and what little infrastructure we had is busted up. Kubrik was one of the few red-hot operators we had in the region, and he's MIA. Kari Morgan was our best intelligence gatherer, and she was only taken off the critical list last night."

"Get someone to guard her."

"She's surrounded by Embassy guards." Kurtzman smiled slightly at the ID photo he had called up. "She's the hottest babe working at the Embassy. The Marines won't let anything happen to her."

There was a pause on the other end of the phone line. "All right, then."

Kurtzman had heard that tone in Bolan's voice before. "So what are you going to do?"

"I can't stay here, and I can't wait for extraction. In my condition, an escape and evade downriver to town would probably be suicide."

Kurtzman asked, already knowing the answer, "And?"

"The only thing I can do is go on the offensive."

BOLAN SNAPPED shut the cell phone. He took a deep breath. Bolan followed the pain radiating through his ribs. He was fairly sure several of them might be cracked. Debi stood to one side holding a paper bag. Her eyes flicked back and forth between the two injured men on the couch.

"I have your gun," she said nervously.

"Thanks."

She stepped forward hesitantly and held a paper sack out at arm's length as if it contained a poisonous spider or a dead rat. "Here."

Bolan took the sack. By weight, he could tell it was less than he had hoped. He reached inside the sack. Debi and Diego watched him as if he were a magician reaching into some terrible magic hat.

Bolan pulled out a snub-nosed .32-caliber revolver.

Diego and Debi jumped as he laughed.

Memories flooded Bolan.

His mind leaped to a place so far away it might have been a dream. The place where Bolan had been born, and the place he had returned home from the war. It was the place he had returned to find his family dead, and an enemy far worse than the Vietcong. It was the place where his war against the mafia had begun. It was the place where Bolan had taken his first job with the Mafia to take it down from within.

Bolan shook his head.

Life was a circle.

Bolan upended the bag, and five round-nosed lead bullets rattled out into his palm. He sighed. Bolan broke open the action and shoved the five ancient-looking cartridges into the cylinder. He closed the action and dropped the hammer on the empty chamber.

Debi looked at the little revolver with trepidation. "Is it all right?"

"It'll do." Bolan smiled at her. "Did you get me some clothes?"

Debi held out a plastic bag. She had done as Bolan asked and gone to a secondhand store in town. Bolan pulled out a pair of beat-up khaki work pants and a threadbare button-down cotton shirt. There was also a wide-brimmed straw hat and some sunglasses. Bolan began cutting the legs of the pants at calf-level. "Diego, you have an extra belt?"

"I have a piece of rope."

Bolan swiftly changed into his disguise. He grimaced as his burns and wounds stuck to the clothing. "How do I look?"

"Like a fisherman." Diego rolled his bloodshot eyes. "And not a very successful one."

Bolan shoved the revolver into the waistband of his pants. He put on the sunglasses and pulled the hat down low. Diego and Debi watched as he taped his boot knife to the inside of his wrist beneath his sleeve. Bolan looked at himself in the small mirror on the wall. The clothes covered the bandages on his body. The sunglasses and hat would camouflage the beaten and flash-burned hamburger that passed for his face at the moment, at least from casual scrutiny. "Diego, I need to ask you one more favor."

"Yes?"

"Let me borrow your machete."

Diego groaned as he pushed himself up off the couch. "You need someone to handle the boat."

"I can handle the boat."

"Do you know how to get to Fredi's from here?" Diego smiled. "Were you intending on asking directions from the policemen you meet on the river?"

The two men stared at one another through broken blood vessels. "Diego, I appreciate what you're doing. More than you know. But this is pretty much a suicide mission."

"Good. You may perform the suicide portion of it." Diego shrugged. "I will just keep the boat running." Diego suddenly stopped. "You know, it is said the grounds of Fredi Vikkers's mansion were badly damaged."

Bolan smiled as he saw Diego's plan. "I need to ask you another favor."

"Oh?"

"Yeah, I need to borrow your shovel."

Rio Lujan

FREDI VIKKERS'S mansion loomed less than three hundred feet away.

The ornamental hedge had been massacred by the APCs, and part of the pier was collapsed, as well. A few men in dirt-and sweat-stained work clothes sat smoking cigarettes at the top of the embankment. Diego scanned the workers from under his hat as he guided the boat upriver. They had motored right past a police boat and another unmarked boat filled with rifle-men in plainclothes. Bolan and Diego were just two more dirty workmen, moving toward the terrorist attack rather than away from it, and Diego's house had already been searched. The trip had taken fifteen uneventful minutes. Diego had waved at numerous neighbors along the way. Diego pulled his boat up to the half-smashed pier. A man sat on the pilings dangling his feet in the water eating a sandwich. He saw Diego and waved.

Bolan picked up the shovel. The pistol was hidden under his shirt. He had wrapped newspaper around the blade of the machete and thrust it down the back of his pants. Diego took up his pick and the two of them walked up the steps of the sagging dock and tried not to limp.

A small army of workers rested in any and all available shade. A few stood in small groups here and there pointing at things that needed doing and discussing various jobs. However, most were either dozing or smoking. The ancient Spanish art of the siesta had been lost in the big cities of most of the Latin countries, but once one was out in the provinces, people still had the good sense to rest during the worst heat of the day. Bolan scanned the grounds. The damage had been extensive. Decorative walls had tumbled and entire sections of lawn needed returfing. Patches of the marsh woods had been deforested. Farther in, men were working on the chewed-up tennis court and the mangled pool. Diego stopped and spoke with a man by the embankment for a moment.

Diego turned to Bolan. "So, what are you going to do?"

"I'm going to find Fredi and shoot him," Bolan responded.

"Ah."

"Then I'm going to try and find out anything I can before hell breaks loose." Bolan shrugged. "It's the best I could come up with on short notice."

"You are right," Diego decided. "This is a suicide mission."

Bolan stared at Diego frankly. "So why are you here?"

"Because I used to live two hundred meters from here on the Lujan. Then Fredi Vikkers moved in and decided he did not want neighbors. He bought out most people. Those who would not sell, he ran off." Diego glowered. "Bambu had a brother. Now he does not. Now Bambu is shot."

Bolan nodded. Shooting a man's dog was a good way to start a blood feud in just about any country on earth.

"I am a pacifist. I can turn the other cheek. But my dogs..." Diego trailed off. His voice hardened. "Fredi has a reputation for taking what he wants. And I do not like the way he looks at Debi."

"Let's go kill him," Bolan said.

"Okay."

Bolan stopped for a moment as they rounded the side of the house. There was a small helicopter pad on the wide expanse of the front lawn. An Enstrom 480 helicopter with civilian markings was parked on it. Bolan smiled. Diego looked at him closely.

"You can fly a helicopter?"

"A bit."

Diego stared at the aircraft. "Are the keys in it?"

"That's an ex-military helicopter. It doesn't use keys."

"You know many interesting things," Diego observed.

"Let's go inside and say hi to Fredi."

They walked back around to the other side of the house and found the servants' quarters. The entrance to the house was standing open. Bolan could smell meat cooking and fresh laundry. They walked past the laundry room and into the kitchen. Two women were working over a massive stove laden with boiling pots and frying pans. They looked up as Bolan and Diego walked in.

Diego put a finger to his lips and spoke softly in Spanish. "You better get out of here. This guy is going to kill Fredi."

Bolan lowered his sunglasses and showed the women his beaten face and bloodshot blue eyes. The women put down their spoons and pots without a word. Like most servants in Argentina, the women were from Uruguay, one of the most impoverished nations in South America, and as Mexicans crossed the Rio Grande to find work in the United States, Uruguayans crossed the Rio Del Plata to find work with their wealthier, more modern neighbors. Most found work as servants or laborers, taking jobs most Argentines thought beneath them. The women knew well what a blood feud was, and they knew all too well exactly what kind of man their employer was.

They disappeared like ghosts.

"Well." Diego lifted a lid and sniffed with interest at one of the pots. "Are you—?"

A man with an Uzi slung over his shoulder stomped into the kitchen, red-faced with anger. Diego dropped the pot lid with a clank and put up his hands as if he had been caught red-handed. The gunman snarled and waved furiously at the servants' entrance.

Bolan bent his shovel blade around the gunman's skull.

The man slumped to the floor.

"Get his gu—" Bolan spun and threw the shovel like a spear. A second man had appeared in the kitchen doorway. He paused for a fatal second as he took in the bleeding gunman on the kitchen tiles. His hand went beneath his coat.

The blade of the shovel was bent but the blunt edge had all of Bolan's weight behind it, and it hit the man just above his collarbone. The hard man wheezed and went white-faced as he fell against the doorjamb and slid down on his haunches.

Bolan's ribs creaked as he grabbed the man under his armpits and dragged him into the kitchen. Bolan could feel the bulge of the pistol beneath the man's jacket as he shoved him in the corner.

An irritated voice shouted from the hallway, *"¡Que pasa!"*

Diego yanked furiously at the Uzi pinned beneath the first man.

Fredi Vikkers stepped into the kitchen.

Bolan drew his revolver and fired.

Vikkers's jaw dropped as the little pistol snapped and the bullet hit him in the belly. Bolan fired again and again. The fourth shot took Vikkers right over the heart. Vikkers's hand came out of his jacket with a Czechoslovakian machine pistol.

Vikkers wasn't going down.

Bolan raised his aim. He put his front sight between Vikkers's eyes for his fifth and final shot. Vikkers jerked his head to one side as Bolan tracked and squeezed the trigger.

Automatic fire erupted from the kitchen floor.

Bolan flung himself aside as bullets ripped through the cabinets by his head. The Uzi was blazing in all directions in Diego's hands. Diego and the fallen gunman struggled over the cycling weapon. Flame spit from the Uzi's muzzle as it jerked and wavered in their hands. Bullets hammered across the kitchen. Vikkers clutched the side of his bleeding head. His left ear was gone. Bolan flung his little revolver in Vikkers's face.

The Uzi clacked open on empty.

Diego pounded his fist into the gunman's head.

Bolan dived into Fredi Vikkers like a linebacker, forcing the machine pistol from his hands. Bolan drove Vikkers into the hall and rammed him against the wall. Vikkers flung his arms around Bolan's ribs and heaved him into the air. He bounced Bolan off the wall like a rubber ball and staggered down the hallway clutching his head.

Bolan blinked at the pulsing stars in his skull. He rose wiping blood out of his eyes and tottered down the hall after Vikkers.

Vikkers lurched into the living room and turned. The double-edged, eight-and-a-half-inch blade of a dagger flashed in his hand.

Bolan pulled the machete from the back of his pants. He snapped his wrist and the newspaper wrapping flew away from the short, beaver-tail blade. Bolan had spent half an hour earlier in the morning with a whetstone and oil on the battered machete. Its edge was quicksilver bright against the pitting and discoloration tarnishing the body of the blade.

Vikkers lunged like a fencer. His body uncoiled with liquid speed. The point of the dagger glittered upward in a ripping thrust for Bolan's solar plexus. His momentum was unstoppable. Vikkers's left arm rose to block Bolan's counterattack. It was a sacrifice attack. Vikkers was prepared to take Bolan's retaliatory cut as long as he buried his dagger in Bolan's heart. Bolan sidestepped and whipped the hard bright line of the machete blade in a vicious arc.

Vikkers's dagger and the hand that held it dropped from his wrist in a wet spray of blood.

Vikkers faltered in his lunge. Bolan stepped past him, and his machete hissed through the air. Tendons parted behind Vikkers's knee as Bolan hamstrung him. The two blows occurred within a heartbeat of each other.

Vikkers sprawled onto the floor. He rolled over and found Bolan kneeling on his chest. "Where's Kubrik?"

Bolan could feel body armor beneath his knee. He could hear shouts outside and feet pounding within the house. The

Executioner put the point of his machete into the hollow of Vikkers's throat and began to lean on it. "Last chance. Where's Kubrik?"

Vikkers looked into Bolan's eyes and spoke through bloody teeth. "Downstairs."

"Matt!" Diego shouted from the hallway. He had liberated the Uzi and it ripped out of control in his hands as he pointed it across the room. A gunman in the opposite hallway ducked the salvo as it climbed toward the ceiling and returned fire. Diego's extended burst cut short as an invisible hand whipped his right leg out from under him.

Bolan rose. His entire body torqued as he released the machete and sent it end over end across the living room. The gunman screamed and fell kicking to the floor as the blade bit into his face.

Fredi Vikkers seized Bolan behind the knees and toppled him.

Bolan's bones jarred as the floor rose up to meet him. Fredi rammed his stump under Bolan's chin and closed his throat. Vikkers's remaining fingers stiffened into a blunt ax as he raised his hand.

Bolan raised his wrists to block Vikkers's hand as it fell with bone-splintering force. The shock of the blow ran down Bolan's arms and rattled his teeth. Bolan pinned Vikkers's hand for a split second. In that second Bolan ripped his fighting knife free from the tape around his wrist and whipped the blade across Vikkers's throat.

Vikkers's eyes went wide with shock. The thin line Bolan had drawn across his throat suddenly gaped. Blood poured out like an oil pan that had lost its cap. Bolan shoved the dying man off of him and rolled over. He picked up the fallen machine pistol and moved to Diego. Blood was welling up on the outside of his thigh. Bolan hauled him up. "Can you walk?"

"I think—"

Bolan ripped away the sleeve of his shirt and bound the

wound and then took the Uzi from Diego. He picked up the machine pistol and set the selector to semiauto. He handed it to Diego and said, "Try this."

Diego looked green at the sight of the severed hand on the floor but he took the pistol. Diego had retained the good sense to take the Uzi's spare magazines. Bolan reloaded. He picked up the dagger and shoved it into his waistband and began looking for the stairs to the cellar.

Bolan's search was answered as a door flung open. Two men erupted through the doorway waving pistols and looking around wildly. Bolan stitched both men with the Uzi. The killers fell back down the cellar steps in a tangle.

"Diego, stay in the stairwell. Shoot anyone with a gun. Let me know if anyone is coming."

Diego was pale with shock. He looked like a deer in the headlights. "Think about Debi," Bolan suggested.

Diego's jaw suddenly set. "Right."

Bolan went down the stairs. Blood kept pouring into his eyes. He wiped at the blood and stepped over the two dead men at the bottom. Vikkers had a well-stocked wine cellar. At the end of it was an open door. The door looked exactly like the whitewash and wood paneling of the wine cellar. If it had been closed, it would have been very difficult to detect. Bolan pushed the secret door open all the way. It opened into a small room. Bolan had seen far too many such rooms before. It was lit by a single overhead light. The floor was concrete with a single drain. There were two folding chairs and a battered folding table. The walls and floor were streaked with both new and ancient stains. It smelled like a slaughterhouse.

CIA agent Kubrik lay shackled in the corner in his T-shirt and boxers. There wasn't an inch of him that wasn't covered with blood. He looked as if he'd been run through a meat grinder.

"Kubrik?"

One of Kubrik's raccooned eyes slit open. It took him several moments to recognize Bolan. Kubrik spit blood from between missing teeth. "You're late."

Bolan nodded to himself grimly. If Kubrik was joking, then things probably hadn't gone further than the usual warm-up rounds of ugliness. He pressed the muzzle of the Uzi against Kubrik's shackles and shielded his eyes as he shot a link of chain apart. "Let's get out of here."

Kubrik groaned as Bolan hoisted him to his feet. Bolan groaned himself. Kubrik could barely stand. Bolan's own cracked ribs creaked. His battered body shrieked with the strain of supporting both of them.

Kubrik's swollen eyes looked at Bolan guiltily. "I told them everything."

Bolan rolled his eyes as the two of them staggered to the cellar steps. "You don't know anything."

"I know. But it's the principle of the thing. I was pretty much already shot and blown up when they dragged me down here. They shot me up with something, and it sure as hell wasn't morphine." Kubrik glanced back at the generator and wires. "I think that was going to be for confirmation."

"Here." Bolan grunted as he bent and pulled a pistol from the hand of one of the dead men on the landing. "Take this. You'll feel better."

"Thanks." The weapon seemed so heavy Kubrik could barely hold it. "Thanks for coming back for me."

Diego sat at the top of the stairs. He looked up blearily at Bolan and Kubrik. "There was lots of shouting outside. Then it quieted down. No one has come in." Diego sat in a spreading pool of his own blood. His leg was bleeding all over the place. His eyes looked glassy. "I'm cold," he murmured.

Bolan's insides fisted with strain as he pulled Diego up and threw his arm over the shoulder Kubrik wasn't using. The three of them gasped, bled and supported each other as they limped out of the house.

Out on the lawn the workmen stood in worried-looking clumps and watched them emerge. Many had fled into the trees at the sound of gunfire. The remaining men held their picks and shovels tightly and stared at the three blood-covered men and the weapons dangling from their hands.

Bolan cleared his throat and spoke in Spanish. "Fredi's dead."

Absolute silence reigned over the grounds.

"No more work today." Bolan jerked his head toward the front lawn. "We're taking his helicopter."

There were no objections. The men standing between Bolan and the helicopter pad parted like a silent sea.

Bolan, Diego and Kubrik lurched across the lawn arm in arm like some dying, five-legged beast.

15

Safehouse, Buenos Aires

Encizo was appalled. "Jesus, Mack. You look awful."

Jack Grimaldi was unfazed. He'd seen Bolan much worse.

"You look like pure hell, Kubrik." CIA Station Chief Marc Dudley shook his head sadly at his opposite number.

Kubrik took in the crutches Dudley was using to stand. "Cripple."

Bolan nodded at Encizo. "They know each other."

Diego looked around nervously at the roomful of dangerous men.

The two CIA colleagues burst out laughing.

Bolan sat on the sofa. Encizo had arranged the safehouse. There were few big cities in Latin America the man from Phoenix Force was not intimate with. Bolan glanced at the laptop computer hooked to a satellite link on the coffee table. "Is Bear around?" he wondered.

"Waiting on you," replied Encizo.

Bolan turned to Diego. "Fredi's dead, but he's only part of the picture. You and Debi are in terrible danger."

Diego peered at his IV unit and the blood expander dripping into his arm. "I knew you would say that."

Encizo smiled. "You should go someplace safe until we

settle things here." He raised an eyebrow. "Have you ever been to the United States?"

"Debi has mentioned she would like to see Disneyland."

Encizo began taking down some notes. "We'll have you both on a private plane within twenty-four hours. I'll arrange passports and money. We'll convalesce your leg in a private hospital, someplace nice with a view." Encizo grinned disarmingly. "Then when you're back on your feet it's off to the happiest place on earth."

Diego was already asleep.

Kubrik had passed out on the couch, as well. Bolan wanted nothing more than to join them. He was done in, but there was still business to attend to. Encizo glanced at Dudley. "You want to take some weight off those legs for a while?"

"No." Dudley lost his good humor as he looked at Bolan. "I need to talk to the big man, here."

Bolan could read the look in Dudley's eyes. "Your family?"

"My brother is a cop. He says he's picked up a tail, and my momma said she saw a strange car outside the house the other day."

"Get them out of there," Bolan replied.

"I did, but we're talking kids, cousins, nieces and nephews. I've got some getaway money, all good CIA spooks do, but..."

"We're going to make them disappear, Marc." Bolan turned to Encizo. "Make it happen."

"They're gone." Encizo snapped his fingers. "How about a nice Dudley family reunion in—" Encizo searched the ceiling and suddenly brightened "—Rarotonga?"

Dudley blinked. "The South Pacific?"

"Well, Antarctica is farther away if you prefer." Encizo shrugged. "But it's cold."

"It is." Bolan nodded. "Trust me."

"Palm trees, blue water, golden beaches, friendly natives, man, at night the Milky Way looks like snowflakes on black velvet." Encizo nodded decisively. "Rarotonga. They'll love it. Everybody does."

"They do," Bolan agreed. "Trust me."

Dudley's eyes flicked between the two warriors. "Just who the hell are you guys?"

Bolan looked at the crutches Dudley leaned on. "I think your family would love to see you there."

"They're after my family, and I don't go anywhere until they're dead," Dudley stated.

"You know I respect you—" Bolan shrugged at Dudley's crutches "—but just what is it you think you can do like that?"

Dudley tossed aside his crutches. His face twisted with strain but he stood unaided. He drew back his suit jacket to reveal a pair of .41 Magnum revolvers. "I'm gonna go Wyatt Earp on their Argentine asses. That's what I'm gonna do."

Encizo laughed. "I like him."

Grimaldi rose, and he and Encizo picked up Diego and went to find someplace for him to sack out. Encizo glanced back at Kubrik's snoring mass. "We're going to need help with him."

Dudley continued to stare at Bolan defiantly. He wanted confirmation.

Bolan rolled his eyes. "Sit down before you fall down, Wyatt."

Dudley eased himself onto the couch with immense relief. Bolan punched a key on the laptop and the screen came to life. Kurtzman sat waiting for him. He was grinning.

"What do you have, Bear?" Bolan was hopeful.

"You asked for the name of the man who could make an amphibious armor assault on the Lujan River happen in forty-eight hours. Well, I've got him." Kurtzman tapped keys and Bolan's screen split.

The photo of a man in a military uniform appeared. He was built like a refrigerator, with brows and jaws that belonged on a Neanderthal. His eyes glared out from under heavy ridges of bone. He seemed to severely disapprove of being photographed.

"General Gustavo Von, born and raised in Cordoba." Kurtzman grinned. "And the highest-ranking military man in the province. Now that's not saying all that much. Most of the generals and admirals spend their time in the capital, currying favor and siphoning funds, but Von isn't part of the old guard, he's—"

"One of the new young lions," Bolan finished. "Just like Del Valken on the political scene."

"Yeah, that's right." Kurtzman called up more data. "General Von has been very critical of the old guard. He's for streamlining the armed forces and cutting costs. This hasn't gone over well with the old men who are taking their personal share out of a bloated, pork-barrel budget, but Von's done a lot in his own province. He's encouraged Argentine involvement in UN peacekeeping missions, and he's founded an antiterrorist unit from the elite of the Fourth Airborne Brigade, called La Fuerza de Paz."

"The Force of Peace." A hard smile passed across Bolan's face. "His own private death squad."

"It's worse than that. General Von was instrumental in initiating training liaisons between the Argentine and United States militaries. In the last five years he's sent men to the United States to train with Delta Force, and United States Army Ranger elements have traveled to Argentina on cross-training junkets. If General Von is using handpicked men from his antiterrorist units as death squads like you say, they're not going to be your usual banana republic thugs with guns. These guys will be certified special forces."

"What else have you got?"

Kurtzman brought up another photo. It looked as if it had been taken from a newspaper. A powerful-looking man wearing wire-rim glasses and an impeccable suit was the focus of the photo. He sat in a restaurant with a bunch of other suits.

Bolan recognized a former Argentine president sitting next to him.

"Who's he?"

"That is General Von's brother, Roberto. Born in Cordoba, went to Harvard and got degrees in law and economics. Came back to practice law and quickly became one of the youngest justices in Cordoba, then rose to become Cordoba's minister of economy. He was noticed, and ten years ago he went to the capital, where he's held a number of positions. Most recently he was a cabinet chief, and he's been a legal and economic adviser to several of Argentina's recent presidents."

"Not exactly a glowing record, given how the country is going."

"That's just the thing. He resigned his cabinet post last year in protest and ceased being an adviser to the president. He's publicly stated that no meaningful reforms can be instituted with the current level of corruption entrenched in the capital. They're calling him the last honest man in Buenos Aires. The papers say his ideas could save the nation, if only they could be implemented."

Bolan saw it coming. "And Roberto Von supports Del Valken for president."

Kurtzman sighed. "Not yet, at least not publicly. But the rumor is he will, if Del Valken runs."

"Bear, what we have is a power grab, and all of Argentina is the prize." Bolan stared at the photos of the Von brothers. "And it sounds like the Cordoban Mafia is moving in."

"Funny you should state it like that." Kurtzman typed more keys. "There isn't too much of what you would call major organized crime in Argentina. Any Argentine will tell you that between the government and the police they have all the organized crime they need. But I was doing research on Cordoba like you asked, and I caught a rumor."

Bolan leaned forward. "What kind of rumor?"

"The ugly kind, about something like an Argentine Mafia. Except that no one will talk about it."

"What do you have?"

"Just a whispered name." The Stony Man computer expert leaned back in his wheelchair. "Los Facons."

"The Knives." Bolan drew the knife he had taken from Vikkers and held it up to the camera. "What do you make of this?"

Aaron Kurtzman's lip curled in disgust. "It's a Waffen SS dagger."

"I took it off Fredi."

Kurtzman's disgust became more evident on his face. "There's another thing Cordoba is famous for."

"What's that?"

"Nazis." Kurtzman scowled into his screen. "During WWII the battleship *Graf von Spee* was cornered in the mouth of the Rio Del Plata by the British Navy. By Hitler's own order they scuttled the ship. Most of the crew stayed in Argentina at the end of the war and headed into the provinces, specifically Cordoba and Misiones. It's always been rumored that after the war a lot of German war criminals fled to Argentina. It's also been an open secret for the last sixty years that if you're a German and you're in trouble, and I mean bad trouble, the kind where you have to flee the country and fast, Argentina is the place to go. If you can get there, and you have money, the local Huns will take you in."

"Vikkers, Von and Valken." Dudley spoke from the other sofa. "Sound like no-account, white-trash Aryans to me."

"Yeah, they do," Bolan agreed. The Executioner leaned back wearily. It was a scourge that just did not seem to die.

Kurtzman had stopped his typing. "So what are you thinking?"

"I don't know." He paused for a moment. "How about third-generation Nazi supermen taking over the most powerful nation in Latin America? For starters."

Cordoba

LOS FACONS SAT in full council.

The room was somber. Even Del Valken was subdued. They had led charmed lives. Since their birth they had been told they were better than other men. They had always known they were special. Their own accomplishments had proved it. Anyone who had stood in their way had been absorbed or destroyed. They were invincible.

Now Fredi Vikkers's chair at the table sat empty.

Robi spoke quietly. "I have reviewed the police interviews. The men who were working on Fredi's house say the man who killed Fredi matches the *yanqui* commando's description. The CIA agent, Kubrik, was rescued. They stole Fredi's helicopter and ditched it somewhere outside of Buenos Aires. There was a great deal of blood in it. A local man identified as Diego Quivon assisted them. He lived near Fredi's mansion on the river."

"Find him," Gusi rumbled. "And cut every piece of information he has out of him."

Robi flipped through a police file in front of him. "Diego has disappeared. So has his girlfriend. I am assuming the American has given them sanctuary, either in a local safehouse or has spirited them out of the country."

"What about the other CIA man, Dudley?" El Negro rolled his eyes as he asked. He already suspected the answer. "What of our operations against his family?"

Robi's frown deepened. "His entire family vanished. Forty of them, living in the Chicago area, all gone without a trace."

"The commando again," Gusi growled. "I do not like his access to United States resources. It stinks of high-level black operations."

"He knows me," Del Valken stated. "He must know you by now, Gusi, and if he has you, then he has Robi. Only El Negro remains a mystery to him."

"What can he do?" Robi tossed his file back on the table. "He has no proof of anything. He is in a foreign country, one we are about to control."

"What can he do?" Del Valken smiled unpleasantly. "He has started by cutting Fredi into fish bait. He has not come here to arrest us, Robi. He has come to kill us."

"No, he has come here to find out what we are up to, and stop it."

Del Valken flung his feet up on the table and leaned back in his chair. "I rather suspect that will involve killing the rest of us."

"Yes," Gusi said. "But the United States is not the kind of government that sends assassins. If the United States wished us dead, we would be waking up in our beds surrounded by navy SEALs, or stealth bombers would be blowing us up while we sat at breakfast. Instead, this *yanqui* has tapped only local CIA intelligence assets and received the aid of locals with antipathy toward us. He is a lone operative. We somehow attracted his attention in Africa, and this commando has been following the trail. He will only now be putting the pieces together."

"He will tell his government." Del Valken spit. "Then the navy SEALs and the stealth bombers will come."

"No, I do not think so." Gusi slowly shook his head. "First, he has no proof of anything, just what he suspects. The United States government will not move against appointed officials and decorated generals of a friendly nation on suspicions alone. Secondly, judging by the way he operates, he is obviously a deniable asset, and expendable. If we kill him, I believe his operation ends."

Robi smiled. Gusi's estimation of the situation matched his own. "So what do you suggest?"

"The commando must be killed as quickly as possible. We will continue to use the terrorist threat to justify whatever political and military actions we deem necessary. I have mobilized my personal units of La Fuerza de Paz, both uniformed and undercover. They are assembled into strike teams and ready to move at a moment's notice. El Negro has brought more men over the border from Brazil. The commando's description has been circulated to the police in every province, and our operatives on the street all watch for him. He must surface to find us, and act against us. When he does, we kill him."

"I do not like waiting." The gleam was back in Del Valken's eyes. "I do not like it at all."

"Then you shall wait no longer, my friend. The United States will have an even harder time moving against the democratically elected government of Argentina." Gusi smiled. "It is time for Robi and the allies we own in the senate to demand immediate emergency elections. It is time for you to become president of the nation."

Del Valken exposed his teeth in the smile that sent women's hearts fluttering. "Yes, it is time for me to become president."

"Good, then we are agreed." He turned to El Negro. "I need you to get the local members of the Facons ready. The commando will be coming to Cordoba, soon."

El Negro was staring into some terrible distance. He blinked and turned his dark eyes to focus on Gusi.

"He is already here."

16

Cordoba City, Cordoba

The Executioner eyed the rust-colored mountains of the Sas de Cordoba range as a sunset like blood slowly sank behind them. Bolan turned and walked into the ugliest bar in the provincial capital. Encizo was already inside. It was a simple sting. Encizo had gone native and asked around. Tips and American greenbacks had led him to the La Zorra pub and its owner, Enrique Schmidt. Encizo told the proprietor he had access to Brazilian cocaine. He wanted to move it into the provincial capital, but he didn't want any trouble and wanted to pay his respects to Los Facons. At first the bar owner had denied all knowledge. Encizo had then paid his respects to the bar owner in a thick stack of one-hundred-dollar bills and begged his assistance.

The moment the owner had said he might be able to do something, Encizo had pressed a button on his cell phone. Bolan had risen from the bus stop outside and walked into the bar.

Bolan took off his sunglasses and the baseball hat shading his face as he closed the door and locked it behind him. He turned, and the bar owner paled as if he had seen a ghost. Bolan smiled. It was clear his description was being circulated in all the wrong places. It was also clear the owner might have something useful to say.

Then Enrique Schmidt began to back up. He nearly jumped out of his shoes as he backed into Kubrik and Dudley. The two CIA men had picked the lock on the back door while Encizo had been wheeling and dealing inside. Dudley held one of his crutches like a club. Kubrik was grinning out of the pulverized meat of his face. Unknown to the owner, Jack Grimaldi was on the roof watching the street.

Encizo produced a Browning Hi-Power semiautomatic. Schmidt froze as the safety flicked off beneath Encizo's thumb. Encizo nodded sympathetically. "My friend, you are in a great deal of trouble."

Schmidt's brow sheened with sudden sweat.

Encizo inclined his head at Bolan. "Do you know who this man is?"

Schmidt would not meet Bolan's gaze. The Executioner continued to smile. The smile didn't reach his eyes.

"This is the *yanqui* who killed Fredi," Encizo explained. "He killed Fredi in his own kitchen, with a machete. Perhaps you have heard this."

Enrique Schmidt trembled with mounting terror.

"P-please..." Schmidt shook so hard he could barely stand. *"Por favor—"*

Bolan produced Vikkers's SS dagger like a magic trick. Schmidt recoiled screaming in fear as Bolan raised it overhead like an ice pick. The massive hands of Kubrik and Dudley clamped down on the bar owner's shoulders as the dagger spiked down into the bar.

"Listen, Enrique." Schmidt flinched as Bolan leaned in close. "I killed Fredi. I'm going to kill Gustavo and Robi. I'm going to kill El Negro and Mariano. The only thing I haven't decided yet is whether or not I'm going to kill you."

Schmidt flinched with every name that came out of Bolan's mouth. *"Por favor*...please, I don't know—"

"I'd like you to tell me what you know. I realize you are only a minor player at best, but this is Cordoba, Los Facons barrio, where it all started, and I bet you know all sort of interesting things."

"They will kill me. They will—"

Schmidt shrieked as Bolan drew the short-bladed machete from under his jacket.

"Last chance," was all Bolan said.

Betrayal and shame twisted across the Facon's face as the words began bubbling up out of him in rapid-fire Spanish. Enrique Schmidt shivered like a rabbit as he spilled his guts.

Cordoba City

BOLAN RIPPED OPEN the crate from Belgium. He looked up in mild disbelief from the FN-2000 assault weapons racked and nestled in packing foam. Kubrik shrugged.

A second crate held spare magazines, rifle ammo and 40 mm munitions. A third, unopened crate held what Kubrik simply referred to as "accessories."

Encizo drove the panel van back from the airport. Enrique Schmidt sat bound and gagged in the back of the van as they drove through the cobblestone streets. Kubrik scowled at him. "You're really going to let this piece of shit live?"

"Made him a deal." Bolan regarded his fear-torn intelligence asset. Enrique Schmidt had not had much very specific to say, but his generalities were intriguing in the extreme. Bolan was particularly interested in the rumor of "Turcos in the mountains."

Argentines referred to anyone from the Middle East as "Turks."

"I'm thinking it's a training ground and sanctuary all in one." Bolan studied a map of Cordoba. "With Gustavo in charge of the local military, he can use military assets to transport and conceal the terrorist cells. His personal Fuerza de Paz troops will be driving the trucks, flying the planes, and I suspect any time the terrorists are in public view they're wearing Argentine army uniforms."

"That still leaves the question of why." Dudley peered over Bolan's shoulder at the map. "Why are Middle Eastern terrorists cooperating with these Facons? I'm not buying sanctuary and weapons in the long run, particularly if these guys are sacrificing themselves to do the Facons' dirty work."

"You're right." Bolan nodded slowly. "It's a lot bigger than that."

"What are you thinking?"

"What's the target of every Middle Eastern terrorist? Who are they really trying to hit, directly or indirectly?"

"Israel." Dudley let out a long slow breath. It was clear his leg wounds were giving him a lot of pain. "Israel, or anyone perceived to be helping Israel."

Bolan reached into a gas mask bag and pulled out Vikkers's SS dagger. There was blood on the handle but the swastika and the SS were still plain to see in the ebony handle. "I think the terrorists and the Facons have something in common."

Encizo brought the van to a halt. "We're here."

Bolan put the knife back in the bag. "Keep the motor running." He pulled his cap low over his eyes and put a cigarette between his lips. He jumped out of the van holding an empty cardboard box and a clipboard. He walked across the street and passed the wooden gate of Roberto Von's town house. Two bodyguards in suits and sunglasses stood like stone Buddhas on either side of the gate sweating in the heat. Each was wearing an earpiece and had a mike attached to his lapel. The bulges under their left arms revealed heavy armament. Their sunglasses tracked Bolan as he walked along the sidewalk.

Bolan smiled like an idiot.

"Hola." He asked for a light as he juggled with the box and the clipboard.

One of the bodyguards scowled and dug his hand in his pocket. Bolan kicked him in the groin and tossed the clipboard and the box at his partner. The man batted the two objects aside and went for his gun. He never made it. His nose broke with an upward rip of the heel of Bolan's hand. Bolan closed his fist and brought the bottom of it down between the man's eyes. The man fell. The first bodyguard staggered with his hands clutched between his legs in agony. Bolan's bottom-fist strike chopped around in a short arc and unhinged the hard-man's jaw.

The bodyguard fell in a heap on top of his partner.

Several people on the street were pointing and exclaiming in alarm at the brief, brutal altercation they had witnessed.

Bolan ignored them as he reached into his bag and pulled out Vikkers's knife. The people in the street shouted as Bolan spiked it into the wood of the gate. Bolan trotted back to the van, and Encizo took it back into traffic.

The Executioner stared at Enrique Schmidt until he started shaking again. He asked, "Where do you find an honest cop around here?"

Cordoba City

OFFICER SANTIAGO Erasquino was dead, and he knew it. His last thought as he desperately fumbled to unsnap the holster strap of his Ballester-Molina duty pistol was that he should have taken the money. Every member of his family and every one of the few remaining friends he had on the force had urged him to take it. He had refused, and with that simple act of honor he had condemned himself to death. He had been sleeping with his shotgun each night waiting for death to come for him out of the darkness.

Death had found him in the middle of the day while he was armed and in uniform. Stepping down a side street to eat a hot dog had been his downfall. He had been surrounded before he knew what was happening.

Santiago froze with his .45 still holstered as the muzzles

of the immense handguns pointed at him like the cold, unwavering eyes of death. Santiago had been so scared for the past week he could barely light a cigarette without shaking. He found himself strangely calm as straightened himself and regarded his assassins.

The immense black man and an equally huge white man with a badly bruised face smiled. But Santiago's gaze was inexorably drawn to the third man of the trio. He was a large man, but not a giant like the other two. It was his sheer presence that was overwhelming. He stood with the machismo of a mountain. Santiago was suddenly aware that there were more standing behind him. It took every ounce of his will not to turn. He met the burning blue eyes before him, and his fatalistic courage began to fail him. He realized with sinking horror that he knew the man's face. He had seen its description circulated at headquarters, and out on the street.

The man facing him was the most wanted terrorist in Argentina.

The man spoke in a friendly fashion. "I'd like five minutes of your time."

In unison the weapons of the three men lowered slightly. Santiago looked back nervously and found two men behind him lowering weapons, as well. He replied in English. "Why?"

The terrorist smiled. "According to rumor you're the last honest cop in Cordoba."

"According to reports you are the most wanted man in Argentina," Santiago countered.

The man maintained his cheerful demeanor. "Well, that's true, but we have something in common."

"Oh?" Santiago found that very hard to believe. "What?"

The man shrugged. "Los Facons."

"What do you know about Los Facons?"

"Come here a second." The man tilted his head conspiratorially toward a parked panel van. "I want to show you something."

Santiago followed the man with great trepidation. The other men fell into a phalanx around him. The man flung the sliding door open. Santiago stared in shock at Enrique Schmidt. Last week, Schmidt had told Santiago that he had wasted all his chances and that he was a dead man.

Schmidt sat staring back, bound and gagged.

The man nodded at his captive. "I know this tough guy is one of them."

Santiago struggled to comprehend the enormity of what was happening.

The frightening blue-eyed man helped him. "Listen, the Facons want you dead. The Facons want me dead. I say we kill them first." The man's face lit in a startling smile. "What do you say, Officer?"

17

Cordoba City, Cordoba

"Fredi's knife! They stuck it in Robi's goddamn door! Here!
In Cordoba!" Del Valken was livid. "His fucking knife!"

Robi sat shaken.

El Negro shook his head. "I told you he was here."

"Then why don't you go kill him if you know where he is!"
the governor screamed.

El Negro rose from his seat with an ugly smile. His hand
went to his dagger. "Nano, I have had—"

"You have had nothing yet!" Del Valken rose grinning to
meet his cousin. "But you—"

"You will shut up!" Gusi thundered. "Both of you!"

Gusi wore his full military uniform. It had required extensive tailoring to fit his massive frame. He was a juggernaut in
khaki. "If you wish to kill each other, do it. Cut each other in
to fishbait. I do not care. But do it outside."

Del Valken waved a hand imperiously. "Listen to me, soldier boy, I am—"

"You are a political pimp. It might take me a little longer,
but I can make Robi president as easily as you, and him I
would not have to worry about."

Del Valken's eyes glittered dangerously. El Negro grinned

maliciously at his discomfort. Gusi turned on El Negro. "And you came crawling out of the jungle, begging for a place at our table. I sponsored you as an equal. Never forget that. You were never part of the original plan." Gusi raised his massive bulk from his chair. "I can make it happen without you, too. As a matter of fact, I can—"

"Do nothing without our consent." Robi rose. He took off his glasses and put them in his pocket. The other three watched as he rolled up his sleeves and held up the Nazi dagger. "We are the sons of the reich. To some of you that means more than to others. But we are all in agreement on one thing. We are fittest to rule. We are now but inches from our goal. In a short time we shall begin to move globally. We shall not fail now due to pathetic infighting and the efforts of one *yanqui* agent. I demand a vote. Either we go ahead with the plan and achieve our destiny, or we step outside and kill each other now."

Robi drew his own knife and stood with an SS dagger in either hand. "I vote on the side of our destiny."

"It is my destiny to be president." Del Valken nodded slowly. "It is all our destiny to rule."

Gusi and El Negro both nodded. "We are the sons of the reich—we are Los Facons. We shall follow the destiny our fathers laid forth for us."

"Good." Robi put his daggers on the table. "We are agreed. Gusi, I suggest you prepare for full military countermeasures. Once Nano and I are the acting government of this nation, the commando will be powerless. He must strike, and strike soon. We must be prepared to crush him with overwhelming force when he surfaces."

Gusi laid down his knife. "I will make all the necessary preparations. He will not survive his next attempt upon us."

Robi was silently relieved as El Negro put away his dagger. "I propose we move up our timetable, and once things go into motion all aspects of the plan must be prepared to move quickly."

"The Turcos will be ready to move within forty-eight hours, Robi. I will see to it personally," El Negro stated.

Robi turned to their guest for the first time. The guest understood little Spanish. He understood the sudden flare of discord all too clearly. Robi smiled and spoke in Arabic. "And you, my friend. All is in readiness?"

Hamza Wahab was one of the most wanted terrorists on earth. There was hardly an atrocity that had been perpetrated in the Middle East or Europe in recent memory that he had not had a hand in. The Egyptian national had been hiding from the wrath of the United States in dusty and obscure regions of North Africa. By contrast his life for the past year in Argentina had been a virtual vacation for him. He and the men he had smuggled into Argentina had enjoyed total protection and anonymity in Cordoba. There were no FBI, CIA or Interpol agents in Cordoba. No one had looked for them here so far. Anyone local who might have had even the vaguest question about their presence was owned by Los Facons or had been ruthlessly eliminated.

It didn't bother Wahab that these men were Nazis. Indeed, Wahab liked these men. He admired them. They had proved their worth a dozen times over. He knew their story. How they had inherited their feelings of superiority from their fathers and grandfathers. They had ruthlessly forged their bodies and their wills to justify those feelings. Even more impressively they had literally made the province of a modern nation their own. From childhood they set about seizing the reins of criminal, political, economic and military power. They were but heartbeats away from taking over the nation itself. Hamza Wahab considered them an iron blueprint for the kind of takeover and control that was needed in many of the politically and religiously corrupt regimes of the Middle East. He smiled.

These men had inherited far more than just their Nazi forefathers' ruthless determination. They had also inherited their hatreds and prejudices.

These men were more than willing to assist in the destruction of the state of Israel. Indeed, they considered it their duty. It was also Wahab's duty, and he had other duties to perform, as well. For the past year he'd had cadres of the most trusted men in his terrorist cells trained in the techniques of special forces soldiers.

Wahab nodded at Robi. "As ever, my friend, my men and I are prepared to do whatever is necessary."

"Thank you, Commander." Wahab smiled at the honorific. Robi stared at the map on the table. "Gusi, have some of your units dispersed throughout the province. The commando may have left Cordoba City."

Del Valken raised a sculpted eyebrow. "But we are all here. Where the hell else could the commando be?"

Sas de Cordoba Mountains, Cordoba

BOLAN MOVED UP the ridgeline. Encizo, Santiago and Grimaldi followed him. Santiago was turning out to be a very valuable asset. He had been an art professor in Buenos Aires until the combination of a professor's salary and the devaluation of the Argentine peso had made his position untenable. It was with some personal humiliation that he had returned to his native province of Cordoba, and his uncle, a sergeant, had gotten him a job in the city police. He had begun as a *suboficial,* but with his education and family connection he had made the rank of *oficial* in a matter of months. He had been issued a gun and become a "real" cop. As a man with an education and family in the force, he was to be afforded some opportunities, and the facts of life were explained to him.

Los Facons ruled Cordoba.

Crime was their business. The local police were their flunkies. It was the job of the police to take the money, look the other way and assist the Facons in driving out any rivals or entrepreneurs in crime who didn't wish to pay their respects to the Facons. Santiago had been offered the money, and he had refused to take it. His fellow officers had come with the money and demanded he take it. Santiago had again refused. He became an instant pariah on the force. No one would work with him. He told his uncle to get him a job writing parking tickets or swabbing out the police station latrines—it didn't matter. His uncle had told Santiago that he was not being blackballed out of betrayal, though many other cops had accused him of it.

Santiago was a dead man.

No one wanted to be associated with a dead man. His uncle said there was nothing he could do to save him. The security of his own family absolutely depended on not getting involved. His uncle had washed his hands. No one said no to Los Facons.

Santiago would serve as an example.

Not surprisingly, when Bolan had shown Enrique Schmidt to Santiago in the back of the van, Santiago had immediately volunteered for Bolan's anti-Facon brigade. They had driven the van to police headquarters. Santiago had gone inside, gone to the armory, shoved his duty pistol in the armorer's face and unofficially checked out a .45-caliber Halcon submachine gun, ten spare magazines, body armor and a tear gas gun along with a satchel of projectiles. The police armorer made little attempt to stop Santiago or to raise an alarm. Santiago was a dead man. Everyone on the force knew it. A man too honorable or too stupid to take the money was also too honorable and stupid to flee the country. Santiago had to eat. He had to sleep. Los Facons were coming for him, and they would come at the time and place of their choosing.

Guns would not save Santiago.

The Executioner had decided to save Santiago. Bolan hunkered down and peered through his binoculars. Both Schmidt and Santiago agreed that something was going on in the mountains of Cordoba. Officially, it was a government water project. Unofficially, everyone knew the military was doing something. However, Bolan suspected that even the Argentine top brass didn't know what was really going on. Only Los Facons knew that.

From Bolan's perch, except for the Argentine flag flying from the command tent, it looked an awful lot like a terrorist training camp.

Bolan surveyed the barbed-wire fencing and the star-shaped complex of observation towers with interlocking fields of fire. The grounds surrounding the base had been cleared of trees and rocks and bulldozed flat into a hundred-meter killing zone around the perimeter. The interior was a small complex of tents and sheds. There was a firing range and several helicopter pads. Bolan examined the camp critically.

It looked more like a terrorist firebase.

Grimaldi lowered his binoculars. "What do you think, Sarge?"

Bolan did some quick calculations. A few men in khaki uniforms lounged about in the heat of the day. Most were probably inside. Bolan counted huts and latrines. The camp could easily house one, possibly two platoons of terrorists and General Von's Fuerza de Paz special purpose troops.

"I think we light the place up," Bolan said.

"Yeah, Dudley can barely walk, Kubrik has multiple concussions and Santiago's fired his service pistol exactly once." Grimaldi's grin grew in wattage. "You ain't exactly tip-top, either. We suck. You know that, right."

"I'll be fine." Bolan scanned through his binoculars again. "We park Dudley someplace classy with a high-powered rifle. Santiago sticks to me like glue."

"Yeah, and what about Kubrik? He's still seeing three of everything."

"As long as he shoots the one in the middle he'll be fine."

Grimaldi shook his head in bemusement.

BRIGADIER GENERAL Paul Gonzalez looked up at his unexpected visitors. They wore army uniforms, but flying medals decorated their chests and both bore the insignia of army aviation. "I am told you have urgent business?"

"We are on extremely urgent business, of national security. Thank you for seeing us on such short notice. I am Colonel Lucas Fabian. This is Captain Tomas Fonzi. We are with army aviation, assigned to the special aviation detachment of Fuerza de Paz, under the command of General Gustavo Von."

The brigadier general's eyes widened. Fuerza de Paz and its actions against the bizarre incursions of terrorists into the Rio Lujan were all over the press and the talk of every military installation. General Von's rapid action against the terrorists had almost single-handedly made the military respectable in the eyes of the Argentine populace. Gonzalez waved at the chairs in front of his desk. "How may I be of assistance?"

The colonel and the captain took seats. "There is little time. As you know, for the first time in our history, there are cells of foreign terrorists operating in Argentina. At first, all evidence led us to believe that they were trying to strike targets in Argentina tied to the United States. However, as you may also know, those terrorist cells have gone active against Argentine citizens and Argentine interests. The strike on the Rio Lujan was their first such action. However, I will tell you, we were lucky on that one. We got an anonymous tip, and were able to deploy in time. From that action, certain evidence has arisen. We believe the terrorists are planning actions within the province of Cordoba."

Gonzalez was genuinely shocked. "What possible targets could they have in Cordoba?"

"We cannot be sure. However, we know they made an attempt on the life of the governor at the American Embassy."

The brigadier general nodded. Governor Del Valken was the pride of Cordoba. All in the province believed he would be the next president of the Argentine Republic.

"General Von is also a man of Cordoba. Both his family

and the headquarters of Fuerza de Paz are here. As the commander of Fuerza de Paz, General Von is the terrorists' greatest foe. His brother, Roberto Von, is our nation's leading economic strategist, if we can just get his plans initiated. It has not been made public, but his life was threatened two days ago." The colonel's face was grim. "The Argentine republic was already in great economic and political turmoil before the incursions of the terrorists, and as you can see, several well-planned strikes in the province of Cordoba could plunge the nation further into chaos. We believe the terrorists intend to destabilize the entire country. Who is ultimately sponsoring them, we do not know. What their true plans for our nation are, I shudder to speculate. All we know is this. We must crush them. Now."

Brigadier General Gonzalez straightened in his chair. "Be assured the complete resources of my base are at your disposal. I will mobilize all fighter, strike and observation wings. I have them rotating in armed-and-ready-to-launch status around the clock."

The colonel frowned. "We believe the terrorists are observing all military installations in the province. If your base goes to full alert, they will most likely lay low or change their plans. We believe their attacks will be small-scale, assassinations and bombings. Our best chance to stop them is to detect them when they act and then strike immediately."

"I understand, Colonel. How may I be of assistance?"

"Fuerza de Paz is dispersed to a number of secret locations in the province and ready to respond at a moment's notice. We have helicopters and heavy weapons. However, even though we believe the predicted terrorist strikes will be small, we believe the terrorists themselves will be heavily armed. Grenade and rocket launchers, heavy machine guns, perhaps shoulder-launched ground-to-air missiles. They appear to have access to a wide range of military hardware. What General Von requests of you is a strike aircraft to be temporarily assigned to Fuerza de Paz. It will be deployed to a secret location near predicted targets and give air support to Fuerza de Paz when and if they go active."

The brigadier general nodded. "I see. Very well, Colonel, I will assign my best pilot—"

"General, I must request that you release the aircraft to myself and Captain Fonzi. I must also request that you do this with utmost discretion. General Von has managed to shuffle units of Third Corps and the Fourth Airborne Brigade to the capital under false orders. It is a slender ruse, but he has made it appear that all units of Fuerza de Paz are in Buenos Aires for an anticipated attack on the capital. Instead, we are here, in Cordoba. The enemy must not know this."

"Colonel, I do not question you or General Von, but this is most unusual."

"General, it pains me to say this, and I believe it is something you yourself must already suspect." The colonel let out a long breath. "No terrorists could act so openly in our country without extensive help from within our own government."

Brigadier General Gonzalez was appalled. "I...see."

"The capital is rotten. We are attacked from without and within. It is up to us, General, the men of Cordoba. General Von was very explicit. This is not an order from the capital. The capital does not know of it. This is a personal request for assistance from General Von and Fuerza de Paz. You are under no compunction to grant it. Indeed, if you find it contrary to the oath you swore, you have the complete freedom to report General Von and place myself and Captain Fonzi under arrest."

The brigadier general blinked. "I—"

"However, General Von was also explicit that I must tell you that should you grant his request, you will have his personal gratitude." The colonel took a silver-handled knife in a silver sheath from within his jacket and laid it on the table. "You understand."

Brigadier General Paul Gonzalez nodded at the *facon* as it glittered on his desk. He was a man of Cordoba. "I understand."

"He also told me to mention that you would have the gratitude of the next president of the republic, as well as her next minister of finance."

Gonzalez nodded again. One did not rise to the rank of brigadier general in Argentina by being a good soldier alone. "I understand completely. Choose your aircraft. My adjutant and his two most trusted men will arm it to your specifications. I will sign orders saying I am having it flown off base for a factory overhaul."

"My thanks, General." The colonel smiled. "You mentioned mobilizing all your aircraft. Have one flight of fighters armed and ready, outfitted for ground attack, under the pretense of weapons training. I will give you a secret radio frequency. Monitor it for the next forty-eight hours. Should it become necessary, we will radio for further assistance."

The brigadier general rose. "Colonel, tell General Von he has my full cooperation and my utmost discretion in the defense of the republic." He pressed a buzzer and his aide came into the office. "Ansaldo, you are to escort these two officers to Hangar 11 and clear it of all nonessential personnel. Then choose two men you trust, and give these officers every assistance. Ask no questions, and carry out your orders in absolute secrecy."

Lieutenant Ansaldo saluted sharply. He turned and led the pair of silent strangers out of the commander's office and across the tarmac to Hangar 11. He cleared the hangar and went to fetch a pair of trusted ordnance men. For a moment the two army aviation officers were alone in the hangar.

Jack Grimaldi turned to Encizo. "Colonel, you are smoother than shit through a goose."

Encizo grinned. "I wasn't bad." He looked at the hangar full of graceful, twin-engined turboprop aircraft.

Grimaldi checked his watch. "Let's get Lieutenant Ansaldo hopping. Striker is going to be moving in two hours."

18

El Negro swept into the tent with Hamza Wahab at his side. El Negro's long black hair was pulled up under a fatigue cap, and both men wore Argentine army uniforms. Aziz Aloui looked up from where he sat cleaning a Brazilian Uru submachine gun. Aloui was Wahab's right-hand man and bodyguard. The Algerian was also a former French foreign legionnaire, and he enforced discipline in the camp with legionary zeal. Even Gusi's Fuerza de Paz troopers gave the grinning, gold-toothed Aloui a wide berth.

Aloui sensed trouble. "Something is wrong?"

"I do not know." El Negro almost seemed to be sniffing the air. El Negro made Aloui nervous. Aloui had been raised in the desert. His upbringing had been very traditional. It was absolutely clear to him that the half-breed was a sorcerer. Aloui was used to intimidating most men he met. He found himself able to meet the Argentine's flat black gaze only with difficulty and had to force himself not to make the sign against the evil eye. El Negro ran a distracted eye around the tent. "Your men will be ready to leave at dawn?"

"All is in readiness. We await one more truck this evening, and we shall be prepared to break camp at dawn, as scheduled."

"You received the final shipment?"

Aloui finished reassembling his weapon and racked the

bolt on a loaded magazine. "It arrived at noon, as scheduled. All components are accounted for and are prepared for your inspection."

"Good." El Negro nodded. "Show me."

Aloui stepped protectively to Wahab's side. The three men left the tent, and soldiers outside fell around them in formation as they walked across the compound. They came to a tent with extra guards around it. The floor within was poured concrete with steps leading down. The three men walked down the steps to the hardened bunker below.

In an open concrete cell with no furnishings, three long, gray-green cylinders lay strapped to a pallet. Well-broken-in coveralls marked with the logo of the Buenos Aires Public Transportation system hung on pegs.

El Negro nodded in satisfaction. "You have picked your men?"

"Yes." Wahab's jaw set with determination. The next step in the plan was his responsibility. "Three two-man teams, as you specified. All six men have undergone full immersion in the last year and speak fluent Spanish. All are among my most trusted inner circle. All are prepared to sacrifice themselves for this endeavor. They have been practicing the mission for a week and are consistently forty-five seconds beneath the allotted time. I can foresee no problem whatsoever with infiltration, particularly with your operatives in the local police controlling the situation for them. The plan is set. All is going according to schedule. There is nothing that can go wrong."

The distracted air passed once more over El Negro's face. His dark eyes roved the ceiling as if searching for something. "There is always something that can go wrong."

BOLAN MOVED through the darkness. They had lost forty-eight hours while the Farm had scrambled to get Argentine army aviation uniforms with appropriate insignia and stripes cut to fit and sent by courier to Buenos Aires and then Cordoba. During that time Bolan, Kubrik, Dudley and Santiago had lain low in the hills around the camp and gathered intelligence. Encizo's and Grimaldi's faces were unknown, and the two men had mingled with the masses in the capital and the countryside, picking up tips and rumors. Encizo had rented a farmhouse outside of the capital as a working base and then picked up the supplies and gear from the airport in Cordoba City. It was a desperate loss of time, during which the terrorist camp had undergone considerable activity and reinforcement, but the prospect of air support could spell the difference between success and failure. It was too good to pass up.

The downtime had also yielded some useful hours of observation. A truck came to the camp both days around noon and again sometime after midnight.

Bolan prepared himself to wait. Despite Dudley's best effort they'd had to take turns supporting him most of the way. They put him in position with a rifle and an FN assault weapon. Dudley was now isolated and unable to move if trouble came his way. Kubrik was creeping as close to the perimeter as he dared. Bolan had to admit to himself that the plan was thin and running toward anorexia by the second. If Encizo and Grimaldi failed, the operation on the encampment would have to be aborted. Bolan's earpiece crackled to life as Grimaldi spoke.

"Striker, this is Cover. One hundred percent success. Cover is secured."

Bolan let out a relieved breath. "ETA?"

"Twenty minutes."

"Affirmative, Cover. Striker out." Bolan switched frequencies. "Polack, you in place?"

"Affirmative, Cooper. Awaiting your signal."

"Chicago?"

Dudley's voice came back. "Affirmative."

"Professor?"

"I am ready and waiting." Santiago sounded nervous, but ready.

The previous day Encizo had bought a car. That car was three and a half miles from the camp at a crossroads in the mountains. The car was up on a jack with a flat tire. Santiago had left his heavier weapons in the back seat and had only his holstered pistol and a flashlight. His main weapon was his blue uniform and his badge. If he couldn't flag down the midnight truck going into the camp, then the mission was a no-go. Santiago had declared his willingness to stand in the middle of the road and let the truck run him down if necessary. It would be much cleaner than anything the Facons had in store for him.

Bolan peered around a rock.

Santiago and his car were fifty feet from his position.

Bolan's earpiece crackled again. "Striker, this is Cover. I have ground traffic coming toward your position, five miles from the west."

Bolan nodded to himself. That was the direction the trucks came from town. "Professor, we are a go, five minutes. Lose your radio."

"Yes, Cooper." Santiago took his radio and threw it beneath the blanket in his back seat. He turned on his headlights and squatted beside the jack and his spare tire. Time ticked in agonizing slowness. Bolan became aware of the ghostly glow of headlights in the distance. Santiago waited a few more moments and then stood. He stepped into the middle of the road and waved his flashlight overhead. The truck came on blaring its horn. Santiago was as good as his word and stood steadfastly in the middle of the road. Dust and gravel flew as the truck driver stood on his brake pedal. The brakes screeched and locked up. Dust flew in clouds in the headlights as the truck ground to a halt. The driver and passenger doors flew open. Men in Argentine army uniforms leaped out. Both men carried sidearms. The man riding shotgun also carried an FN rifle with the stock folded.

Santiago took an intimidated step back as the two men advanced on him, roaring in blistering Spanish about military priorities and idiot local police.

Bolan moved.

Santiago's orders were simple. He was not to look for Bolan. If he managed to stop the truck, he was to buy Bolan one minute, no matter what. Santiago lowered his flashlight and shone it in the eyes of one of the soldiers. The soldier screamed to get the light out of his face and Santiago dropped the flashlight and continued to let the soldiers back him up all the way to his car.

Bolan slid under the truck. He had no climbing gear, only rope he had knotted into a makeshift harness. He looped the rope around a strut beneath the truck and took up the slack so that his hips would be suspended. His weapons were strapped to his chest. Bolan waited while the soldiers chewed out Santiago. They spent nearly a minute spewing venom. They took his badge number and his name and then leaped back into the truck and slammed the doors.

Bolan pulled his gas mask over his face and braced himself against the bottom of the truck. Gears ground and the truck lurched forward. The truck turned and took the road that led to the camp. Bolan spoke into his mike. "All units, I am inbound."

The roads in the mountains of Cordoba were rough, and the driver was clearly pissed off and driving fast. Bolan bounced and jerked in his makeshift harness and his gloved hands and feet were yanked from their bracing positions with every pothole. Dust and gravel tore into him from under the tires. Only his gas mask allowed him to breathe. It was a backbreaking three miles to the camp. The dark dust storm came to an end as the truck entered the light thrown by the camp and stopped at the gate. The truck was hailed by guards. Bolan clung like a spider to the bottom of the truck as it rumbled through the gate.

Dudley's voice spoke in Bolan's earpiece. "Cooper, I have you confirmed through the gate. Awaiting your signal."

"Affirmative."

The truck drove a short way into camp. They parked next to a pair of similar trucks and a group of jeeps and motorcycles. The engine clanked off and Bolan pulled his gas mask up from his face. The two soldiers stepped out of the cab. Bolan heard the chink of a lighter and watched their boots as they moved off. Bolan heard them speak to one another in Arabic.

The Executioner drew his knife and cut himself free from his ropes. He crouched beneath the truck listening. There was a tent a few yards away from the front of the truck. Over the popping and ticking of the hot engine Bolan could hear more voices speaking in Arabic.

Bolan emerged from beneath the truck. He was wearing a plain khaki uniform and fatigue cap. No one in the camp would be carrying an FN-2000 weapon system or belts of grenades and web gear, but he would just have to brass that out. He had raided Kubrik's crate of accessories. His weapon now sported the long black tube of a sound suppressor and was loaded with subsonic ammunition.

The multiple-munitions, antipersonnel round loaded in the 40 mm launcher below it would make significantly more noise.

Bolan walked around the tent and ducked beneath the flap.

AZIZ ALOUI and the two men with him looked up at the stranger who walked into the tent. He wore a khaki uniform, but the weapon he carried was of a kind that Aloui had never seen before, much less around the camp. Dust made dark outlines around his face where he had obviously been wearing some sort of face cover. Every instinct earned in a lifetime devoted to war, terror and murder spoke to Aloui now.

Something was wrong.

Aloui smiled and exposed gold teeth. He spoke in Span-

ish. "Are you lost? The Fuerza de Paz mess is two tents over."
He turned slightly to one of his men and spoke in jovial Arabic. "More tea, Ahmad?" He lifted the kettle. "Shoot that man—he is—"

The weapon in the stranger's hand barely whispered. The click-click-clicking of his weapon's action cycling was the loudest noise in the room. Aloui sat frozen in place as his men slid from their chairs to the floor. Aloui's hand was inches from his submachine gun, but he didn't move his hand.

The smoking black eye of the suppressed muzzle trained itself on Aloui's single thick black brow. The man's disturbing blue eyes narrowed as he spoke in Arabic. "I know you."

Aloui felt a terrible sinking feeling in the pit of his stomach as the man switched to English.

"You're Aziz Aloui. You're a wanted man, and wherever you are one finds Hamza Wahab." The man's cold eyes never left Aloui's. "Where is Wahab?"

Aloui's eyes strayed against his will toward the table where his submachine gun lay. The man smiled at him. "What's in the larger tent with the guards around it?"

Aloui swallowed. The man's terrible gaze continued to bore into Aloui's as if he could read his mind. "You're not the suicidal type. Here's what you are going to do. With your left hand, with two fingers, I want you to eject the magazine of your weapon. Empty the round in the chamber, then eject all the rounds in the magazine and replace it in your weapon. Do it all slowly."

Aloui followed orders with molasses-like slowness. "Now what? You will never leave this camp alive," he challenged the intruder.

"You and I are going to take a walk over to that tent I was asking you about. You make one false move, and I put you in the bone yard." The man inclined his head at the table. "Light a cigarette."

Aloui rose from his seat woodenly. The man had read him

like a book. Aloui was a terrorist, a murderer and a torturer of men, women and children. But he was not suicidal. That he left to other men. Aloui slung his empty weapon over his shoulder. He lit a Parisienne. The tandem muzzles of the stranger's weapon never wavered. "Let's go for a walk," he said.

The two men walked across the camp talking as Aloui smoked a cigarette. No one made any attempt to stop them. Aloui fought for an out. "I must give the recognition signal."

The man brooked no argument. "We walk right in."

Aloui gnashed his teeth as his men saluted sharply and held the tent flap for him and his guest. The flap fell behind them. The stranger stared at the steel door at the bottom of the concrete stairs. "Open it."

"I do not have the code."

The man brought his weapon to his shoulder and lowered his aim to Aloui's knees. "I'll blow your legs off."

Aloui's hands itched for the tiny .25-caliber Walther pistol in his pocket. He walked down the stairs as if he were descending into his own grave. The voice behind him was iron. "Open it," he demanded.

Aloui keyed the numbers and the steel bolts slid back with a thunk. He pushed open the door and the single overhead light automatically came on. Aloui entered and the stranger followed. The man stopped and stared at the three cylinders and the inscriptions on them.

Aloui lunged.

Bolan's finger squeezed the trigger. He had been stabbed, burned, beaten and blown up in the past week. Grimaldi had warned him that he was not one hundred percent. Aziz Aloui was the larger and stronger man, and in the moment that he lunged he was also the faster.

The action of the FN-2000 rattled in Bolan's hands. Bolan's reactions were a half step too slow, and the extra foot and a half of sound suppressor on the barrel of his weapon gave Aloui reach and leverage. The Algerian slapped the muzzle skyward, and Bolan's silent burst chipped concrete from the ceiling. Bolan grimaced as Aloui buried his fist into his middle. Bolan's ribs cracked. Aloui's fist was filled with a small stainless-steel pistol.

Aloui began pulling the trigger as fast as he was able.

Bolan wasn't able to wear full armor on his infiltration, but he was wearing concealable soft body armor beneath his army uniform. He prayed his armor would hold as Aloui shot him six times in the stomach. Bolan swung his knee up between Aloui's legs but the Algerian managed to block it. Bolan struggled to bring the muzzle of his weapon in line with Aloui's head. The Algerian's massive hand held the suppressor like a vise and kept the muzzle pointed up past his head as Bolan fired another burst. Aziz exposed his gold teeth and flexed his fist. The aluminum tube of the suppressor crumpled and twisted. The light, subsonic, .22-caliber bullets tore into the suddenly misaligned baffles and springs of the suppressor and piled into one another. The expanding gas behind the bullets choked off. Bolan's 5-round burst failed to exit the barrel and his weapon jammed up solid.

Aloui grinned triumphantly. Bolan saw stars as the terrorist drove his empty pistol between his eyes. An elbow rapidly followed it in a blow to the side of Bolan's skull. The Executioner's battle instincts took over. He couldn't beat Aloui in hand-to-hand combat in his current condition. Aloui's elbow clouted Bolan along the side of the skull a second time. Bolan kept both hands working on wresting control of his weapon. Bolan's vision tunneled as the Algerian's elbow ripped into his jaw.

Bolan suddenly ceased fighting Aloui's grip on the weapon. He went with it and twisted the rifle with both hands. The weapon went vertical between the two men. Aloui's gold-toothed grin froze as the much shorter muzzle of the grenade launcher was suddenly twisted beneath his chin.

Aloui's head disappeared in a 40 mm eruption of yellow flame and buckshot.

Bolan shoved the corpse away. He swayed and caught himself as his vision swam.

Kubrik's voice immediately spoke in his earpiece. "Cooper, I heard some sort of muffled detonation. Please confirm."

"That was me." Bolan stared back at the cylinders. Chemical hazard warning stickers were emblazoned on each one. The letters HCN were stenciled in bold black letters beneath the warning markers.

"Cooper, I have movement within the camp."

Bolan didn't doubt it. He looked at the Buenos Aires Public Transportation coveralls hanging on the wall. There was also a map of Buenos Aires hanging on the wall. The central train station of the capital was highlighted. There was a second schematic of the station itself. Bolan glanced back at the cylinders. They were filled with hydrogen cyanide gas. It was known as blood gas in military circles. It was instantly lethal to anyone who breathed it.

It was the same gas the Nazis had used in their gas chambers in the concentration camps.

With total clarity, the Executioner understood Los Facons' plan. There was going to be another terrorist attack in Buenos Aires, a massacre in the capital's busiest train station. There would be a demand for emergency elections. Mariano Del Valken would be unanimously elected president, and he would immediately appoint General Gustavo Von as supreme military commander. Martial law would be declared. They would miraculously stop the attacks. The "terrorists" would be rounded up and executed.

Then with an entire nation in their fists, the real fun would begin.

Bolan's lips skinned back from his teeth. "Professor, are you in position?"

"Yes, I am in position."

In their two days of downtime they had located the cables supplying electricity to the camp. Assuming Santiago survived stopping the truck for Bolan, his secondary mission was to get to the wire and cut it.

Bolan pulled his gas mask on and pulled his night-vision goggles over the lens adapters. The lights in the bunker blinked off as he powered up the goggles. Bolan unscrewed the mangled suppressor from his rifle and cleared the action.

An alarm began to howl through the camp.

The Executioner slid a fresh magazine into his rifle and aimed it at the first cylinder. "Professor, cut the lights. Polack, wait for the generators to kick in—then hit them."

"WHAT THE HELL was that?" El Negro looked up at hearing a vague, hollow, thumping noise.

Wahab glanced around. "I heard nothing."

El Negro's instincts screamed up and down his spine. His face split into a snarl of hatred. "He's here!"

"Who?"

"The commando!" El Negro scooped up his Brazilian submachine gun. He whirled on one of Gusi's Fuerza de Paz troopers. "Sound the alarm! Contact General Von and tell him the camp is under attack!"

The trooper sprinted out of the tent. Seconds later the raid sirens began to howl across the camp.

"Wahab, get your men together! Follow the plan! A fighting retreat and then dispersal into the mountains! I will take the troopers and secure the ga—"

Generator engines roared into life, and lights blinked back on in the camp.

"We have been infiltrated." The recognizable thump of a 40 mm grenade launcher boomed from outside the perimeter. Machine guns answered from the towers. El Negro's worst suspicions were confirmed as he heard a high-explosive grenade detonate within camp. The steady pulse of the emergency generator howled off kilter, and the lights of the camp sputtered and failed as the stricken diesel died. "Have your men put on their night-vision equipment. Get to the trucks."

El Negro powered up his goggles and stepped out of the tent. The machine guns in the eastern two guard towers sent tracers into the perimeter like blind feelers. Turcos ran around the camp waving their rifles and trying to find Wahab and protect him. Gusi's troopers were better organized. They ran to their assigned emergency positions. A squad was already armed and outside El Negro's tent waiting for deployment.

"There is an intruder in the camp. Follow me!" The men fanned out behind El Negro as they sped to the concealed bunker. El Negro whipped his hand in a short circle, and his men surrounded the tent. He knifed his hand forward, and the two men beside him broke off and silently moved to the tent flap.

The first man's knees buckled. He made a stricken sound and fell to the ground. The man beside him suddenly staggered and clutched at his throat, gurgling. A man at the far corner of the tent hunched his shoulder as if he had been stabbed and fell forward onto his face.

"Back! Back! Back!" El Negro roared at the top of his lungs. "He's released the gas! He's—"

El Negro's submachine gun rattled in his hands as the tent flap fluttered and a grenade bounced out into the dust. He threw himself down. The lenses of his night-vision goggles solarized as the magnesium flares of the flash-stun grenade blazed into their incandescent millisecond of life.

THE EXECUTIONER LUNGED from the tent. The blinding effect of the flash-stun was amplified by the light-gathering power of his opponents' night-vision equipment. However, the Fuerza de Paz troopers had indeed been trained by some of

America's finest. Even blinded, they dropped and put the tent into a withering cross fire. Bolan chose a lane between the muzzle-flashes and ran for his life. He staggered as a bullet struck his armor and his already besieged rib cage screamed in protest.

Bolan threw himself down beside a man blindly firing into the tent and screamed in Spanish. *"¡Donde!"*

The trooper blinked his eyes against the pulsing after-images of the flash grenade and shouted back. "He's in the tent! An infiltrator! He—"

Bolan drove the knife edge of his right hand down into the blinded man's neck. The trooper collapsed on top of his sub-machine gun.

Bolan ripped off his gas mask. The hydrogen cyanide was dispersing rapidly away from the bunker and it was a chance he would have to take. He couldn't afford to be the only man in camp with a gas mask on. Besides, blood gas had the unfortunate side effect of instantly beginning to degrade the filters of gas masks.

Bolan pulled his fatigue cap around and became a Fuerza de Paz trooper. He fired a burst from his submachine gun at the empty tent. The rest of the troopers were blinking and shaking their heads to clear their vision from the grenade. Trucks and jeeps were grinding into life, and armored men were spilling out of tents like ants.

Kubrik's grenade launcher continued to thump in the darkness. The machine gunners in the towers tried to respond to his muzzle-flash. A high-powered rifle cracked in the distance, and one of the tower gunners fell over the rail and tumbled to the ground.

Dudley was in the game.

The threat had been identified and the enemy engaged. It was time to call in the cavalry.

"Jack, I need you."

"Confirm position, Striker," Grimaldi replied instantly.

Bolan glanced around. The spare fuel drums for the generators were burning nicely. "Forty yards due south of burning fuel. Moving south."

"Affirmative, Striker. Inbound."

Bolan broke cover as the sound of a twin-engined turboprop started to rumble in the distance. A voice roared in Spanish. It rang with the unmistakable tone of command. "You! Come with me!"

Bolan broke his course and ran toward El Negro and the two troopers with him.

"Quickly! Get my jeep and come back here! See that—"

El Negro's jaw dropped as Bolan raised his stolen submachine gun and began firing. Bolan then swung his muzzle onto the two Fuerza de Paz troopers. The weapon buzz sawed in his hands as he put a burst into one of them. An answering burst hammered Bolan's armor. The Executioner stayed on target and gunned the second man down.

Bolan swung his muzzle back.

El Negro stood with three bleeding holes in his chest. His left hand clutched a tent rope to hold himself up. The Uru submachine gun in his right hand had Bolan dead to rights. The two men exchanged fire. Bolan was driven backward as El Negro held his trigger on full auto. Twenty of the thirty rounds in the magazine hit the left side of his torso. Bolan's heart and lungs fisted in his chest. His own aim was driven off track and his burst went wide. Sonic cracks whipped past Bolan's left ear as El Negro's muzzle climbed and he burned the rest of his magazine into the night.

Both weapons clacked open on empty chambers. Bolan gasped and nearly fell backward. He couldn't tell if his armor had held or not. His limbs felt as if they belonged to someone else.

The thunder of turboprops in the distance rose to a roar.

El Negro heaved himself off the rope and came in for the kill. He dropped his spent weapon and his dagger appeared.

His hand whipped upward in an underhand throw. The flashing steel flew like a dart straight for Bolan's face.

Bolan brought up his empty submachine gun, and El Negro's gleaming blade clattered off the still smoking receiver.

El Negro came on. His long hair flew behind him. The front of his khaki shirt was bloody from collar to belt. The fires of the burning diesel fuel backlit him in lurid orange. El Negro came on like the end of the world. Bolan had no strength to exchange blows with the killer. He didn't bother. El Negro's stiffened fingers shot for Bolan's eyes and throat. Bolan didn't try to block. He did what his body was screaming to do anyway and simply fell down.

He managed to grab El Negro's wrists and put his boot into his belly as he fell and rolled backward.

El Negro soared over Bolan. His flight was rudely interrupted as he collided with a tent rope and folded around it. Bolan rolled over and pushed himself to his hands and knees. If he had the strength, he would have sworn at what he saw. El Negro rose with inhuman vitality. He reached over to a pallet beside the tent and picked up a crowbar.

Bolan's fingers closed around the handle of the fallen SS dagger. He pushed himself up and swayed.

El Negro's bloodstained smile was hideous as he stepped forward. The killer stopped only when Bolan brought up his blade between them. A strangled wheeze escaped El Negro's lips as he was impaled on his own knife.

Bolan threw himself back from his adversary.

El Negro fell on his face in the dust.

The roar of the turboprops overhead rose to a scream.

The camp lit up like Hell on Earth as the napalm detonated.

THE PUCARA'S ENGINES howled as Grimaldi pulled up out of his attack run. It was a joy to fly.

Grimaldi banked his plane around to survey the damage. Encizo was serving as spotter from the second seat. "Just keep her steady," he said to Grimaldi. "We'll switch to rockets. Head for the main tent complex."

"Affirmative," Grimaldi said.

"Striker, what is your position?" Encizo asked.

Bolan's voice was labored. "I'm on the southern edge of camp."

"Good, stay there."

Grimaldi flicked his weapon selector. "Going to rockets. Going in."

Grimaldi was pushed back into his seat as he shoved his throttles forward and dived to attack. He put his reflector sight in the middle of the main complex of tents and depressed his trigger. The 2.75-inch rockets rippled out from pods beneath the wings. The thirty-eight rockets screamed down into the tents and detonated. Grimaldi cocked his head as the very air around the tents suddenly lit up in yellow fire and pulsed outward around the larger orange blooms of high explosive.

Encizo cocked his head. "Striker, I am observing peculiar secondary explosions."

"The enemy had hydrogen cyanide gas. I deployed it. The gas is igniting. You're getting secondary fuel-air effect."

"Well, hot damn!" Grimaldi pulled out of his run.

The enemy was rallying. Tracers were reaching up into the sky from the camp. Worse, the machine guns in the towers were hammering lead up at the Pucara.

"Pull out and orbit at one thousand feet. That's an order!" Bolan commanded.

"Affirmative, pulling out."

Grimaldi banked his plane. Their estimate of the camp had been too conservative. There had to be at least three fully armed platoons of terrorists and troopers, possibly a company.

There had to be another underground bunker.

There were also about ten trucks and at least half a dozen jeeps. Machine guns were popping up like mushrooms by the second, and tracers streamed into the air from all around the camp.

"Rafe, call in your friends. Let's light this place up for real," Grimaldi said.

"Affirmative," Encizo replied.

Grimaldi brought the Pucara in line and switched his selector to guns. The Pucara mounted four .30-caliber machine guns and two 20 mm cannons in her sharklike fuselage. "Striker?"

"Affirmative, what's your status?"

Grimaldi grinned. "My status is going to guns. You better get the hell out of there. There's about to be a hellstorm."

LIEUTENANT ANSALDO BURST into the room. "General! I have an urgent communication on the radio frequency you told me to monitor!"

Brigadier General Gonzalez shot to his feet. "Pipe it in!"

Lieutenant Ansaldo adjusted the radio. Static crackled and a voice spoke in Spanish. "General! This is Colonel Fabian. We have engaged the enemy in the Sas de Cordoba Mountains and met heavy resistance. Captain Fonzi's plane is damaged. I am nearly out of munitions. Can you assist?"

"Yes, Colonel. This is Brigadier General Gonzalez. My second wing is armed and hot on the tarmac as you requested. Please send me your coordinates."

Lieutenant Ansaldo wrote down the coordinates. "Colonel, what is the situation?"

"Enemy in brigade strength and attempting to disperse. They are disguised as Argentine army personnel. Be advised they have heavy machine guns. Possible rocket launchers. Intelligence tells us that they are being led by Hamza Wahab and Aziz Aloui. They are known terrorists wanted by the United States and Interpol. They cannot be allowed to escape."

Brigadier General Gonzalez punched a button on his intercom. It piped into a room where six Argentine air force pilots waited for word of their undisclosed mission. "Wing 2! All pilots launch!"

Out on the base, the ready room of Wing 2 burst open, and men ran across the tarmac toward six Mirage III fighters. Rockets, bombs and missiles festooned the hardpoints beneath the wings. Near the trailing edge of the wings, the nozzles of rocket-assisted takeoff bottles gleamed. The pilots leaped into their planes and powered up the already warmed engines.

They began to roll down the runway, and the rockets suddenly screamed and plumed fire beneath their wings. The French fighters shrieked into the air at almost impossible altitudes. The air above the base shook as the pilots shoved their throttles full forward and lit their afterburners.

Lieutenant Ansaldo rapidly read them the coordinates.

Gonzalez punched his intercom. "Colonel! Wing 2 is airborne and going supersonic! Estimated time of arrival—" the general checked his watch against the map of Cordoba on his wall "—five minutes! What is the status of friendlies in the area?"

"No friendly forces in area. Captain Fonzi and I were the first to respond! Only a skeletal force of Fuerza de Paz were in the area. They have been murdered. General, the enemy is attempting to extract in jeeps and trucks! We have local police attempting to set up a roadblock while Fuerza de Paz reaction teams move in on the area. They are thirty minutes out. The terrorists cannot be allowed to escape and disperse into the mountains! Their targets are confirmed. Governor Del Valken, General Von, Economic Minister Von. If they disperse, they can still carry out their assassinations. All vehicles on the road within three kilometers of coordinates are hostile. They must not escape! I repeat! They must not escape!"

"Colonel, I have six Mirage III fighter planes fully loaded for ground attack, inbound." The general's fists clenched.

"Colonel, I will have Wing 6 airborne in ten minutes. I shall also put every airman qualified with a rifle into helicopters and secure the area after the fighters have made their attack runs." The brigadier general spoke with iron certainty. "Not a single terrorist shall escape. I give you my word."

Rafael Encizo's voice spoke back with similar certainty across the radio. "General, this night you shall be the savior of the republic."

Sas de Cordoba Mountains

"WHAT IS HAPPENING!" Gusi's voice thundered over the radio.

Hamza Wahab nodded at his driver to get the jeep moving. "We had an intruder. Then we were attacked by an aircraft."

"Aircraft?" Gusi was shocked. He couldn't believe the American government would dare attack Argentine soil, no matter what their suspicions. "Bomber?"

"No, it was a twin-engined attack aircraft of some kind. Turboprop. Armed with rockets and—"

Gusi's voice went cold. "Pucara!"

"If you say so," Wahab agreed. "There was only one. However, it did succeed in destroying the blood gas and in setting fire to half the camp. We have lost nearly two platoons of my men and your Fuerza de Paz troopers. We succeeded in driving it off with ground fire. We believe there is also at least one sniper and a grenadier out beyond the perimeter. The chemical agents are destroyed, and the camp is burning. I am evacuating."

"The *yanquis* must have stolen the plane." Gusi considered. "No matter. We can turn this to our advantage. Tomorrow's newspapers will say that terrorists have dared to attack an Argentine military installation. It will help to justify our takeover."

Wahab motioned a truck forward, and his convoy began to rumble toward the gates of the camp. Every truck and jeep had one or more heavy machine guns mounted on it. Their muzzles swung out in all directions searching for the telltale flash of the sniper or the man lobbing grenades. "I am evacuating as planned," he told Gus. "Once away from the camp, we will go to the dispersal points and break up."

"Pucara." Gusi was speaking more to himself. "They would have to have gone to the air base, but nothing has been reported stolen. No alarm has been given. If they had broken onto the base and taken off from the runway, General Gonzalez would have sent supersonic fighters to destroy it. How could—?" Gusi cut himself off. "Where is El Negro?"

"Missing, General Von." Wahab glanced up at the sky distractedly. "Presumed dead."

"What?" Gusi's voice tore into rage. "How has—?"

"General Von," Wahab interrupted.

"Find him!" Gusi roared. "Find him or find his body!"

"General Von!" Wahab looked up into the night sky. The very air itself was rumbling. "General, have you ordered any—"

The lead truck of the convoy and the front gate of the camp flew apart in a ball of orange fire. The expanding fire and flying wreckage annihilated the next jeep in line. Wahab watched in horror as the night sky strobed alight and twin 30 mm cannons began chewing a straight line through his convoy. The air vibrated with the scream of fighters passing overhead.

Wahab never saw nor heard the 500-kilogram bomb that obliterated his vehicle. His convoy was lined up to exit the gate. They formed a perfect target for the six Mirage IIIs.

The bombs fell like rain as each of the jet fighters completed its attack run. The jets soared into the sky, and their pilots eagerly switched their selectors from bombs to rockets. The six-plane formation broke up into three two-plane elements and spread apart as they thundered back toward the camp. The pilots of Wing 2 were known for their discretion and their patriotism. Their orders were explicit. Their targets were terrorists—foreign enemies of the Argentine republic.

None could be allowed to escape.

The Mirage IIIs dipped into their attack attitudes. Rockets bloomed into streaks beneath their wings.

19

Cordoba City, Cordoba

Roberto Von could not believe what he was hearing, much less what he was reading in the morning paper. He sat having breakfast in the inner courtyard of his town house. An attack on the mountain camp was inconceivable. The entire nation would be in a furor by noon. "The camp has been completely destroyed?"

Gusi's voice was arctic over the phone. "Yes, I have lost seventy-five percent of my inner cadre of Fuerza de Paz troopers."

"And the Turcos? How many—?"

"There are no more Turcos. They have been annihilated. Wahab and Aloui are both dead. Our stock of blood gas has been destroyed."

Robi prepared himself for the worst. "And our cousin?"

There was a long pause on Gusi's side of the phone. "Negro is, missing...presumed—"

"He is dead." Robi's face was a frozen mask. "Or he would have contacted us." Robi shook his head in disbelief. "Brigadier General Gonzalez attacked the camp? With jet fighters?"

"Yes." Bitter amusement crept into Gusi's voice. "On my orders."

Robi nearly choked on his coffee. "Your orders?"

"It was news to me—but that is what he told me. To control the situation I had no choice but to confirm it. I suspect I will have to give him a medal." Gusi's voice dropped an octave. "He was extremely thorough. He wiped the camp from the earth with 500-kilogram bombs and then occupied it with armed airmen from his base. He is being interviewed on television right now. It is being hailed as a great victory for the republic."

"But…" Robi tried to calculate the magnitude of the disaster. "How did this happen?"

"Somehow the *yanqui* got agents onto the air base. They posed as Fuerza de Paz pilots. They requisitioned a Pucara on my orders. They also told Gonzalez to monitor a certain radio frequency and keep a wing of fighters heated up on the airfield. The *yanquis* penetrated the base, discovered the gas and destroyed it. When my troops rallied, the *yanquis* called in Gonzalez. They broke off their own attack and let fighter wings from Gonzalez's command finish the job."

Robi's brows drew down. "Right now, it is a great victory against terrorism, and as you say, will assist us in the takeover. However, we must control the investigation. When people begin to look more closely it will be obvious that large numbers of Fuerza de Paz and terrorists were cohabiting."

"My soldiers are already relieving Gonzalez's airmen on the scene."

"Gonzalez is a patriot. What if he becomes suspicious?"

"I suspect he will." Gusi's voice was a low rumble. "But before that happens he will die a tragic death, a casualty in the war against terrorism, and be replaced by someone more tractable. I already have an air force officer in mind."

Robi frowned in thought. "Where is the stolen Pucara aircraft now?"

"We don't know. Before he died, Wahab told me they had driven the Pucara off with ground fire that damaged the aircraft. The *yanquis* will not be able to rearm or refuel it. The *yanquis* also know we are looking for them. The plane is a nonissue."

"Very well, I will contact Nano, and—" Robi looked up at a fluttering noise from above.

A skydiver was descending at dangerous speed into his courtyard. The commercial parachute flared like the wings of a hawk. Robi just had time to rise to his feet and reach for his pistol.

The Executioner landed on him with both feet.

Robi went flying beneath Bolan's boots and bounced violently off the courtyard fence.

Inside the house bodyguards were shouting and responding to the sudden crash.

Bolan wearily pushed himself up out of the ruins of the breakfast table. He drew a white-phosphorus grenade and pulled the pin. Inside the house he could see men in suits with pistols in their hands running toward the open door to the courtyard. Bolan hurled his grenade. White fire erupted within the house and filled the interior, allowing Bolan a few moments of privacy.

The Executioner returned to his first order of business.

Roberto Von rose. His left arm hung at a horrible angle from his shattered collarbone. Blood poured down the side of his head, and he blinked his eyes rapidly. He came up with his SS dagger in hand.

Bolan drew El Negro's dagger and plunged it into Von's belly.

The son of the reich gasped as the steel went in up to the hilt. His own dagger fell.

Roberto Von went limp and collapsed to the paving stones. Bolan reached down and picked up Robi's fallen blade. Robi's phone lay on the ground, and someone was shouting in frenzied Spanish. Bolan picked up the phone and listened a moment. "Robi! Robi! Brother! Answer me! Robi!"

Only one man would be calling Robi "Brother."

Bolan spoke cold, slow Spanish over the phone. "Robi's dead, Gusi. I just killed him and burned down his house. Now I'm going to kill you and Nano."

Bolan clicked off the phone and spoke into his radio set. "Santiago, get me the hell out of here."

"Yes, Cooper." An engine gunned on the street. The boards of the side fence smashed inward beneath the front bumper of a Ford Falcon. Bolan gathered up his chute as the car lurched to a halt. He stepped over smashed fencing and slid into the passenger seat. Encizo sat in the back with a rifle. Grimaldi would be flying the Pucara Bolan had jumped from back to the farmhouse outside the capital. Encizo leaned out the window and peered at Roberto Von and the SS dagger sticking out of his chest. "You got him."

"Yeah, I got him." Bolan closed his eyes as Santiago threw the car into reverse. He was utterly spent. The town house was burning. Smoke poured out of every window, and flames licked the eaves. Bolan opened his eyes and considered Robi's dagger.

There were two more deliveries to make.

Sas de Cordoba Mountains

SANTIAGO WHEELED the car up the road to the farmhouse Encizo had rented. The Pucara aircraft sat beneath the trees. The counterinsurgency aircraft had been designed to be able to take off and land on country roads or rough field strips and so far had done yeoman's service.

Grimaldi stood beside the plane he had flown over Robi's house. Bolan's aching muscles remembered the jump well. Bailing out of the attack craft had been an exercise in itself. The pilot had beaten Bolan back to the safehouse by two hours. Bolan grunted with fatigue as he pulled himself out of the car and joined the pilot in examining their air assets.

The planes had taken some damage.

"How are we for armament?" Bolan asked.

Grimaldi snorted. "Well, now, there's the rub. We're low, and we don't have extra munitions or the tools to open up the gun bays and transfer munitions. It's also leaking oil and down to half a tank of fuel. If they go anywhere at all, it ain't going to be far or fast."

"Fair enough." Bolan shrugged. "It will have to do." Bolan turned to Kubrik. He and Dudley sat in the shade monitoring the radio. "What have we got?"

"It ain't good," Kubrik replied. "Governor Del Valken has declared martial law in the province of Cordoba. The capital is locked down, and there are roadblocks throughout the mountains. From now on, moving around is going to be difficult if not impossible. General Von is getting credit for destroying a 'massive terrorist threat' up in the mountains. Del Valken's party is saying that the terrorists could not be operating so boldly in Argentina without either government collusion or massive incompetence. His party and the majority of the population are demanding emergency elections. The ruling party buckled an hour ago, and next week Argentina's going to vote. Del Valken's national approval rating is sky high." Kubrik paused and looked around unhappily. "I hate to say it, but next Tuesday, the Facons take over Argentina, and I'll tell you this, Cooper, I don't know who you answer to, but I work for the CIA, and assassinating the freely elected presidents of American allies is above my pay grade, no matter how evil they are."

"I can respect that." Bolan considered his options. He was running out of them. His team was wounded and exhausted. They were still free, but they couldn't move from their hiding place without being discovered. Their air assets were questionable in the extreme, and only had two seats. They had done an admirable job of cleaning up the Facons, but Del Valken and Gustavo Von were still viable, and they were the biggest threats. Becoming the president and supreme military commander of the nation would make them almost unassailable.

Not that this would stop Bolan.

The Facons went down. With official sanction—or without it.

"I'm with you." Dudley rose from his chair as he read Bolan's mind. "They went after my family, and if we can't get a legal hunting license for these assholes, then by God we go poaching."

"Well, I am a dead man." Santiago gave a supremely Latin shrug. "So I am with you for the duration."

Bolan looked at Encizo, who was smiling. He considered himself an international man of Latin America, and everything below the Rio Grande was God's country. His country. No one messed with it on his watch.

Bolan looked at his ace pilot. Grimaldi let out a heavy sigh. "Oh, all right, but you're flying in the death trap with me."

"Deal."

The team turned their eyes on Kubrik.

The CIA man rolled his eyes toward heaven. "Oh, what the hell. No one burns off my girlfriend's eyebrows and gets away with it. But I'm going to lose my benefits, I can tell." He shook his head as he abandoned his better judgment. "Just tell me you have a plan."

"I have a plan," Bolan replied.

Kubrik raised a mangled eyebrow. "Tell me it's not as jackass as the plan you hatched on those armored personnel carriers on the Lujan."

Bolan nodded. "It's worse."

20

Stony Man Farm, Virginia

"Striker!" Aaron Kurtzman shouted. "Where the hell have you been?"

"Here and there. You know, out in the provinces."

Kurtzman glanced at the glaring Latin American headlines scrolling across his computer. "That wouldn't have been the province of Cordoba, would it?"

"Yeah, as a matter of fact. Listen, Bear, I'm kind of stuck out here in the sticks. What's the political situation?"

"Both countries are in an uproar. The U.S. Embassy in Argentina has been attacked twice. There have been two battles with terrorists in Argentina since then. Of course it turns out those battles were with you. You have the President's trust, but he is starting to wonder what the hell is going on." Kurtzman sighed unhappily. "Are they really Nazis?"

"Oh, they're Nazis, all right. Third-generation South American Nazis, but they've got the mentality down pat. They're true believers, and they've been groomed to rule. Los Facons are absolutely for real."

"So what do you intend to do?"

"There's going to be emergency elections in Argentina next week. We have exactly three days before these guys take over. I have very limited resources. What is the tactical situation on your end?"

Kurtzman stared at his map. "The country is buttoned up tight, at least as tight as a South American republic can be. Police and military roadblocks have been set up throughout the provinces. Every military installation from the border with Brazil to Tierra del Fuego is on the highest state of alert. They're waiting for the terrorists to make their next move, which means they're waiting on you."

"Tell me something I don't know."

"Governor Del Valken is on television every day making speeches. Denouncing terrorism and directing thinly veiled blame on the United States for what is happening. A lot of other nations are getting upset at the idea of the war against terrorism spilling over onto their shores. Politically, this is turning into a goat screw."

"What about the battle at the training camp? What kind of fallout is being generated?"

"Brigadier General Gonzalez was found with a bullet in his head in his own office. They're saying he was assassinated in retaliation for his destruction of the terrorist base."

"He was, but not by terrorists. His men were holding down the base. General Von will take over, and no investigation of the camp will come to anything. Once Del Valken and Von come to power, no investigation of anything will come to anything. We have seventy-two hours before these guys go legit. Then they go after Israel and God knows what else."

"Striker, if you do anything, you'd better make it fast. I don't know if the President will support a termination once the elections are a done deal. The United States has always been very leery about removing elected heads of state."

"I know that, Bear, but these guys go down. I don't care whether they're wearing a uniform or a crown, or whether it's tomorrow or after Super Tuesday. Nazis go down. Wherever I find them. With or without sanction."

"Mack, you assassinate the freely elected president of Argentina, and your official status could be persona non grata."

Bolan's relationship with the United States government was an arm's length affair. There was always the lurking fear that sooner or later the President of the United States would decide that Mack Bolan had gone too far or become a liability.

"Tell me you have a plan," was all Kurtzman could say.

"I do. But I have to find Del Valken and General Von first, and my recon options are severely limited."

"Finding them won't be hard." The Stony Man cyber whiz considered the problem. "But getting at them, that's going to be the trick."

"Where are they?"

"Governor Del Valken and General Von are conducting high-level meetings to present their new national security plan before the assembly. They're going to publicly present them Monday."

"And Tuesday they get elected. I don't want to try and take them in the capital. Way too much can go wrong. Where are they now?"

Governor Del Valken has a mansion in the hills outside of Cordoba City. It's isolated, which is in your favor. But the governor is surrounded by an army of bodyguards."

"That means Facon street muscle."

"True, but General Von is there, too. He's got the place surrounded by his Fuerza de Paz troopers."

"Any word on numbers?"

Kurtzman glanced about at the vast amount of data he had collected. "I can't get any hard intel on that. Barb's working every angle she can, but we just don't have anyone in position in Cordoba or an available satellite. I'd say you have to plan to run into the enemy in platoon strength. They probably have at least one or two helicopters on the premises, and if they're Fuerza de Paz, they'll be armed and hot on the pad."

"Any more good news?" Bolan asked.

"Yeah." Kurtzman glanced at his map again. "Like I said, there are roadblocks all over the province. I can see only two roads that lead to the Del Valken mansion. Those will be blocked at least a mile out, and I would count on encountering armor at both points if I were you."

"What's the situation on friendlies?"

"Well, that's about the only real good news. Del Valken made a big, televised show of giving his staff paid time off until after the elections, 'for their safety.' The public is eating it up. They're calling him the savior of the nation, and he hasn't even been elected yet."

"They know we have to hit them before the elections. Von and Del Valken are daring us to come and get them."

"Yeah," Kurtzman replied. "They're waiting for you."

"Let's not keep them waiting." Bolan's voice dropped into mission mode. "Send me the coordinates and any intel you have at all on the surrounding area."

"You going to let me in on this little plan of yours?"

"You really want to know?" Bolan challenged.

Kurtzman considered the question and Bolan's tone very carefully.

"Yes." Kurtzman's eyes slowly widened as Bolan revealed his plan. It didn't take long. It wasn't much of a plan at all.

It was suicide. Spectacular suicide, granted, but suicide nonetheless.

"Striker, you need professional help," Kurtzman pronounced.

"What I need is a regiment of United States Marines, but I'll be happy to put in for a Section 8 when I get back."

"Get back?" The computer expert snorted. "So far you haven't said jack about how you intend to extract."

Bolan's voice grew amused. "You really want to know?"

Kurtzman thought about that, too. "No."

Bolan told him anyway. Kurtzman stared at the map of Cordoba on his computer screen.

"Jesus H. Christ."

Sas de Cordoba Mountains

BOLAN CLICKED OFF the line with Kurtzman. He turned to Kubrik. The CIA man held an ice pack to his face. His contusions were slowly diffusing from purple and black to blues and yellows. "How many FN-2000s do we have left?" Bolan asked him.

"Well, not to be a dick about it, but you slagged two of them." Kubrik sighed. "Ammo we've got, but we're low on grenades. For that matter, the batteries for the integrated firing systems are low on all of them, and I have no way to recharge them."

"All right. You keep yours." Bolan turned to Encizo. "You take Dudley's." Bolan took the map the Farm had faxed him. He tapped the two marks Kurtzman had made with a pencil. "We're here. Von and Del Valken are here. They'll have at least a platoon around them. I'm expecting helicopters and armor. I want to break us down into two teams." He turned to Grimaldi. "Jack, you're with me."

The Executioner tapped the map. "The rest of you are going to be team two." Bolan glanced meaningfully at Dudley. "How are your legs?"

"Not good. I wish it was different, but not good." Dudley glared helplessly at the aluminum crutches by his side. "These escape sticks aren't going to get me anywhere far or fast. Put me in a car or park me behind a rock with a rifle. I'll do my best for you."

Bolan shook his head. "I need you more mobile than that."

Dudley's eyes widened. "Well, I am open to suggestions."

"Yeah." Kubrik eyed Bolan warily. "And I'm still waiting to hear what this plan of yours is."

"I know, but I needed to work out the details first." Bolan gestured behind him at the Pucara counterinsurgency plane parked beneath the trees. "It's pretty simple, really. Jack and I will be in the plane."

"Okay." Kubrik nodded. "That's all well and good, but what exactly is the plan?"

"Yeah." Dudley leaned forward. "And what are the rest of us supposed to do? How do we sneak through the Argentine military checkpoints?"

"I agree." Santiago scratched his head. "My uniform will not get us past a checkpoint, and there is probably a warrant out for my arrest by now. We won't get anywhere in a car."

"No," Bolan agreed. "You guys aren't driving."

Kubrik frowned. "We only got one plane and two seats."

"That's right, and it's over a hundred miles to the Del Valken mansion from where we are now, and all the roads are all covered, so—" Bolan grinned and stabbed his pencil into the map "—here's what we're going to do."

Bolan laid out his plan.

There was absolute silence until he was finished. Grimaldi and Encizo glanced at each other. They were both very familiar with Bolan's improvisational skills. But the big guy's plan caught even them flatfooted. Kubrik, Dudley and Santiago did not have the same luxury. This was their first experience of a Mack Bolan rolling war.

They were absolutely appalled.

Kubrik stared at the map and then at Bolan. "Mister, you are nuts."

"Right." Bolan grinned and looked at Dudley. "Dudley?"

"Momma always said white folks was crazy." Dudley shook his head. "But, mister, you *are* nuts."

"Good." Bolan nodded. "We're all in agreement, then."

21

"He won't attack." Governor Del Valken stood on his balcony and gazed out over the grounds. The stars were fading, and the sky was beginning to turn purple. The mansion was built like a Spanish colonial fortress. It was nestled against the side of a hill. Beyond the cleared land and the corral, forest-land and hills stretched in all directions. A pair of armed Huey helicopters currently occupied the corral. An M-113 armored personnel carrier dominated the circular drive and was flanked by a pair of gun jeeps. Armed men swarmed the grounds.

"Of course he will." Gustavo Von swirled the cognac in his glass meditatively. "He has to."

"They will fade away." The governor nodded to himself. "It is just another failed *yanqui* secret operation in South America."

"Ordinarily, I would agree with you, Nano, but this *yanqui* is not just another operator. He discovered us in Africa, and followed us halfway around the world to our own back-yard. Fredi, Robi and El Negro are dead. You and I remain. Today we go to the capital, and you will address the assembly and the nation, proposing Robi's economic plan. Tomorrow you will be elected president. Trying to take us in the capital would be extremely difficult. His job is not finished, and he has a very tight schedule to keep."

"He did not attack yesterday, nor the day before. He did not attack last night." Del Valken tossed back his drink. He let the fire of the brandy take off the predawn chill. "He is out of time."

"The day has yet to begin." Von gestured meaningfully toward the view with his drink. "And I would not stand out on the balcony like that if I were you."

Del Valken made a derisive noise and stood silhouetted where he was.

Von's eyes hardened beneath his Neanderthal brow. More and more, the governor was becoming uncontrollable. In the past few years Von had been forced to spend more time coddling Del Valken while at the same time devoting inordinate amounts of time, effort and finances to covering up the results of the governor's moral failings. God only knew what kind of president he would make. Being the mind behind the figurehead was to have been Robi's job. Gusi's eyes closed at the thought.

His brother was dead.

Los Facons had been based on a democracy. They were superior, and destined to rule. That destiny was about to come to fruition. The inner sanctum of Los Facons had always operated as equals. Gusi considered his cousin.

Fredi, El Negro and Robi were dead, and Nano was becoming a liability. Gusi believed that it was possible that terrorists might assassinate President Del Valken, and in the face of such a threat, a military junta would be the only reasonable form of government to deal with the threat.

The democracy was over. It was about to become a patriarchy. The next generation of Facons would be molded in Gusi's own image.

"Is that one of yours?" Del Valken inquired.

Von looked up as his train of thought was interrupted. "One of my what?"

"Planes." Del Valken pointed. "There."

Von stepped onto the balcony and squinted into the first orange rays of the sun. A plane was flying over the eastern hills. It was flying straight at them, and at high speed. Von straightened.

It was a Pucara counterinsurgency attack aircraft.

Von seized his radio. "All units! Engage the incoming plane! Shoot it down!"

Tracers began to reach up into the dawn. The plane roared toward the mansion like some immense avenging insect. It made no attempt at evasive maneuvers. Its guns were silent. Infrared flares blossomed out from under its wings as one of the Fuerza de Paz troopers below fired a shoulder-launched surface-to-air missile. The missile streaked into the sky. Von watched as its infrared seeker was distracted and veered into one of the flares. The missile detonated behind the incoming Pucara.

The plane didn't even wobble.

It just came straight on.

Von grabbed Del Valken's arm and yanked him back inside the mansion as the roar of twin engines shook the windows in their frames.

"HERE WE GO!" Grimaldi said.

The engine howled in protest, and every last warning light on the console flashed as Grimaldi pointed the Pucara's nose at the corral. A pair of helicopters was parked there, and one of them was already starting to take off. The second helicopter's rotors began threshing the air. Grimaldi put his reflex sight onto the first helicopter and squeezed his trigger. Flame erupted all around the fuselage as the machine guns ripped to life. Tracers streaked from the Pucara and converged on the rising helicopter. Grimaldi triggered a burst from his 20 mm cannons, and the chopper shuddered and broke apart under the barrage. The Stony Man pilot kept the Pucara's nose pointed in the same line and engaged the second helicopter.

Tracers flew toward him as the helicopter's door gunner fired back. He had one .30-caliber machine gun.

Grimaldi had four.

The helicopter rose a few feet in the air and listed to one side as Grimaldi hammered it. Grimaldi put a short burst from the cannons into the chopper, and it burst into flames and fell. The Pucara shook and bucked. Tracers streaked from the riflemen on the ground. It sounded like hail hitting a tin roof as bullets struck the armored cockpit. The rest of the plane was standard aircraft aluminum, and it rent and tore with the bullet strikes. Grimaldi ignored the incoming fire as he pointed his plane at the armored personnel carrier parked in front of the blazing mansion. Its three machine guns poured fire into the air. Sparks shrieked across the fuselage, and the cockpit glass cracked and spiderwebbed as the heavy machine guns sought to hammer the Pucara out of the sky.

Grimaldi lined up his nose with the armored vehicle. He poured tracers into the APC and was rewarded with sparks as the .30s bounced off the welded aluminum armor. Grimaldi unleashed his cannons.

Blossoms of 20 mm armor-piercing incendiary fire blew the APC out of existence.

"Missile!" Bolan roared from the back seat.

Grimaldi fired his flares as a streak of smoke and fire flashed up at them. The flares bloomed out to either side. The Argentine army's antiaircraft missiles were twenty-year-old British technology and exactly the kind of weapon the flares were made to defeat. The missile caromed off course as the infrared seeker was drawn irresistibly like a moth into the blinding sun of the flare.

The missile detonated a hundred yards behind them.

Bolan's voice was calm as he craned his head. "Another missile!"

They were out of flares and the Pucara was in no shape to maneuver. Grimaldi aimed the plane at the mansion and judged the distance.

Grimaldi put the reflex sight on the burning mansion and hit the autopilot.

"Eject! Eject! Eject!" the pilot ordered.

BOLAN REACHED DOWN and ripped the ejection lever upward. The ejection bolts in the cockpit frame fired, and the battered canopy cut loose. The open cockpit instantly became a two-hundred-mile-per-hour maelstrom. Bolan reached behind his head and yanked the face screen down. The seat fired. G forces rammed Bolan against his seat as he rose up and away from the aircraft. The Pucara roared toward the mansion, trailing smoke and fire, and crashed into the balcony.

The Pucara's fuel tanks ignited. The gunmen on the grounds in front of the mansion scattered as pieces of the plane rained down on them in a meteor swarm of flaming ruin.

The chair beneath Bolan yanked as his chute deployed. He craned his neck around and saw Grimaldi descending toward the front of the house. Bolan grimaced as he looked forward again. The ejection seat he was occupying was also twenty-year-old British technology. The seat didn't detach once the chute deployed. The seat and the chute were intimately committed to one another, which meant that the parachute was almost totally unsteerable. Bolan reached for the ropes anyway as he drifted down toward the burning mansion. His efforts did almost nothing to alter his course.

Bolan sucked in a breath and yanked up his heels as he went straight into the flames.

Instantly Bolan's world was a burning orange and choking black hell. Heat seared him. There was no sense of direction as fire and smoke enfolded him. Bolan collided with something solid and spun violently. He burst out of the smoke and the sky twisted crazily. The seat tumbled and skidded across part of the remaining roof and Bolan suddenly fell a dozen feet as he went over the side. The seat yanked against him as the chute took his weight again.

Bolan looked up and saw that his canopy was on fire.

The silk above him blackened and parted, and Bolan suddenly lost lift. He and his metal chair struck the ground with bone-crashing force. The Executioner lay stunned. Instinct took over as the remains of his parachute drifted down upon him like a burning ghost. Bolan hit his buckles and rolled as fiery silk sought to enshroud him. He rolled to his feet, slapping at the shreds of burning fabric that clung to him.

The sun spilled golden light over the hills. The mansion was burning out of control. Guns were firing out front. The .44 Magnum Desert Eagle and the Beretta 93-R machine pistol filled the Executioner's hands as he spoke into his throat mike. "Jack! Sitrep!"

"Enemy KIAs in squad strengths!" Grimaldi replied. "Enemy scattering beyond my position! Unknown number of hostiles still in the building!"

"Affirmative. Can you enter from your side?"

"Not from this side! She's burning like a Roman candle!"

"Affirmative, I am holding the rear of building. Can you assist?"

"Cooper, this is Chicago." Dudley's voice crackled across the link. "ETA thirty seconds!"

"Affirmative, I am on the west side of mansion."

"Inbound, west side, Cooper."

Men came boiling out of the burning building. For the next thirty seconds Bolan would be on his own. The expensive suits and handguns revealed the men to be Facons, high-level muscle and bodyguards. Bolan's pistols bucked in his hands as he put them in a one-man cross fire. Facons fell. Argentina was cattle country. Bolan drifted to his left and put a massive stone grill between himself and his opponents. More men burst from the house. They knelt and fired and forced Bolan to take cover. So many pistols were firing it sounded like one sustained roar.

Bolan threw a pair of frags over the top among the shooters. Men screamed as first one grenade detonated with a crack and then the other. Bolan rose with both pistols spitting lead and flame. Those who still stood toppled and fell. Bolan couldn't allow himself to be flanked out in the open by the next rush from the house.

He had to put a cork in the bottle.

Bolan ignored the writhing wounded on the ground and moved to the momentarily clear back door. "Chicago! Am entering the house! Rear side!"

"Affirmative, Cooper! ETA fifteen seconds. I got delayed."

Smoke crawled up from under the top edge of the doorframe and billowed upward. Bolan pulled his next-to-last frag and hurled it through the door. The oozing smoke pulsed with the detonation and earned Bolan a wounded scream from within.

Bolan entered running at a crouch.

The kitchen was clear save for a man on the floor, kicking and screaming and clutching the red ruin of his face. A foot of black smoke covered the ceiling. Heat washed through the room. Bolan leaped over the man and moved deeper into the burning mansion. He caught movement in the corner of his eye and fired through the open doorway of a living room.

Multiple automatic rifles chewed the wall where his head had just been.

"Chicago!"

"Cooper, back door is burning up! Where are you?"

Bolan glanced back. The kitchen behind him had lit up like kindling and he couldn't go back the way he had come. Bolan drew his last frag and went forward. "Chicago! There's a floor-to-ceiling window thirty feet from the back door. Try busting in there. I am closing on it."

"Affirmative."

Bolan threw his grenade into the living room and leaned back to put a wall between himself and the lethal swarm of fragments. He lunged into the room with his pistols hammering in his hands. Two Fuerza de Paz troopers went down. A third ripped at Bolan with his rifle on full auto. Bolan threw himself down as bullets cratered the wall behind him.

The Executioner glanced up as the lone horseman of the apocalypse came through the living room window in a storm of shattered glass.

With only seats for two in the plane and the roads blocked, Encizo, Kubrik, Dudley and Santiago had been forced to cross the one hundred miles between the rented ranch and the Facon's mansion on horseback. It would have been a particularly rough ride for Dudley, with a bullet hole in each leg, but the man was here and came through the window like a one-man wrecking crew. He held the reins in his teeth. His horse screamed as twin .41 Magnum revolvers rolled like thunder in his hands.

The remaining two riflemen fell with their skulls crushed by .41-caliber flatheads.

Dudley's horse rolled its eyes and shied and snorted beneath him. Bolan rose and slid fresh magazines into his pistols. "What's the situation outside?"

Dudley's smile was ugly. "Total chaos, but little more than mop-up. When the plane took out half the house, most of the remaining Facon muscle outside beat it for the bushes." The CIA man shook his head with grim finality as he started shoving fresh shells into his pistols. "And they ran right into me and the professor. Santiago linked up with Jack and Rafe and they're taking out the remaining the Fuerza de Paz by the corral. Kubrik should be here with us any second—"

Bolan was already firing.

A bullet hit his armor as Facons came out of the opposite hallway. They wept and choked from smoke inhalation, but they spilled into the living room shooting. Dudley snapped his partially loaded pistol closed but his horse reared and screamed as a bullet struck it, and the CIA man was nearly thrown. Bolan kept his front sights on the open hall. The gunmen dropped as Bolan shot them down.

Bodies piled up like cordwood in the living room as Bolan grabbed the reins of the rearing horse. Its eyes rolled in panic with the smell of fire and smoke and the pistol bullet that had creased its withers. The hallway beyond flickered and glowed Halloween orange as the fire crawled through the house. Bolan held the horse's head down as it bucked and spun. "Dudley, we've got to—"

Mariano Del Valken bounded out of the hallway. His hair was on fire. Half of his movie-star handsome face was bubbled and burned. His white teeth flashed, and his eyes gleamed with insanity. Backlit by the burning hallway, he looked like Satan himself.

Bolan released the reins as the horse spun between himself and the governor of Cordoba. Del Valken raised a .45 automatic and shot Dudley seven times in the chest. The CIA man jerked and sagged in the saddle as he took hit after hit. The governor reached him in a single leap. He clouted Dudley upside the skull with his empty automatic, and the CIA station chief toppled from the saddle right on top of Bolan.

Bolan twisted aside beneath Dudley's weight and struggled to bring up his pistols. The slide of Del Valken's pistol chopped down into Bolan's left forearm, and the 93-R fell from his hand. Bolan saw stars as Del Valken backhanded him with his empty automatic. The governor wrapped one blackened and blistered hand around Bolan's right wrist and the other around his throat. He already had the strength of a world-class athlete. That strength was redoubled with his unleashed insanity. Bolan drove his knee into Del Valken and felt the body armor he wore beneath his charred suit. The rearing, screaming horse slammed into both of them with its shoulder.

Bolan's gun hand came free. Del Valken's fingers vised down and pulled as if to tear Bolan's throat right off of his neck bones. Bolan caught motion out of the corner of his darkening vision. He shoved the muzzle of the Desert Eagle into Del Valken's midriff and pulled the trigger as fast as his failing fingers would obey him.

Del Valken was wearing armor but he was still accepting over fourteen hundred pounds of energy with each bullet that struck him. The grip on Bolan's throat weakened but not enough. Bolan brought his gun up for a headshot, but Del Valken grabbed for his wrist. Bolan let him. Del Valken pushed the pistol toward Bolan's head with insane finality. Bolan let the pistol come in, then twisted the muzzle beneath the wrist of the hand choking him and fired. Bolan squeezed his eyes shut against the spray of blood and bone.

The slide of the smoking Desert Eagle locked on empty.

Del Valken staggered a step and blinked uncomprehendingly at the shredded stump of his right wrist.

Bolan's burning lungs sucked air past his bruised trachea. He stepped forward and whipped his empty weapon across his adversary's temple. Del Valken's head rocked on his neck, and the insane light in his eyes went glassy. The Executioner raised the four-and-a-half-pound pistol like an ax and brought the butt down into the crown of Del Valken's skull. His eyes crossed as Bolan raised the pistol again, and bone splintered with the second blow.

Mariano Lopez Del Valken fell with his blown pupils looking in two different directions.

Bolan bent and put his hands on his knees as they began to buckle. His brutalized throat gagged as he sucked smoke.

"Your pistol appears to be empty."

Bolan looked up. General Gustavo Von stood in the living room. The last Facon threw aside the sodden blanket he had covered himself with to escape the fire. Bolan considered the spare magazine for the Desert Eagle in his webgear. His eyes flicked to the fallen Beretta where it lay on the floor a few feet away.

Gustavo Von's inhumanly large hands opened, and his lips twisted into a smile that lit his brutal face.

They both knew Bolan would never live to bring either gun into play.

Bolan dropped the Desert Eagle.

Von's lips twisted in a sneer as he stepped forward. "Mercy?"

"No, you don't get any."

Von halted as Bolan drew the eight-inch blade of a Nazi SS dagger.

"This belonged to your brother, Robi." Bolan matched Gusi smile for smile. "I think you should have it."

Von's smile froze on his face. His eyes narrowed to slits. His hand went to the ivory-handled dagger beneath his belt. "Oh, how I shall carve you."

"Eat shit." Dudley teetered on his wounded legs. Blood soaked both his pant legs where his wounds had opened. His thumb shook as he cocked back the hammer on his .41 Magnum. The muzzle leveled two feet from Von's eyebrows. "And die."

The hammer fell with a dull click.

Dudley began squeezing the trigger as fast as he could to find one of the rounds he had reloaded before being thrown. Von's hand closed around Dudley's wrists and yanked the muzzle aside. Flame spit as the revolver roared.

"Dudley! Cooper!" Kubrik came through the shattered remnants of the window with his FN weapon system leveled.

Von slammed his hand up into Dudley's crotch and lifted him over his head with grotesque ease. The giant station chief hurtled through the air like a three-hundred-pound sack of potatoes and smashed Kubrik off of his feet. The two CIA men fell in a tangle of limbs. The rifle went spinning across the floor.

Bolan flung his dagger and dived for the rifle.

The ebony-handled dagger revolved through the air. Von moved with a fluid speed that was horrible in a man so large. He jerked his head to one side and the blade sliced across his cheek. Bolan's hand closed around the grip of the FN-2000 as Von's boot hit his ribs with horrific force. The blow smashed Bolan upright. His vision went white as Von's right hand hit him in the chest like a train wreck. Bolan's body folded around Von's fist and he sailed backward. Only his armor kept his rib cage from shattering like kindling. Bolan bounced off the wall and sat down hard on his haunches.

Von smiled again and drew his dagger. "Now."

Bolan reached down to his ankle. His skeleton-handled boot knife came out with a rasp. He nodded as he tried to push himself to his feet. "Now."

Von laughed.

Douglas Kubrik blindsided Gustavo Von with every ounce of his 275 pounds like the all-American noseguard he had been back in his school days in Buffalo. Von grunted with the impact. Kubrik slammed a forearm up under Von's chin, and the dagger slipped from the giant Nazi's hand. Kubrik followed up by crashing his elbow across his jaw.

Von reached out his left hand and enfolded Kubrik's face like a catcher's mitt. He lifted Kubrik up into the air by his head and heaved him into the horse. Kubrik thudded into the already panicking animal and fell beneath its flailing hooves.

Bolan rammed his knife between Von's ribs.

The blade grated on bone and stuck. Von swung his fist around. Bolan put up both arms to block and was thrown back against the wall again. He landed on his feet and came forward again. Von ignored the knife in his side. He opened his fists as if he held a gift for Bolan in either hand.

Bolan's hands stiffened into blunt spears as he closed.

"Cooper!" Bolan's earpiece was gone but he could hear Santiago shouting from outside the burning house. "Cooper!"

Von seized the reins of the rearing stallion. For half a heartbeat Bolan was afraid Von was going to throw the horse at him. Instead the strongman scooped up his fallen dagger and vaulted himself into the saddle. The horse tried to throw him, but Von held on and dug his boot heels into the horse's flanks.

Von spurred the stallion straight at Bolan. The dagger rose glittering in his hand for the kill.

Bolan lunged for the fallen rifle. The horse's hooves smashed the floor tiles as it bore down. Bolan's hand closed around the barrel of the fallen FN-2000 as the horse's mass blotted out the rest of the room. There was no time to shoulder the weapon or even get his finger on the trigger. Bolan swung the eight-pound rifle up and around like a bludgeon. The buttstock and action of the bullpup rifle shattered against Von's skull. The charging horse buffeted Bolan aside with its shoulder and sent him spinning to the floor.

Von lay back in the saddle and nearly fell. He grabbed the saddle horn and righted himself. Santiago appeared on horseback in the empty frame of the window. Von swung out an arm like a fire hose and clotheslined the police officer out of the saddle.

Von rode off into the dawn.

Kubrik wheezed from the floor.

"Get Dudley out of here before you both burn to death." Bolan lurched to his feet, clutching the FN, and staggered to the window. Santiago lay on the ground gasping for air. Bolan levered himself up into the saddle of Santiago's horse and spurred after Von. He examined his rifle as he rode. The stock was cracked and the butt was gone. The bolt handle stuck out at an unnatural angle, and the magazine was dented and bent.

The 40 mm grenade launcher appeared to be intact.

Bolan cracked the breech and his insides grew cold. Kubrik had loaded a CS gas grenade for clearing rooms. Bolan glanced down at the makeshift saddle scabbard Santiago had fashioned out of a blanket. Santiago had been carrying his Halcon submachine gun when he had been unhorsed. The saddle sack held the Arwen 37 mm tear-gas launcher he had liberated from police headquarters in Cordoba. Bolan was beaten and exhausted, and he was down to irritant gas. Gustavo Von was one of the most powerful human beings the Executioner had ever faced, and he had a blade. If he got away, he would become the undisputed dictator of Argentina.

Bolan couldn't let that happen.

Von was riding a wounded and exhausted horse, and the stallion was bearing a burden well over three hundred pounds. The Executioner spurred his horse toward the rising sun and swiftly began to eat the ground between them. Von turned the bloody mask of his face to look back. He veered his horse for the trees.

Bolan raised his broken rifle to his shoulder. The rifle mechanism was useless, but when he punched the button the electronic fire control module blinked to life. The range between them appeared in the reticule of the laser range finder. The elevation blinked with every jostle of the galloping horse, but elevation was a nonissue. All Bolan had to be was close.

Von spurred his horse mercilessly into the treeline.

Bolan closed to forty yards and fired.

The broken rifle bucked against Bolan's shoulder, and yellow flame shot from the muzzle. A second later the CS grenade burst beneath Von's horse. The stallion screamed in terror and spun as the skip-chasing bomblets shot out in four different directions from underneath it, hissing and spewing gas. The horse reared up and toppled over in terror and exhaustion, taking Von with him.

Bolan tossed away the spent FN and drew the gas gun from Santiago's saddle. The revolving cylinder held five rounds of 37 mm gas grenades. They were undoubtedly much less powerful than the hardcore CS rounds Bolan and his crew had been carrying. Bolan wrapped the sling around his arm and shouldered the weapon.

General Von rose to his feet. He looked at Bolan bearing down on him. Von reached out and closed his hands around a six-foot sapling and tore it up by the roots. Bolan fired the Arwen. The grenade bucked and struck Von in the chest and detonated. Gustavo Von's massive form was enveloped in gas.

General Von stepped out of the gas cloud and swung the sapling.

He didn't aim for Bolan. The six-foot tree trunk scythed around and snapped across the knees of Bolan's horse. The mare screamed and plunged nose downward as her front legs collapsed. Bolan's boots left the stirrups, and the Executioner flew through the air before he met the dirt with an ugly impact.

Bolan lay sprawled in the leaves and stared up at the sun shining through the branches overhead. He turned his head dazedly at crunching noises close by. His horse was pushing itself back to its feet. Both front legs were bloodied. The mare limped feebly and shook all over. Bolan felt about the same as he pushed himself to his knees.

Gustavo Von stood a dozen feet away. He reeled on his feet. The Arwen's munition was a police, not a military round. However, the 37 mm aluminum grenade had struck him in the chest at close to six hundred feet per second. He had staggered out of the gas cloud, but a deep, bloody divot the size of a tea saucer oozed blood and gray gas where CS element had been imbedded. Tears streamed down his face, and his eyes were a mass of reddened veins. The hatred burning behind them was palpable.

Von pulled his dagger from his belt and stalked forward.

The Arwen was still attached to Bolan by the sling. Bolan's legs felt as if they belonged to someone else as he levered himself to his feet. He brought the Arwen to his shoulder and squeezed the trigger. The weapon bucked against him and Von jerked and staggered as tear gas detonated against him. Bolan pulled the trigger three more times in rapid succession.

Gustavo Von disappeared in a gray cloud of gas.

Bolan stepped back as the cloud rapidly expanded outward. He waited with the fifth and final round in the cylinder.

Gusi staggered out of the cloud like a drunk. His torso looked as if someone had teed off on his chest with a nine iron. His eyes were nearly swollen shut, and his breath came in a strangled wheeze.

He raised the SS dagger overhead like an ice pick and came for Bolan.

The Executioner let him get within six feet then shot him in the face. Von's head snapped backward on his bull-like neck. His head vanished in a violent gray cloud. The giant stood for a moment within the expanding cloud and then toppled backward like a felled oak.

Bolan stumbled away to put a safe distance between himself and the gas. He'd nearly had his throat ripped out and had inhaled way too much smoke. If he were caught in the tear gas, he would probably pass out and choke to death. Bolan leaned heavily against a tree and concentrated on the usually simple act of breathing. His horse shambled up to him and he put a hand on its shaking muzzle.

"Girl, I know how you feel." Bolan looked back the way he had come. The mansion was belching black smoke into the sky.

Horsemen were spurring across the open ground between the mansion and the trees.

Encizo had bought enough horses for each of them plus several spares. Santiago, Kubrik and Dudley sagged in their saddles. Grimaldi and Encizo led the battered little cavalry detachment. Bolan took his horse's reins.

General Von lay where he had fallen. The flesh of his brow from his eyebrows to his hairline had been brutally peeled back to bloody bone. His face was blue from strangling to death on the tear gas. Bolan stared into his glassy dead eyes.

Encizo reined his party to a halt beside Bolan and surveyed the scene. "We've got to get out of here."

Bolan nodded at the obviousness of the statement. "What's the situation?"

"The mansion is burning to the foundations. A lot of the bad guys were bunkered inside. Not very many got out alive."

Bolan nodded. "The Fuerza de Paz?"

Encizo shook his head. "There are no more Fuerza de Paz."

Bolan took the reins of one of the spare mounts as Encizo

tended to Bolan's horse. It took every last ounce of strength Bolan had to pull himself up into the saddle. "Los Facons?"

Encizo's face was tight. "Like I said, not too many got out alive. They're Nazis. We didn't think taking prisoners was appropriate." He glanced at General Von's corpse. "I think you got the last one."

"Choppers are probably on the way." Bolan glanced up at the rising sun. "And it's five hundred miles to the Paraguayan border." He spurred his horse wearily. "We're out of here."

Bolan let Encizo take the lead. He led them into the trees in a ground-eating trot. In his career Bolan had learned to sleep in almost any situation. He'd learned to sleep during hurricanes, shell bombardments, hanging from a sling attached to a flying helicopter at two thousand feet or at eighteen thousand feet pitoned to a mountainside. Sleeping standing up and marching had been cake since boot camp.

As he closed his eyes, he found sleeping in the saddle was no trouble at all.

James Axler
Outlanders®

ULURU DESTINY

Ominous rumblings in the South Pacific lead Kane and his compatriots into the heart of a secret barony ruled by a ruthless god-king planning an invasion of the sacred territory at Uluru and its aboriginals who are seemingly possessed of a power beyond all earthly origin. With total victory of hybrid over human hanging in the balance, slim hope lies with the people known as the Crew, preparing to reclaim a power so vast that in the wrong hands it could plunge humanity into an abyss of evil with no hope of redemption.

Available November 2004 at your favorite retail outlet.